The Connecticut Fault

Tracy Lee Sargis

ISBN 978-0-578-87185-1
Cover design by Germancreative

Printed in the United States of America

To my daughters, my living legacies. The two greatest miracles that could ever come from my existence. No matter what glorious beings you each grow to be and no matter what different lives you may lead, love each other. Unconditionally. As I will always love you.

I love you more than ever,
more than time and more than love.
I love you more than money
and more than the stars above.
I love you more than madness,
more than dreams upon the sea.
I love you more than life itself,
you mean that much to me.

Bob Dylan, "The Wedding Song"

Prologue

I can see the house clearer the tighter I close my eyes. My eyelids shut, and my memory starts filling in all the holes, the gaps, the light and dark corners. At the end of the long, hilly driveway, there is a house. A brown, deep-wood-colored house. Its wings spread across two acres of beautiful, green, well-maintained lawn, hugged by wild, twiggy woods and frog-filled ponds. The air rattles the dry, dead leaves over the ground like nature's symphony, and I can hear their song linger through the distance. The heavy, motorized garage door heaves itself upwards, and the faint smell of dried car oil spread across the ground creeps into my nose as I draw in a deep breath and step inside. Inside the garage there is a short set of stairs, carpeted and covered with stains, leading up to a dark brown door, the doorknob cool to the touch and gleaming gold. I can see a blurred version of myself as I turn the shiny knob, open the door, and step inside the house.

The smell of my mother's weekly veal dinner strikes my memory first as I close the door behind me. To the left is an antique armoire with a diamond-shaped mirror and coat hooks over a large seat reserved for my father's coat and briefcase. It's the first thing visible upon entering the house, a quiet, beautiful, inconspicuous piece of perfectly good furniture that just melts into the background. The "sitting room," as the

1

one-percent refer to it, is the first room on the left, and keeping in sync with the monochrome colors of the house, a body-sized, brown couch sits positioned across from two antique sitting chairs. A timeless oriental rug covers the floor right up to the ashy brick fireplace. To the right is the music station.

In my mind, my feet shuffle over the red rug, past the hearth tools, to the shelf, and I run my fingers along the weathered vinyl sleeves until my fingertips stop on a worn, faded copy of the film Grease's soundtrack. Flashes of our hair flying around the room as young girls flicker in and out. I stifle the nostalgia and turn around to face the screened-in porch, the first room to the right of the door. I can see my father asleep in the hammock with a heavy book on his chest. I can also see myself in the hammock, swinging, not sleeping, and my father yelling at me to stop putting holes in the screens with my feet. I see myself listening only when he is watching.

I step out onto the wooden slats of the porch and place my hands on the large, round, white table where I spent many hours playing gin rummy with my mother. At that same table, I spent many hours drinking gin and rum, not with my mother. The cross breeze on the porch draws out the smell of my mother's veal, beckoning me back inside the house. There is a runner underneath my feet, leading straight into the kitchen. The busy kitchen is sanitized and bright. The lights bounce off the white-

and yellow-patterned vinyl floor, highlighting the dark-stained cupboards. Another round table of similar monochrome wood sits in the entryway of the kitchen, and a large butcher block island dominates the middle of the room.

The nostalgia returns, and I see her and me as children, sitting on the floor, fingerpainting on the metal shelf underneath the butcher block. Shaking off that image, I see another: my father comes home through the brown door and places his briefcase on the empty armoire, hanging his coat up and heading straight for the butcher block. He sorts through the mail, pouring a glass of wine from the bottle on the counter before sitting down for his meal.

My mother is putting the final touches on her famous veal as I set the table and place the trivet in its center. The pan goes straight on the tabletop; we dish it out ourselves. My mother is done for the day. I don't have the heart to tell her how much I hate that veal. How once I leave her house, I will never eat veal another day of my life. How once I leave this house where I am allowed to do only certain things, I will find a world that also allows me to do only certain things. Because then my mother would be right. I could never let her know that she was right. Life has limitations no matter where you are or who you are. I wish I would've known this then.

At the table, with the soggy, salty veal center stage, I

sit across from my father with his glass of wine, full again. My mother, to my left, shamelessly unbuttons her pants and drinks from her cloudy water glass, food stuck underneath her nails. My sister, to my right, obediently eats her meal in a silence interrupted with spurts of monotone, one-word responses. This is family dinner. Every night. With my eyes closed, my adolescence seems to make much more sense now.

After family dinner my memory takes me through the kitchen to a surprisingly cramped yet formal dining room that holds years of fond memories of holiday meals featuring our own family drug dealer, a family friend, whom we all pretended was a starving artist. Not many starving artists live in the city and drive Porsches, but then again what did I know? I was only a kid, but he would let me sit on his lap and drive the car. I remember once when I was barely twelve, sitting on his lap, barreling down Sturgess Drive at 100 mph, when he told me to put my nose to the steering wheel. No vibration, *he said. Maybe that's when the trouble started.*

Leaving that room behind, I enter the family room. At its threshold is another priceless antique. It is a dresser, lovingly adorned with framed snapshots of fond times, against a wall that speaks the same. To the left is a large, light tan, L-shaped couch that has noticeable divots of wear and tear. The couch is positioned across from a large screen tv, and my mind

4

shows me more images of her and me. We are leaping off the couch in full princess costumes with plastic guitars strapped over our small shoulders, wearing oversized, star-shaped sunglasses that covered our faces. No fear. No shame. Doing all the things we love at once.

Exiting the opposite end of the family room brings me into the foyer, laid with cracked, mauve-colored cobblestone tile abutting a heavy, dark-stained oak door. Smoothing my feet over the uneven tile, I have come full circle on the main floor. I find myself standing in the middle of the sitting room where I began, and here is my favorite part of this house. Standing in the middle of the sitting room, I look up. The ceiling vaults up to the roof, opening the house from ground level up to the sky. I can hear "Trois Larmes Et Un Grand Sourire" coming from the piano upstairs. I see her chasing me, and me chasing her back and forth along the upstairs hallways. I see our bodies wrapped around the stair's large banister, laughter echoing through the house as we slide down. I walk away from the sounds of joys past and once again shuffle my feet across the timeless oriental rug, back around the monochrome couch, and down the runner to the gleaming gold doorknob. I see my blurry reflection once again in the knob leading me back out to the garage. The crisp leaves scraping against the ground tell me I'm back outside again, standing at the foot of the long, hilly driveway of our house, The Connecticut House. Then comes the rain, the break in humidity coming in crocodile-tear-sized raindrops patting my head. Wake up, *it says.* Wake up.

Stanton

The rusted crane groaned as it pulled the bloated body out of the water. The pouring rain fought the large, unstable hook, and the water that cascaded off the corpse created odd patterns as it broke the surface of the river below. The corpse hung upside-down as more liquid rushed out over its dark blue lips and whitened eyes. There was panicked commotion from all directions. My heartbeat flooded my ears and suffocated the boat's siren. The body had been in the water for a while although I couldn't be sure how long. Not long enough to become rigid.

The body dropped onto the boat's deck. Despite the shock of pulling a corpse from the water, the men automatically went to work trying to revive it as though they had been trained for just this. I stood and watched as a man twice the size of the bloated corpse pumped on its chest while another leaned over to give it mouth-to-mouth. I don't know what was more disturbing, the sounds of breaking ribs or the white foam that came bubbling out of the body's lifeless lips. That didn't keep them from pounding over and over again on the dead man's chest. The man holding the corpse's head repeatedly cleared the white foam from its mouth and then put his own mouth over the corpse's; its stomach bubbled up and down, but nothing happened. No reaction from the dead body. Certainly not the reaction they were looking for.

People gathered from every corner, hovering over the bridge, straining to get a glance of the bloodless scene unraveling beneath them. The men on the boat tried desperately to protect the scene from the gawking stares above while working to revive a body that was not going to come back to life. I never understood why people are so drawn to death. If I had a choice, I would wish myself into a dark corner with a soft light and my favorite book.

Life was very different then from what it had been; that's what I'm told and what I've read. Before, the world was filled with violence and savagery, but there was order, and there was hope. There was humanity. This world, our world, was a horrible nightmare of an afterlife, but it wasn't the afterlife: it was our reality. We'd just been forgotten there. The rest of the world...maybe it wasn't their time yet. Either way, we'd been forcibly emancipated from the rest of civilization. Families torn apart. The young taken from their parents. After the Great Superstorm exiled us, the daunting dilemma of rebuilding everything was forced upon us. Everything became a matter of survival or surrendering to death. Where we lived was known as the Den. We were considered a plague of evil.

I knew I'd had a different life once. I knew it, and I felt it in the way you feel a shadow following you only to disappear when you turn around to confront it. For someone who no one expected to remember anything, I knew much. I'd always suspected there had to be more than that place—more than just the Den—and not by instinct alone. Things about the Den didn't add up, like the structures that already existed when we arrived. Shelter was scarce and insufficient, but it was there. Albeit limited, there were some resources. No plan was in place, yet some people seemed to know their role, such as the Procreates. They stepped forward as the Den's leaders, and no one questioned it. Limited forms of technology existed as well from the first day we arrived, but there was never any explanation of how those technologies remain maintained. Many things about that place didn't make sense.

So, I listened. I listened to the coffin-dodgers tell their stories of death and destruction before being exiled. I listened to the parents and guardians tell their stories of how life was so much simpler once. I listened to the Procreates tell their unapologetic and ruthless stories of struggling to create law and order so that they could chart a new way of life for us all. I listened, closely, and I remembered.

I took a closer look at the mob still lingering above us. I searched the faces, looking for any tell, any giveaway. I was searching for some explanation of truth. The lines on faces were far more revealing than the piercing sounds of hyperventilated screams. Some faces showed fear, some showed sorrow, and some showed nothing at all, like they knew this had been only a matter of time. I tried to get a clear view of as many faces as I could. It was difficult, though, to get an accurate view between people manically running around and others visibly ill from the events occurring beneath them. I needed more time to evaluate, time I didn't have. The Den's warning sirens raged in the distance, shaking the boat's frame. The militia would be there soon.

One could now begin to understand that for this dead, bloated man on the deck of this decrepit boat, it wasn't the crime that was most shocking or disturbing. Rather, his very presence meant change to a life we had all forced ourselves to accept. I didn't believe the people in the Den were resilient enough for any more adapting. We all hung on to the same last thread of conformity. Today, however, was supposed to be a special day. Today would have marked the fifteenth year that the Den was murder and suicide free.

***

I knew what was going to happen next. Although it had been fifteen years since a death from violent crime, people still died in the Den, so this wasn't the first dead body I'd seen. It wasn't the first dead body any of us had seen.

Every year for the last fifteen years, the people of the Den had made a sacrifice, and this year would be no different. It had been law since the creation of the Den, and everyone partook. People of the Den made peace with the act of sacrifice because they didn't recognize the sacrifice as a human being. We'd rid ourselves of any connection to the chosen sacrifice, and it was usually easy for most because the sacrifices came from the isolation chambers.

I'd searched for the isolation chambers. I'd asked about them, but no one could or would confirm where they were located. I'd searched every inch of the Den I had access to and had never found a trace of their existence, but I felt them. And every year, a sacrifice emerged from them. It was a place they took people to hold in darkness and isolation, where prisoners were starved and forced to watch images of all the violence that ensued before the Den became free of violence. The Procreates' entire foundation was built upon a violence-free society, yet they treated violence with violence, and no one had ever questioned their hypocrisy.

To be sent into the isolation chambers meant a person was a traitor to the Den, and that meant they must also be a high-risk threat to our violence-free beliefs and way of life. Whoever was sent down there may be human when they go down, but they are something else entirely if they ever come back out. Which is why it was believed that a prisoner's true value culminated in their final act of sacrificing themselves so that the people of the Den could enjoy another year of living violence-free. The sacrificial ceremony was traditionally carried out three days after the annual anniversary. Day one was to celebrate. Day two was to prepare. And day three was for execution.

Upon confirmation that the body could not be brought back to life, it would be temporarily kept in holding cell 5468. The holding cells were one of the structures that were there when we arrived. We used them as waystations for the dead, like morgues. Over time, though, the body count well exceeded the amount of holding cells, and the romanticism of preservation became a relic. Since then, the bodies had been disposed of elsewhere. After that we used the holding cells to keep a body for further inspection or until the cause of death had been declared. To holding cell 5468 the body would go.

The militia arrived, and the crowd scattered as though just by being there they implicated themselves in some sort of crime. Nets were thrown out on the crowd like cattle. It was loud and messy, and in the relentless downpour very injurious. Bodies climbed over each other, limbs outstretched between the netting, heads ripping through the string cages trapping their bodies. The militia had their job to do to mitigate risk factors. The men on the boat with me weren't militia; they were laborers, fishermen, not militia but the ones who found the body, so it was up to us to decide what to do and quickly.

Before long, I'd be the last face this John Doe would ever see. I thought of him as John Doe, but the cruel truth was that there were no John Does in the Den; everyone had to be *somebody*, and everybody was accounted for, dead or alive. In an early effort to rein in the chaos in the Den, the Procreates, the group that governed the Den, devised a count system. It was elementary and consisted of nothing more than the name, birthdate, and sex of all the Den's citizens, though entries were often incomplete. There was no exact certainty or science to it, but no one else had much of a better idea. In the Den, if your name was not in the count system, there was a problem.

The Procreates passed another law: no one came in, and no one left. I'd always suspected and hoped there was a way out of the Den and that the inability to leave was another lie the Procreates created to keep us contained, but as long as I'd been alive, I'd never heard of either an entrance to or exit from the Den, another reason to distrust both the laws passed there and the ones who created them. Clearly, aspects of our world were kept from the people of the Den.

And therein lay a question: Where did John Doe come from? And how did he get to the Den?

The lost life that was discovered today would signify more than just another death, although no one was privy to this yet. Sound came flooding back into my ears as my eyes, blurry, strained to keep hold of everything around me. The men lifted the pale, blue, waterlogged body onto their shoulders. If you have ever tried to lift dead weight, you know how cumbersome a task it can be. The body slithered out of their hands and hit the deck of the boat with a muted thud. I winced at the sight of the body struggling to be carried, like the dead man knew where he was being taken and refused to go.

More rain came, and more men arrived to assist in transporting the body. It was a quick and decisive decision that John Doe would be taken to the holding cells through the valley. Everyone wanted to keep the focus of the militia off him, and no one wanted the bridge scene following us while we dragged this dead body through the city's streets. It was bad for the people, and we didn't want to be responsible for anyone not making it home that evening. That meant we needed more men. The trip down into the valley was not an easy or favorable option. There would be no gurneys or pulleys or brakes. The valley was not a place anyone wanted to be, and that was why it was the only way we could transport John Doe. Whatever we could do to start making John a bad memory was what we needed to do. The Procreates would want John to disappear just as quickly and with as little warning as he'd appeared. They wouldn't want anything to interfere with or overshadow the sacrificial execution. We needed to turn John into a ghost.

It took over two hours and five healthy men to carry

the body to holding cell 5468. As if carrying the body wasn't hard enough, the terrain through the valley to the holding cells gave no reprieve. I followed the dead body up through the slick and muddy man-made paths and then down into the overgrown forest marked with slaughtered willow trees. The forest floor was angry and unforgiving, filled with sinkholes and vines that waited in the forest's shadows to sabotage the men.

By the time the body reached the holding cells, it was mangled and disfigured, riddled with postmortem lacerations and punctures as a result of being dropped repeatedly and being used as a human shield against the angry arms of the forest's soldiers. One of the dead man's shoulders had become dislocated in the transportation, and the arm hung awkwardly, cocked back in a position of retaliation. The sight of it all was terrifying and ironic; even in this man's death, he still was not able to rest.

When we arrived at the building for holding cells 5000-6000, we were allowed entry by a boy no older than twelve. His Uzi waived us through. I always thought it odd that our weaponry appeared shiny and new while everything else in the Den felt old, smelled rotten, and looked filthy. The likelihood of the submachine gun being loaded was slim since much of the Den's arms and ammunition were stockpiled by the Procreates. I often questioned why the guards even had weapons if the Den was, in fact, violence-free, but nobody was eager to confront the Procreates about such things. So, it became just another thought lingering in my mind. I was always taking stock of the Den.

The men dragged the body to the elevator, leaving a wet trail behind them. I stared at its slimy glare and pretended it was like one of the fairy tales my mother told me about children who left breadcrumbs in the woods so that they could find their way back home. The pleasantness of the thought did not last long. As soon as the elevator doors closed, the stench was unbearable. The smell of men soaked in their own filth, covered in days of sweat and grime, permeated the already rank air. John Doe was the only man unaffected by the box of poison we all stood in. The dead man's expression, even after being dragged through the forest and used as a human deflector, was calm. The men exchanged concerned glances as the elevator began to move.

The holding cells were underground. The coffin-dodgers called them *sunken skyscrapers*. Once upon a time, in the old world, buildings like the holding cells were aboveground and stretched all the way up to the sky, they say. Since the buildings had sunk underground, the elevators had been rewired to descend versus ascend. The silver door crept closed, offering a cloudy image of whatever was inside. The four walls were stippled with small dents and holes, and in the upper corner, camera guts tangled up amongst themselves. I counted the dents, the holes, trying to imagine all the different people and scenarios that camera had once captured. The metal box crept down the shaft, yet it never seemed to take as long as it should. *Like a bullet train heading towards a brick wall*, the coffin-dodgers said. It seemed fittingly ironic.

The sounds that came from the elevator made me think about the scary stories the coffin-dodgers retold when they'd had one too many drinks. Who knew if their stories were true, but most people believed the Den was haunted. The theory didn't surprise me, and in a place used only to keep the dead, the rumors felt truer with every passing floor.

The sound of water trickling down all around us called out to all the critters and tiny bugs that manifested out of thin air every time a dead body was brought into the elevator. So when the door opened, everyone let out an audible sigh of relief, even John, it seemed. Upon first breath, the air tasted stale and damp; it reeked of old earth and rotting flesh, but it was the most honest place in the entire Den. The dead didn't lie.

The five men in the elevator with John and me began filing out. Two stayed behind, and they each grabbed one of John's legs and pulled him out of the elevator, dragging his body along the torn-up floor.

"Jesus Christ!" I heard one of the men carrying John yell out behind us. I turned to look. John had managed to get his clothes caught on part of the uprooted floor. The laborer's mind must have thought the dead man had come back to life and was trying to resist. It was enough to unsettle even the most fearless, and he'd stumbled back onto the floor. The man drew his hands in close to his chest to cover up that they trembled out of control. The other men, incapable of properly expressing their fear, audibly ridiculed their colleague for his behavior. I held my hand up to ease the men that were too scared to admit it and leaned down to meet the man's eyes.

"It's okay to be scared," I told him. His eyes held mine. "But grab his goddamned legs." I reached my hand out to him, but he shoved it out of his way and got to his feet on his own.

"Fuck you, kid," he threatened, but the fear was still in his eyes. He took a second to collect himself, but after that second, he picked up John's dead legs again and finished dragging him to holding cell 5468.

The men hoisted John up onto the examination table. At that point any respect for the dead had been left back on the deck of the boat. The men swatted the insects on their faces and wiped the sweat off their foreheads with dirty hands just like at the end of any hard-labor-driven chore. To them, carrying a dead body was like carrying a sack of potatoes, only there was no meal afterward to reward them for their hard work. The men cast cold glances over the dead body as though John had been responsible for ruining their afternoon. A couple of the men grunted as they left, but in hindsight I knew that they were all just glad their part was over. My job was about to begin.

I waited until I heard the elevator coax itself back to life; that way I was certain I was alone with John. I circled the examination table, looking over his dead body. He was a sight not to be seen. John looked as though he had been desecrated in every way imaginable. His bloated and maimed torso and limbs reminded me of zombies in the old comic books the coffin-dodgers thought they hid. John was no zombie, though; he was just a dead man. I looked closer at his face. His eyes were almost entirely white, even his irises. I couldn't tell what color his eyes once had been, but I sensed that they were just as tired and beaten up as the rest of him and that they had seen one of two things: everything they needed to see, or something they should never have seen.

I tried to close his eyelids, but they crept back open. I ignored his stare and looked at the rest of his face, pretending his eyes were closed. Most of my days were spent with the dead, and there were times when it became difficult for me to decipher whether someone was dead or alive. To me, the dead seemed more alive than the living.

Even though his head and body were waterlogged, I could still make out a fine bone structure. Whoever John was, he had been a handsome man. He had a defined jawline that protruded out into a stern chin, high cheekbones, and a strong brow that suggested deep-set, thoughtful eyes. The physicality of this man did not really matter, to me or to the Procreates. What mattered was what was inside John; what mattered were his secrets.

I wasn't the medical examiner, as it may have seemed I was. True, I was often the last with the bodies. True, I was the one who cleaned the dried blood from their wounds and reset their broken bones. I did those parts by choice. I did them because the day I die, I hoped someone would have the dignity of sending me to my grave with hands clean and limbs straight. No, I was no doctor. In the Den, they called me the Interpreter. I had a talent.

My talent was speaking with the dead, but the conversation with John was one I was not prepared to have.

There was a presence of shame in the air. I looked at John, wondering what had happened to him. I asked aloud, "Where did you come from?"

"Somewhere you know," John offered. Cryptic. I was intrigued to say the least. His voice was calm and soothing, too calm in a moment like this. Calm like he knew me, like we were old friends.

I unbuttoned his shirt and discovered something peculiar underneath it: a scar, several inches long and lying right in the middle of his chest. The mark was thick with scar tissue as though his chest had been opened repeatedly. I put my ear to it, hoping for a heartbeat I knew would never come.

I quickly drew my head back at the sound of his voice again. "You have one too?" he asked.

"I do," I replied, feeling my chest in the same spot where John's scar was. *How odd,* I thought to myself. *What are the chances?*

There was little time to waste. The Procreates were waiting, impatient as ever, for some explanation for John's death. I looked down at his hand, dangling off the side of the exam table. Being amongst the dead was never easy, but I took an odd comfort in knowing that the deceased had no reason to be untruthful. I had a standard set of questions. For some reason, however, I didn't want to know what John knew; it felt indecent and invasive. I had no choice but to continue.

"What happened to you?" I asked. He didn't respond. I took his dangling hand in mine, reminding myself not to be alarmed by the coldness of death settling into his body. I was still surprised, though. I was every time. His hand wasn't cold; it was clammy and moist, like it was alive, like it was nervous. I told myself that his hand was clammy because he had drowned, and his body was still secreting excess water, but I wasn't truly convinced. I regained focus.

I asked John again, "What happened to you?" No response. I asked a different question, a baseline question. "Do we know each other?" He answered with more silence. I was just about to repeat myself when he spoke.

"I know you," he said.

I winced, and my hand tightened its grip around his. That was not the answer I was expecting. *The dead don't lie,* I reminded myself. How could it be true though? I would remember a man with a scar like that. "You know me? Should I know who you are, too?" I asked John.

"Look for the Trojans," he said. Another enigmatic comment. "Where they roam is where you'll find your beginning. When you get there, look for the brown house at the bottom of the hill. It's hidden by the trees, but you'll know it when you see it. Don't be fooled by imposters."

"Imposters? What do you mean?" John was silent again. "John, what are the Trojans?" Nothing but silence from John. "What are you trying to tell me?" I was losing connection. I placed his moist hand over my beating heart, and placed my hand where his heart used to beat.

The visions were murky, undefined, like I was underneath the water with him in his final moments. The images became a little clearer and then clearer still, and then I saw something I had never seen before: nothing. Every person has a beginning, middle, and end, but John's life was just blank, like he was blocking his memories. I stood still with his hand in mine and mine in his as the realization set in that I had failed. Realization turned into worry as I thought about how I was going to explain to the Procreates that the cause of death was unknown. I thought about the uproar this would cause, the punishments to be endured, the never-ending questioning and investigating that would rip right into the little amount of privacy and trust the citizens of the Den had scraped together. I thought about it until the anxiety made my heart feel like it was going to give out.

At that moment my hand fused to John's, and the last pieces of his life exploded in vivid visions...and I swear I felt his heart beat. The last moments of John's life came and went fast, representing with razor-sharp clarity exactly how blurry and chaotic and final his last seconds were. Through the haze of his memories emerged something familiar and horrifying. In his visions, he showed me something—someone—close to home. Too close to home. They didn't belong there, in John's last moments. They shouldn't have been doing what they were doing, and it was clear John was asking me for something I wasn't sure I'd be able to give him: justice.

I felt tiny droplets of water bouncing off my forehead, like water torture. I opened my eyes, stunned to find I was flat on my back. I looked up and saw

John's hand reaching down as though he were trying to help me up. I must have blacked out. I stood up and looked around the small room. I had no idea how long I had blacked out, yet everything around me seemed to be in place except John. It looked like someone had sat John up and then had laid him back down again. His muddy, torn-up clothes were tangled around him. His shoes were missing, and I was imagining all those inconsistencies. I was almost convinced, but then I saw that his eyes were closed.

John had not closed his own eyes. Someone else had been there.

***

With the hollows of the valley at my back, I began making my way to the Procreates. They had been waiting for an update on John, and I was certain by then they knew they weren't going to get much. Usually, the longer it took to hear from me, the less information there was. When it was easy, and the visions were clear, they came quickly with no need for further interpretation.

As I walked towards the Procreates' grounds, I found my mind begging for my earliest days to return. When I was a young boy, I realized I could make sense out of what I feared, but just because I mastered what I feared, it didn't make me fearless. A part of me was always afraid. I remember as a young child telling my mother that I wished I wasn't different, that being different scared me and kept me up at night. She would say, *Stanton, it's not the fear that we want to rid ourselves of. The fear is good. We need to learn how to control the fear.*

I'd read that memories begin as young as three years old, but I remembered being haunted well before then. There was still violence then; I was born into it. Violence had its ebbs and flows. It didn't stop overnight, but it became less prevalent every year, every month, every day until one day it was just gone.

The best way I could describe my earliest memories was that they were like daytime nightmares. I was awake, and I was lucid, but I saw images that I knew didn't exist for others, heard voices I knew others didn't hear. Back then, interpreting was exceptionally simple. My mind was young, uncluttered, unpolluted, and uncompromised. I was pure. Everything came easier then. I was only five when the Procreates suspected I was different. At first, they couldn't quite put their fingers on it. They tried to figure me out, figure out my gift. To them, I was an anomaly, an unbreakable vault filled with unknown possibilities, and they wanted whatever was inside even without knowing what that vault held. They had to have it. They too were scared though. Scared of the unknown. Scared of what they couldn't control. Scared of their own envy. Scared at the possibility that someone may know more than they were willing to share. I was a risky asset. Surely there were debates on whether or not to find a way to make me go away, but they were too greedy.

I remembered the first time the Procreates confronted me about my powers. Two years had already passed with no violence, but infection-free never meant death-free. Plenty of deaths occurred after the violence ended. I still believed the Procreates were disappointed death continued even after the violence stopped as though they believed they would somehow become immortal if they eradicated the infection. They forgot, though, that even in violence's absence there were still many ways to die.

When I was five, the militia responded to a death claim in my sector. Mrs. Rappaport had evidently choked while eating dinner with her small child. A neighbor noticed the young daughter, Melanie, standing outside their shelter, tears streaming down her face, with no guardian responding. When she asked the little girl where her guardian was, the child just sobbed uncontrollably. The neighbor went inside, and when she found Mrs. Rappaport, she flipped the sector siren on to call for the militia. By the time they arrived, Mrs. Rappaport's daughter had run out of tears and sat limp from exhaustion in the arms of her neighbor.

My mother saw me watching this from our front door. She saw me watch my father, already a militia commander, pull an old, stained gurney from the back of a battered emergency vehicle, and she slipped a small, purple- and cream-colored shell into my hand. My eyes widened at the sight of it; it was beautiful. I had never seen a shell like it before. I ran my fingers over the small lines, rubbing my fingertips into each groove, scraping my nail along its surface. The shell hung on a thin string, like a necklace. I held it up by the string, staring at it in awe.

My mother gave me an expressionless nudge and nodded at Mrs. Rappaport's daughter. I walked the short distance to the Rappaports' shelter and sat down next to Melanie and her neighbor, whom she remained glued to. Dirt clung to her face and her hair and her small hands. She had a look of emptiness in her eyes that no child should ever have. She didn't acknowledge my presence, and that was okay by me. I put the small, purple, ribbed shell in the open hand that sat on her lap and then stood up to head back to Mother. When I got up, I looked back down at Melanie and saw that she had wrapped her tiny hands around the shell. A dim glimmer in her eyes silently thanked me for the token.

I looked over at my house and did not see my mother; I sensed she didn't mind me paying my last respects to Mrs. Rappaport. I wasn't shielded from death. Mother and Father felt death shouldn't be hidden as it only made it more difficult to accept, and in the Den, where famine and illness took lives daily, it paid to be accustomed to it.

Father and his men were standing above Mrs.

Rappaport's body, discussing her cause of death.

"She clearly choked to death," said one of the militiamen. They nodded together, including my father. "Poor woman. No one here to save her."

I caught a glimpse of her dead body, and that was all I needed. "Daddy, she's got rocks in her."

My father and his men, startled at the unexpected sound of my voice, turned around and closed the gaps between their legs to cover the sight of Mrs. Rappaport's dead body from me. In one quick swoop, my father had me in his arms.

"Son, Mrs. Rappaport choked, and sadly no one was able to help her before she stopped breathing."

One of my father's men pointed at me. "No, no, Lyman. Let your boy say what he's got to say. Go on, Stanton."

Father sternly put his hand out, staring hard at his men. "Stanton, go to your mother. Now."

"You're such a hard ass, Lyman," I heard his man say as I walked out. "He's a good…"

That's all I heard. My mother was now waiting for me outside our house as though my father had telepathically communicated to keep an eye on me. She put her arms out and gestured for me to hurry to her, and I did.

Later that night, I heard my mother and father talking about Mrs. Rappaport. I heard Father say, "She's next, Jan. She deserves to know the truth, too."

Mother replied, "Yes, yes," followed by a loud shushing sound. She obviously did not want me to hear this part of their conversation. "One thing at a time, please."

Father's heavy steps strode back and forth. "Mark my words," he said, pacing outside the bedroom door. "It's going to come back on us if we aren't honest with them both."

I opened the door just enough that the creak would call their attention.

"Father," I said, trying my best to prove to them I wasn't a little boy. "Jo will be okay, trust me. I'll never let anything happen to her."

"That's not your job, Stanton. And it's not her I'm worried about," he said, staring at my mother.

The lingering silent stare between the two of them was broken up by five unmistakable knocks at our door. Five knocks were the Procreates' knock, one knock for each of them, every knock louder than the last.

"God damnit," I heard my mother say. She quickly motioned for me to go back into the bedroom and close the door. I sat on the bed where Jo slept, watching her belly rise and fall as she peacefully dreamed. I really did mean what I'd said, that I was never going to let anything happen to her. I was her big brother. I was her protector. That was what my father always told me.

I listened to the muffled voices of the Procreates and

my mother and father and tried to imagine it was a distant radio. After a few minutes, their footsteps approached the bedroom door.

"Stanton, come on out here," my father said on the other side.

The Procreates stood in our common room, making our already small house that much more claustrophobic. There were five of them, three men and two women. They didn't look like they belonged in the Den, yet they were the ones in charge. Their clothes weren't worn through like ours. Our clothes were thin and patched in the same spots repeatedly, and years of wear had muted the colors. But their clothes were bright, clean, and colorful. They had socks that came all the way up to their knees. Having socks was a status symbol. We were lucky to have shoes that fit properly, let alone socks. Over their comfortable socks, they wore sturdy, fitted shoes that were clean and dry with new soles and no holes. They bathed regularly. I could tell because their skin wasn't discolored with the dirt as ours was. No odor followed them around. Their hair was shiny and well kept, especially the women's.

The two female Procreates stood on either end of the three men, giving the impression they were all equals. But I could tell in the way they held their hands clenched below their waists, and in the way they pressed their lips closed, that it was just that, an impression. It was clear who was in charge. It wasn't male versus female, but there was a clear alpha among the Procreates. It didn't matter who you were; everyone answered to the alpha Procreate.

His name was Lester. He was the tallest, the skinniest, and the ugliest. Looking back, I saw him as the Slender Man from the tales coffin-dodgers recited to get a rise out of small ones. Lester had long, brittle, twig-like fingers. His skin was pale with a greyish tinge, and his facial features were oddly obscured and unnaturally animated at the same time. He loomed over the other Procreates, and it was clear they were under his thumb just as the rest of us were. But the other Procreates figured they were in a better spot than the rest of us.

Lester, sitting down to look me in the eyes, folded his twiggy fingers across his lap and pointed his feet in my direction.

"Stanton, we are here to talk to you about Mrs. Rappaport. Did you know her?"

Even at five I knew this was a silly question. "Yes," I responded, looking at my father. He nodded back at me. My mother stood beside my father as they again seemed to pass telepathic messages to one another. Mother kept her eyes on the women across from her until the Procreate broke the stare.

"Your father said you saw her right after she passed. Is that right?" Lester resumed.

I once again gave a nod.

"Why did you go inside her house?"

I looked at my father, who gestured in reluctant approval. "I wanted to see Daddy," I said.

The stick-fingered man leaned close to me. "In my previous life, I was called Lester the liar because I told and knew every lie there ever was to tell and know."

I knew I was supposed to be afraid, but I felt something different from fear. I felt anger. I again looked at my father.

"Let's try that again. Why did you go inside Mrs. Rappaport's house?"

"I wanted to see her," I said, my face slack.

Lester stood and flashed his disgusting, filthy smile. "And do you remember what you said?" He ran one of his discolored stick fingers over his lips.

"I said she had rocks inside her."

Lester looked at my father and mother, impressed by the strong-minded boy they were raising. "What a peculiar thing for such a little boy to say," he said aloud. "And what a tone to take." He paused, waiting for an apology that wasn't going to come. "What did you mean when you said that Mrs. Rappaport had rocks inside of her?"

"Nothing. She just had rocks inside her," I said.

Lester lowered himself to my level to make sure I heard his every word. "Mrs. Rappaport choked on her dinner, and her child was too young to save her. That is what the report says." He leaned in toward my father.

32

"But when we had the medics analyze her body at the holding cells, they found several malignant tumors inside her body." Lester looked back at me. "Do you know what tumors are, son?"

"He's not your son," my mother broke in. Father held his hand up to her chest; she stared down at it.

"Tumors, Stanton, are like little rocks." He pulled a small, harmless-looking, grey pebble from his shirt pocket, holding it between his fingers so that I could see it. "Some of them are harmless nuisances, like a small pebble in your shoe. Some are bad. The bad ones can be small too, like pebbles, but then they spread, invading your body in a quiet, hostile takeover. Mrs. Rappaport had the bad ones. A lot of them. Turns out, she was already dying, but nobody knew. Except you." He waited for me to respond, but all I did was look to my father and mother for a hint about what to do next. Neither of them made any motion or sound, so I did the same. I used silence as my best response.

Lester stared at my father and said to me, "Okay, Stanton. It's late. You ought to be heading off to bed now, son." He smiled and tossed the pebble at my feet. My father clenched his jaw as the Procreates turned to leave.

Father walked the Procreates to the door where I had no doubt the conversation continued. My mother swiftly turned me around and rushed me off to the bedroom. We all knew that night would be the last night my secret would be kept.

We repaired to bed for the night, but the moment I closed my eyes, Jo began crying. I remembered my mother slipping out of bed, careful not to disturb Father and me. She leaned over Jo, and Jo immediately hushed. The two of them left the room, and I fell asleep.

When I woke up the next morning, the sun had just peaked over the horizon. Mother was already awake and had made breakfast and tidied up the kitchen, just like any other day. She helped me get dressed and then helped my father get his supplies ready for the day. For a long time, I was certain my mother was magical because she never slept, yet she always had the energy to take care of us all. I learned over time that magic takes sacrifice, so she really was the most magical of us all.

Once father left and our breakfasts had been cleaned up, I sat back down at the table as usual, prepared to begin school. But Mother, looking over her shoulder to make sure Father had left, bundled Jo up in blankets and grabbed a small bag from behind the ice box; without a word, she grabbed my hand, and we were out of the house, running in the opposite direction of the rising sun.

We made it to the valley, past the holding cells, and were nearly at the Den's shores when Mother stopped us dead in our tracks. I looked into the distance and saw Father standing on the shore alone. I didn't know at the time why Mother had tried to take us to the shores as it was forbidden. I didn't know why Father was there waiting for us either, but in that moment, I knew I didn't belong in the Den. None of us did. In that moment, I understood there were secrets to the Den. Secrets that Mother and Father both knew, and some maybe they did not know, even about each other. Secrets that everyone hoped I wouldn't figure out.

***

John, like everything else in the Den, had secrets, secrets that could only be described with intrusive clarity, and the Procreates weren't the open or analytical type. Many things were better left unsaid, and I'd found it useful to reveal only what they needed to know. But at that moment, the information that would satisfy the Procreates wasn't available.

My legs thanked the forgiving ground above the valley. The earth was different in the hollows. When I stepped, each movement took more effort as though I was trudging through quicksand, and the land was trying to swallow me one small bite at a time. Above the hollows, though, it was firm and stable, even with the aggressive rain challenging each step. One more landslide, though, and the ground could be swept out from under my feet.

In the near distance, I saw the columns that held the walls of the Procreates' grounds together. The Procreates chose their headquarters with purpose. Yes, it was the strongest structure aboveground. Yes, it was central to the Den's surroundings. More important, though, than foundation and proximity was what was within its walls. Their headquarters was in the Den's only access point to knowledge: the library.

It wasn't just any library. It was the only library the Den had, and it was the only library that made it through the Great Superstorm, the same year I was born. That was the most violent, most destructive, and most devastating storm our country had witnessed in the twenty-first century. Its turbulence couldn't have come at a worse time in history. Mother had told me about the storm surges in the years leading up to the Great Superstorm. She told me she watched people change. She watched the world changed.

At first it wasn't apparent. People initially were more helpful and empathetic than usual. They lent their neighbors flour and eggs. They helped push cars dead in the water. They brought meals for neighbors with small children. They made courtesy visits to the elderly. When the storms didn't show any sign of slowing and people's household goods and amenities dwindled, and that shortage extended to the stores, empathy quickly turned to apathy and panic and paranoia. The same neighbor who lent flour and eggs now bought out the store and kept the items under lock and key. People put physical distance between themselves and others, which ultimately expanded everyone's emotional distance.

Everyone isolated themselves. The world became a very small place for many. Mother said people aren't built for being alone.

Then came the rolling power outages that took out all technology-based communication along with their power sources. Schools and universities were forced to close their doors as in-person education became obsolete, along with any virtual options. The economy imploded as business and industry titans folded like poorly-stacked card houses, leaving millions without ways to feed their families. The prison systems collapsed as the prisons' personnel became affected by the storm surges; the prisons, already run by skeleton crews, found new ways to make ends meet. They made deals with criminals for access to resources in exchange for freedom. Outside the prison walls, home invasions ravaged communities, rioting and looting left nothing but scraps of scraps, and the black market became the only place people could turn to for what they needed. Mother said the number of displaced people was more than the shelters had room for, and people didn't want to open their homes to strangers after the prison systems began leaking criminals. The streets were filled with angry, hungry, lost vagrants fighting for survival and criminals desperate to hold onto their freedom. Violence hit its peak with our country on the brink of lawlessness. The nation was further tested when its leader proved ineffectual at handling any sort of crisis situation.

Then, the outbreak of the twenty-fourth gene happened. It was the perfect storm.

The country's leader at the time of the Great Superstorm pulled the rug out from under the nation in a weak attempt to bring the country back from the brink of cataclysm. He ordered the infected to be rounded up like sheep and interred at an unknown location. Those affected by the twenty-fourth gene, the illegitimately-released criminals, and every single displaced vagrant, regardless of age, gender, or status, was taken. That began the great disparity of cultures between them and us here in the Den. They stayed in their world, and we, disposed of, were banished here. It was intentional segregation: the supernatural phenomenon of the Great Superstorm just moved things along in the eyes of the old world.

The story continued. Mother said they packed all the infected into large shipping containers. However, the cops couldn't contain the hordes. The criminals clawed, stabbed, sliced, shot, gouged, and climbed out, and everyone else followed. The screams of the dying created a hellish symphony amongst the sounds of the Superstorm. The Superstorm ripped up the earth under their feet, swallowing up anything and anyone it wanted. The waters from the nearby shores birthed waves larger than the breaker walls could handle, and electricity pulsed through the open sky in jagged flashes of brilliant, blinding light.

There were a few structures nearby, the closest being the library and the hospital. As people scattered, the water's fingers pulled in everything in their reach. Mother and Father and some others made it to the library. They took refuge in the basement. Criminals, vagrants, innocents, infected, elderly: all were one as they held their breath together and prayed for survival. A deafening clap in the atmosphere gave way to unearthly tremors that moved the very foundation beneath them, and a burst of extraordinary light blinded them. Then there was nothing but silence and darkness.

Mother said she and Father awoke in the same clothing, soiled with blood and filth, that they'd been wearing before running into the library, but when they emerged from the basement of the library, everything was off. Not off in the way that a Superstorm had ripped through the city; that was a clear notion. Off in the way where everything seemed right but at the same time not right. They exchanged accounts of what they remembered with others right before the deafening clap and blinding light happened, but no one seemed to remember anything after that.

The only people in sight were those who had been in the library basement with Mother and Father. Mother said there were around seventy people, but the way she always avoided talking about the exact number made me believe she wasn't telling me something. They searched for other survivors, but in the following days found no one but themselves. An entire city of people just...gone. This cityscape, this place, did not belong to them. It resembled a demented version of where they'd come from but was not their city; it was not their home. What used to be the downtown area of the city had been swallowed up by the earth, and greenery would soon turn the giant crevasses into the valley I knew. The city's shoreline finally hemmed them in, revealing no other land in sight. Provisions were limited, and a relentless rain settled in.

In the first days of their new reality, Mother and Father kept to themselves. They didn't trust anyone, and they had a newborn, me. Many people died in those first few days, some from dehydration, some from existing illnesses they'd carried with them to wherever they were now, and some from injuries they'd sustained during the Superstorm. Then there were those who were suffocated in their sleep. Those who's throats were slit.

Mother and Father never slept at the same time; they took shifts and even then slept with one eye open. It wasn't long before the virus started making its way into Mother and Father. It started as dreams in which they carried out justice with their own hands. One day those thoughts didn't end when they awoke, and they found themselves consciously contemplating how they would protect their own. Would it be with their hands? Or would they use a weapon? Would they do it face to face? Or would they do it while backs were turned? When they couldn't stop asking themselves these questions, they realized just how dangerous a grip this infection had. The only way to do their part was to commit to not committing any violence. Mother said she had been a nurse before the Superstorm, so she did what came natural to her and tended to the wounded and the sick. My father was a strong man, and he used that strength the best way he could think of: protecting those who were targeted by the virus. Father never talked about what he had to do to keep Mother and me alive, but whatever it was, I trusted it had to be done.

Father raised me to do the same. He raised me to do whatever I had to do to keep the virus away, even if it was something I couldn't be proud of. There are worse things a father can teach his child and worse manners in which to raise a child. So, I obliged because Mother taught me everyone's definition of *good* was different.

***

I finally reached the Procreates' grounds where another child soldier stood guard docilely, expressionless. The library was once a landmark in the coffin-dodgers other world. In the Den, it was still a landmark but not one anyone wanted to venture to. It should have been a safe place for quiet contemplation, growth, and discovery, but the Procreates had their claws in deep, making sure that if anyone learned anything, it was only at their discretion. Makeshift barbed wire surrounded the library grounds. They sealed off every entrance and exit except for the small back door—easier to guard, I suppose, than the large set of double doors in the front. A widow's walk on the top of the seventh story was Lester's favorite spot. He was often spotted on the widow's walk, looking down on us all.

The boy waved me in without a word. In any other circumstance, I would have been happy just for an opportunity to get out of the relentless downpour, but there the clouds only multiplied.

Once inside, I stared at the seven stories of empty shelves. I always found myself asking the same question when I entered their headquarters: *Where were all the books?*

Mother did the best she could for Jo and me with what she remembered. She tried her hardest to improve our intelligence, but I hadn't been intellectually challenged by Mother in years. So, I'd worked out a deal with the Procreates that I kept secret from Mother and Father. It was difficult enough for her, relinquishing part of me to the Procreates, and I was certain she'd send herself to an early grave if she knew I'd given Lester more of what he wanted.

Speaking with the dead was my inherent gift, but I acquired the ability to foresee when others may die. It wasn't a sure thing, and it happened infrequently, but I'd been lucky on more than one occasion when it really mattered. I hadn't perfected it—far from it. I didn't quite understand how or why I received that secondary gift, but I didn't let it go to waste.

Unfortunately, I couldn't use that ability on command, and the information I received came in disjointed waves. I imagined watching television through a snow screen that was being turned on and off; that was what those visions were like when they came to me.

The deal I made with the Procreates was this: whenever I saw an impending death, I revealed it to them and only them. Of course, they tested me, and up to then, I hadn't been wrong once. In return for reporting a pending departure, I was allowed two hours with any books of my choosing. There were restrictions, of course. I had to be in the same small room, supervised the entire time. I wasn't allowed to physically choose the books: I told the Procreates what I wanted to read, and when I arrived, a stack of preselected books waited for me. Often times, the books weren't what I asked for, and other times they left me the same books, intentionally, I'm certain, but I didn't say a word. I read and reread until I remembered every word. There is no such thing as wasted knowledge. With these restrictions also came the threat of repercussions if my visions failed to come to fruition. I'd successfully evaded being sent into isolation eleven times.

I entered their chamber. Disdain floated freely in the air as the Procreates whispered back and forth, looking at me with disapproving eyes. The relentless rain outside the library walls wasn't loud enough to drown out their sharp whispers. They'd wag their bony fingers at me, begrudging the time they had to spend listening to the ramblings of a "dead talker." Even if it were a burden to listen to my conversations with the dead, it was their only link to the truth. I knew they would listen, and I knew they would wait. In this room, I let them believe they were in control. In reality, when it came to what they wanted to know, I held all the power.

"I need more time with John," I said, breaking their tense, back-and-forth hissing.

The Procreates laughed with impatience. They turned their noses up, forced the corners of their mouths down, and looked the opposite way.

"He has named it. He has named it! I want to ask you a question, boy," Lester said. Lester, the first elder to begin the Den's re-civilization, was past his prime, but he was still the Den's leader, and his ruthless ways of ruling had everyone under his command. "Can you feel pain, son?"

I nodded.

"Does your body provoke a sense of carnal need?" Lester flashed a dirty smile and licked his lips. His crudeness was offensive but true; I nodded again.

"Do you need to breathe and eat? Do you need

44

shelter when the storms will not relent?"

I gave a solitary nod.

"And what is your name, boy?"

Lester knew my name and knew it well, but I answered obediently, "Stanton."

Lester flashed another dirty smile because I had justified what he was going to say next. "Well, Stanton. I call you by your name because, as you have agreed, you can feel pain. You crave human touch. You need to breathe, to eat, and to rest your head after you have done all of this." He looked down into his lap, pausing for added effect. "That dead man you call *John*, he neither does nor needs any of the things your beating heart requires. His name is not *John*. It is number 0155468, and that is all. Go back and finish your job, Stanton."

I turned my back in obedience, but in my mind, I fantasized about confronting Lester and the other Procreates. I thought about what it would be like if I were in their shoes, if I had both their control and my powers. The Den would be a different place: people would know the truth rather than only what the Procreates decided to tell them.

Outside, the rain had slowed, but the sun hadn't come out. It never did. The bugs, however, trying desperately to avoid their watery graves, crept out in abundance. The sky was a muted purple hue, littered with clouds that hung low. The scent of rotting earth filled the air. I had to spend more time with John; I had to get more answers.

I went back to the holding cells alone, once again waved in by the young boy and his gun, and took the long—yet somehow not long enough—elevator ride back down to John.

***

When the sun set and darkness descended on the Den, the holding cells became colder, less familiar, and more disorienting. This wasn't my house; it was John's, and I felt his presence pulling me in his direction as my eyes struggled to adjust to his lighting. I didn't make a habit of visiting the cells at night. It was hazardous enough getting around with the ambient light that filtered in from the few levels aboveground, but at night, the earth closed in and swallowed the holding cells in darkness. I relaxed my eyes and let the light go out to make room for the dark.

I held my arms out to either side and every now and then felt them brush lightly against the walls' peeling paint. I ran my fingers over the numbers on each door as I passed by in the blackness until I felt the numbers 5468. By the time I found my way back to John's room, my eyes could see as though I belonged there.

John was as I had left him this time, unlike when I had awoken from my blackout. His eyes were still closed, his garments still tangled around his battered and soiled limbs. I circled his table, waiting again subconsciously for him to sit up and open his eyes.

"Just wait one more minute," I said to myself aloud.

I stood with John in the cold long enough that my toes began to tingle. Time didn't exist down in the holding cells. I had to trust my body to know when it was time to go.

I put my hands on John's chest, again startled by the frigidness that had taken ahold of him. My longing for him to come back to life left me, reluctant as I was to accept John's reality. He was dead, as dead as they came and as dead as they went.

His skin was still moist and slick like a frozen fish at the end of its thaw. *Fish can swim though*, I thought to myself. I wondered if John could swim. I wondered how he found himself in the waters of the Den because by then everyone knew John wasn't from there.

"How did you get here?" I asked out loud.

I straightened out his torn shirt as best I could, covering the scar on his sternum. His feet looked worse off than mine, and that was saying something. They were blackened and bloated; I wondered if they were like that before we found him. A belt held up his tattered pants. I tried to wrap the torn pants back around his legs; the fabric was dry and stiff between my fingers. I patted his sides; nothing there, unsurprisingly. Then I had a thought. I slowly rolled John a few inches onto his side and felt his back pocket. Nothing. I pulled him toward me and reached for the other pocket on the back of his pants.

I felt an object. My fingers didn't recognize the shape, but something was there. I pulled John closer, almost entirely on his side. My grip was slipping, but I managed to unbutton the back pocket before he slumped onto his back. I wrestled with John and pulled him with all my strength so that I could get to what he was hiding.

I had what I wanted, and John could finally have what he wanted: to be left alone.

The object was small; it fit in the palm of my hand. I ran my fingers over the cover and down the side, feeling a familiar binding. It was a notebook of some kind, a journal maybe, with letters embossed on the front in gold: a simple *J.D.*

I laughed a bit. "You really are John Doe," I said, rubbing my thumb over the letters.

I couldn't believe what I held, the endless possibilities this journal could represent. Heat spread through my body, warming me from my face down to my frigid toes. I thought, *I now know what euphoria feels like.* Had John been an angel sent to us to show us the way? Or was he the devil sent to solidify our damnation? Or was he just something to distract us?

I felt liquid in the pages when I pressed on the book. The holding cells were too dark to make any sense of the object. The conditions of neither the journal nor the holding cells would be conducive to reading its pages.

It needed to dry out, and I needed to find a safe place to store it and read it. I smiled to myself, as yet unaffected by the unknown content in the pages I held between my fingers.

***

I raised my hand, ready to knock hard and fast, but stopped myself. I didn't want to call attention to myself. Nothing could seem out of place. I breathed in slow and deep, envisioning a calm, white light flowing through my nose, down my throat, and into my heart, slowing everything down. When I regained focus, I knocked three times, softly, on the door. On the other side, I heard a chair creak, and I hoped it was just her. I held the journal tightly under the edge of my ripped shirt and felt the soggy pages press together under the pressure of my anxious grip. The door opened, and it was her, thank God. I let out a cloud of invisible white light, and she felt the release too. She would know what to do without me having to tell her, she always did. Without unlocking our eyes, I handed her what I had taken from John. Her expression didn't change; she just gave me a quick, small nod and shut the door.

Liv

Sweet pea body spray mixes with the rotting scent of a single cream-colored rose dying on her desk, filling me with sweetness and sorrow. She is here, yet she isn't. I can't remember the last time I was in her room. I can't remember the last time I saw her. The flower on her desk says it's been a few days at least. Teenagers don't like parents in their space; I should have remembered that.

Her room is very neat, everything in order. You wouldn't know that a sixteen-year-old girl lives in this room. That's how neat she is. Is this normal? No pictures or posters on the wall. No dirty laundry lying around or school books spread across her room. Nothing of the sort. Her walls are bare, her desk tidy, her chair pushed in. Even her bed is made with dull grey sheets. Did I buy her those sheets?

My fingers drag along the empty shelf above her desk. Not a speck of dirt. My life has been plagued by doubt, my years of motherhood even more so, but with all certainty I realize that I don't have any idea who my daughter is. When I close my eyes, I see her. I smell her. When I open my eyes again, her image fades quickly. The muffled voices and footsteps of strangers throughout the condo sound like a conversation underwater. Everything is muddled, but though I can't make out all the words, I still have a good idea of what's going on.

Oddly enough, despite the recent events, our home isn't any quieter. I imagine in a situation such as ours someone saying tritely *Oh, it's so quiet without so and so*, but Dani is a quiet girl. It's difficult to say you feel someone missing when you really never felt their presence.

It was only a matter of time before I'm interrupted from my thoughts. Detective Pete Ryan stands at the threshold, waiting to be invited in. I walk to him and extend my arm toward the hallway, shutting Dani's door behind us. Pete holds the silence until we reach the living room, where he motions for me to sit.

"Pete, you don't have to be so formal. It's me," I say as I wait for him to sit first.

Pete makes sure his guys are spaced apart in their stations. He gestures for them to keep their masks on.

"This is my house. My rules," I say, looking at his mask.

Pete keeps it on but gives me a nod and holds his hands up in surrender. He lays out all the customary paperwork but skips over the explanations. We both know what's going on here.

"I'll make this easy for you, Pete. I need you out there. Now. Last time I saw Dani was forty-eight hours ago. Last time I spoke to her was over three days." I throw out numbers that I hope are right; I just need to give him something to work with. "We haven't had any contact, and I haven't had the opportunity to contact any of her friends yet." We both know that last part was true because this is the first time I've been off the clock in days. I'll finish in her room while you guys wait for forensics. Make sure to check her hard drive and get that back to me yesterday and—"

Pete holds up his hand. "Liv, I know you. You got to let me take the lead. You know that," he says, looking back over his shoulder. He slides a folder across the table to me, flashing me a piece of paper hidden under it.

He sighs through his mask. "You're to observe only. If you come across anything, you call me. If you speak to anyone who has seen or spoken to Dani, you call me." He pauses to make sure I'm still listening. "You call me. Me only. And I know I don't need to tell you how imperative it is that you don't go public. We are only a couple days away from the parade. Keep the circle tight."

"I know, Pete. I know the rules," I remind him.

Pete leans in. "Have you talked to Steve?"

"The only time I talk to Steve is through his articles. You know that," I reply.

"I know, I know. But he's her father. Is there any chance she's with him?" Pete asks.

He's doing his job by asking. I would do the same, and yet I find it intrusive. I don't like being on this side of the table.

And…inside I know I'm not sure of the answer, but how would that make me look?

"You know he only cares about his work." Pete gives me a look that says *sounds familiar*. I shoot back first. "But I'll check. It's unlikely, but nothing is ever impossible." Neither of us is convinced I'm telling the truth.

Pete double taps the folder and gives the signal for his guys to leave. I wait on the couch until they're all out of my condo; then, I pull the paper out from under the folder Pete left. It's some type of report. There are two pieces of paper, but the page numbers are 1 and 4. I head toward Dani's room but remember Pete's men took her computer.

Tablet, I say to myself and head back into the sitting room. Her tablet is in the entertainment system, right where she always leaves it. I pull apart the two thin rods like a scroll, and the screen projects in midair. I swipe through the air, and the screen announces, "Password please."

"God damnit," I say, frustrated. "God damn password. What's the password, Dani?" I air type TrailsEnd11.

"Access denied," the air announces without emotion.

I try Warriors18. Wrong.

My fingers stiffen as they air type the letters M I C H A E L 3 5.

"Access granted." Everything unlocks.

The Journal

There are dark corners in everyone's mind. We all find ourselves going to these corners once in a while. We must remind ourselves how to be human. Like a bad wreck, we don't want to look, but we can't help it. It makes us more grateful for who we are and what we have. But what if we don't feel like that after? What if, when we go to the dark places in the back of our mind, we like it there? There are two things in life I've always wanted to do: create a life and take a life. It's dark, but it's true. No one would know just by looking at me. It helps that I'm exceptionally good at lying. Lies are what we're built on and what protect us. Lies keeps people together when they're too stubborn or stupid to accept the truth. So we lie. We all do it, and the best of us get away with it while the rest let it get the better of them. Lying has made me stronger. I learned to lie at a very early age to protect myself, and here I am today, thriving.

Liv

New Chicago's 15 Year Crime-Free Era
By Steven Roberts

9 July: To what does New Chicago owe its 15-year crime-free era? To whom are New Chicagoans indebted for a near decade-and-a-half violence-free era? A city once in shambles. A city once referred to as Chiraq. A city once broken and broke. A city once on the rebound, torn and riddled with insufferable wounds, now thriving with fortune and life. A city that, 15 years from its last violent crime, continues to hold fast as the nation's number one power, coast to coast.

As the financial dominator of this nation, New York said it was impossible, but today the city of broader shoulders looms over New York's markets, proving itself to be the only city that truly never sleeps. California said New Chicago could keep the riches because they had the masses, and the west coast would always be where people dream of going. New Chicago begs to differ as we continue to urbanize surrounding suburbs to create more room for our growing population.

New Chicago was once a city the worst criminals fled in fear of even worse criminals. Now, there are no criminals to run from. Once a city with a devastating unemployment rate of 25%, leaving those at the top mingling with bottom-dwellers, New Chicago now boasts an unemployment rate of 2% and is the only city in the nation with a mandatory minimum wage of $35/hr. Once, New Chicago's real estate market forced families out of their homes only to leave empty houses to crumble and decay as the unforgiving market wagged its fleshy finger at any who dared enter. Now, a record number of New Chicago residents are in the top 1%, and we all live the American dream.

So, what do we owe? And whom do we owe it to? The answer is we owe nothing and everything to each and every one of us. The city will hold its annual Crime-Free Era parade Saturday, July 14th, beginning at Mercy Square. This year's special guests will include Daniel Kang, Elliot Lyons, and Sara Schwartz, with a keynote speech by the head of Novyx, Hannah Kerwin.

This is the first window that opens on Dani's tablet, a sensationalist piece her father wrote.

"Fucking coward," I mutter to myself. Fifteen years ago, Steve wouldn't be caught dead with his name on a piece like this. He used to be one of the good ones.

I look at my cell; today's date is July 11th. *When was the last time I saw her?* I keep asking myself as I struggle to find the beginning of a timeline.

If Dani read this article the day it was released, Monday, July 9th, then she was here within the last forty-eight to twenty-four hours. Dani isn't one for theatrics, but she is following in her father's footsteps, a born investigator. There's no chance she'd miss out on a good reporting opportunity like the city's Crime-Free Era Parade.

The parade is in three days. That means three days for the city to get itself prepared for another possible outbreak. Every year we've gone without violent crimes or suicides, the government has reduced official law enforcement. In the government's eyes, they're killing two birds with one stone. With no violent crimes or suicides, there's a lot of excess on the city's payroll. They've scaled back on law enforcement and opened up the city's budget. Initially, they vowed to put it back into the city, and in the beginning, the intention was good. Layoffs were made slowly so as not to shock the system or raise any alarms.

The government offered our guys good pensions since it cost them less to offer decent severances than to keep people they didn't need on payroll. They provided alternative career paths, too, but over time the replacement system began to collapse; cops aren't built to be businesspeople or teachers. The city saw less and less money, which had everyone asking where all that extra payroll money was going. So, people started looking for it. When they couldn't find it, they got even hungrier for it.

Dejected cops were starving for their old way of life, and suddenly everyone was turning on them. So, they started going after everyone else. It could've been boredom, or ego, or the need simply to fulfill their family role, but they created a problem for the city. To the government, it became clear quickly that these disbanded officers threatened the new way of life free of violence and suicide, and they had no plans for allowing the infection back in. Over time, all my old colleagues began disappearing, and the government had us payroll cops too busy to pay attention.

The government is convinced that their plan has worked, and why wouldn't they be? Law enforcement still on payroll are damn good at their jobs, but while the number of violent crimes and suicides dwindled down to nothing, it actually increased our workload. Those old colleagues of mine may have faded away from our society quietly, but what the general population sees is far from what I see. From what Pete sees. We are busier than ever, but our purpose is different now.

My job is to contain the absence of those "forgotten," to stop the wrong sorts of questions from being asked or at least asked too often. It's made my job particularly difficult when the entire city lives with a veil pulled over its eyes. A very delicate veil. The false sense of security that this city has adopted proves what I've always known: ignorance is bliss.

With the reduction of the police force over the last decade and a half, normal men play dress-up in what used to be a uniform of honor. The government thinks it's the smartest plan. Nobody knows the difference between the real cops and the ones who just dress up as us. To the government, they see it as getting extra, unpaid help, and everyone gets to play the hero for the day. It's fucking ridiculous. A bunch of nobodies pretending to keep this city's violence at bay. Most of them haven't lived through or seen a violent event, and none of them has actually dealt with a live violent event in their entire lives and wouldn't know the first thing to do if there was an outbreak. It's a fucking liability. They are all fucking liabilities. I just don't understand how anyone can sleep at night. Fuck it, though. It's worked. It's hard to remember things you're committed to forgetting.

Maybe Dani will come to me, I think, hopeful.

In our day and age, one could ask why a mother would even be all that concerned with her child missing. With no violence or suicide, what harm could be lurking out there to predate a child? But laws are made to be broken, and most mothers aren't like me. Most mothers haven't lived through or seen what I've seen. Most mothers haven't done the things I have done. For the last fifteen years, I've been granted permission to be somebody I'm not. But at my core, I've always been someone drawn to violence and disaster. It exists in my core, and if it's possible it never left me, then it's possible there are others out there who have suppressed the infection as I have. This is why I will never stop worrying about my child's safety and wellbeing. Nothing lasts forever.

However, I do live in our world as it is today, and in our new world, the new rules have to be followed very closely. One slip-up could call attention to a situation or a person who may not want to be brought into light. I am no saint, and with all the research that Novyx has conducted regarding epigenetics, it's only a matter of time before the lab coats come to take my daughter for testing. I want to give my daughter a fighting chance; to do so means taking care of this on my own. The more noise I make about her disappearance, the more focus it puts on her and me, which is exactly what I've tried not to do for the last fifteen years.

Images of old crimes flood my mind, Dani's face floating through each crime scene as my mind plays out all the sick scenarios that shouldn't happen but can happen.

I can't risk it, I tell myself.

I am surely unsure. I tap the air showing the blue mail icon on Dani's tablet, and an update alert pops up. The little, empty time bar quotes forty-five minutes until an update completes. Sparking all this bullshit has my leg jumping up and down. What's the point of all this technology if you still have to wait forty-five minutes to read a god damned email? I need to sooth my nerves and get my head back in the right space, but I also need to get into Dani's email. The timeline bar hasn't budged, so at an anxious tempo, I get my shoes and lace them up.

I know everyone is used to the new running machines. You really don't even have to run; the machine does all the movements for you. Just another way to make us believe all these changes are improvements. Dani likes accusing me of acting like I'm already dead, but I delicately explain to her that change does not always make something better. I prefer to use my own legs while I still have control over them, before the world finishes brainwashing me and turning me into a robot.

I'll never get used to leaving my home without feeling the weight of house keys or a wallet. I put my micro ID tablet in the lining of my shorts. It feels like a hair pin poking me in the side, another annoying reminder of all the wonderful changes. Cash is something from another life, but nobody ever lost cash. People are constantly losing bobby pins.

"Change does not always mean making something better," I say into the small vent on my door and hear the deadbolt lock.

When I get to the lobby, a young boy is being shooed away from the front door. Even with the lowest unemployment rate in the country, homelessness still exists, even right outside my luxury high rise doors. I don't feel like getting into it with the concierge, so I dismiss his overbearing assertiveness toward the young boy and figure I'll make it right once I get back. Outside, the oppressive heat warms my limbs and sends a bolt of electricity down my spine. I run a quick 3.5 miles, and when I get back to my corner building, I slow.

The young homeless boy hides in the shadows of the side door alcove. I walk up to him and discreetly display my micro ID tablet. He takes his out, and with one quick tap, he has a thousand-dollar surprise waiting for him when he opens his tablet next. He doesn't yet know how much I transferred, but the gesture alone lights up his little face, and I feel human.

He jumps out onto the sidewalk and, with no care of being re-shooed, he proudly walks me to my front door and sweeps it open with one hand behind his back. His form is better than the grossly-overpaid concierge's. The glorified doorman and I make eye contact, and I nod to the boy to take off. He smiles and flees before the concierge can get to him again. I stare right through the concierge to make it clear that I don't give a fuck what he thinks about me or about my slipping a homeless little boy a grand. Or that I will to do it again if I so please, and there's nothing he can do about it. He stops advancing before he's even begun. His head drops back down, and the glow from his computer screen throws shadows across his face.

Computer, I say to myself. *Email.* I speed to the elevator corridor. I push the up button with my elbow, an old habit. The ride up to the twentieth floor to my condo feels longer than it should. I look up into the corner of the elevator and see the digital eye stripping me down, reminding me that I am always being watched. I don't realize I'm holding my breath until I reach my floor and finally exhale.

My legs feel heavy as lead from my run, and my shirt is soaked straight through the worn letters spelling *Trojans*, my high school's mascot. Memories of fonder times, less confusing times. More fun with fewer questions and expectations.

My mind is always five steps ahead of my body. It feels good though, to feel the fatigue, to feel the way my blood changes when I have a lead, to feel the race of time bearing down on me.

Email, I remind myself. I speed to the living room, grabbing Dani's tablet. *Update complete.* I air tap the complete button, and a bright red dot pops up in the corner of her email icon.

My finger hovers over the small blue icon. I draw in my breath and touch my fingertip to the transparent screen that floats in the air. A bold black headline reads "Your Next Steps To Finding You – 24andMORE" and underneath is a greyed-out title: "Your DNA Connections – 24andMORE." At that moment, the light in my head blinds me. I trip over my own feet, trying to get to my burner cell.

The call goes to voicemail. "Hannah, it's me. Liv. I

know it's been a long time. A long...time. But I need—I'm using that favor. If you still remember, you owe me one. Tomorrow, my place. 500 N. Michigan, Unit 2000, 7 a.m. You owe me, Hannah. You owe me."

I hit end on my burner and see a similar red dot on Dani's photo icon. Without hesitation, I press the gallery icon. What my eyes see has to be a mistake. I quickly close the two rods of her tablet, hoping that turning it off will make the images go away, but I know better. It's always different when it's your child. Knowing there's no turning back, I ease the rods apart and turn her tablet back on, returning to her photos.

Photos filled with blood. The violence is unspeakable.

Stanton

It smelled better at home than it had in while. It had been two days since our family had had food, but today it smelled like we may get to eat.

"Where have you been?" my mother pressed.

Why is she asking if she already knows? I asked myself. I looked worse than usual. My clothes had been soaked through twice, and it seemed as though the filth from the day's events had stained my skin.

"I was in the holding cells. There was an event today."

She glared me, unresponsive. "Get decent." She nodded toward the makeshift bathtub. Steam rose from the hot, fresh water. The thought of being clean, of bathing, of feeling human, sent a funny feeling through my bones. I wasted no time, stripping off my clothes and getting into the steaming water without testing it first. The water wasn't unbearable, but having contact with hot water made my skin and blood feverish in the best way. I pulled the tied-together rags that made up our makeshift curtain around me. I was a man and had been for a while, and it was no longer appropriate to be naked in front of my mother. She never seemed to understand this.

I sat in the bath and watched steam rise from my fingertips. I thought about John. I thought about where he came from, when he had his last bath, and if his mother had been behind a curtain cooking dinner for him. I shook my head clear of him. Before long, the water became frigid and tainted with grime. I got out and began cleaning the tub.

"Leave it," my mother said.

"But, Mother, it's filthy."

She stared a hard stare. "The water's good, son. It's good."

Mother went back to her cooking. She was a good woman but had a difficult time coming to terms with this fact. In the Den, the harder you are, the easier it is to get by.

This hadn't been the longest we'd gone without a good meal, but a good meal was rarely preceded by a warm bath. Something was happening.

"Where's Father?"

"On a trip," she said quietly.

When I was a young boy and my mother said Father was on a trip, it was usually a story put in place so that my father didn't have to be present because something bad was going to happen. In our family, as in many families in the Den, the female ran the house, not the male. This was for one unmistakable reason: women could create life; thus, women made the decisions. It was quite ironic seeing as men made the rules and women followed, so with this small allowance, women took their homes very seriously.

"Put those on," she pointed to clothes hanging on the

rafter.

The shirt was a button-up, not my size but clean. There was also a pair of pants the coffin-dodgers called slacks; they were rare to come upon. Confused but cautiously delighted at the new wardrobe, I put on the clothes.

"Let me have a look at you," my mother said.

I turned around so that she could see me. She pulled out a broken mirror, which she kept stashed within a large crack in the wall, and held it up so that I could see my reflection. I hardly recognized myself. Mirrors were as uncommon as slacks, and they were always kept hidden and brought out only for special occasions. I couldn't recall for certain the last time I'd seen myself, but it was clear I was a man now and no longer just a boy. I stood a full foot above my mother. I knew I had facial hair; I'd had it for a while but never got to see it. My dark brown hair sat restless on top of my head. My eyes were a clear blue; I asked my mother when I was a child why my eyes were so light when her eyes and my father's were so dark. *You're special* is all she would tell me. As I grew up, I stopped asking.

As I stood examining myself, my mother propped the mirror up against the wall and took out a small package.

"Happy birthday," she said, handing me the package.

My breath stopped, and my heart missed a beat. *My birthday,* I thought. A wave of heat surged through my body from my hair through my toenails. My nervous hands fumbled the small box. I opened the package; inside was a long, slender piece of black cloth. I didn't know what it was and just studied it, feeling the fabric between my fingers for a few minutes. Mother watched patiently as I admired the gift. When it became clear I didn't know what to do with it, she moved behind me, taking the black cloth into her hands and wrapping it around my neck. She told me to stand still and tall and to pay attention. I watched in the mirror as her graceful fingers made loops and shapes with the black cloth. I imagined this was what it would be like for a normal man to learn a normal thing from his mother. After a few swift movements and one firm tug, Mother stepped away to look at me in my entirety.

"Looks like I still remember," Mother said with a small smile.

I hadn't seen her smile for a long time. I looked down at the ordinary black cloth now wrapped around my neck, making me feel and look like a gentleman. I held the end of it in my hand, still confused.

"It's called a tie, son," she said. She pulled herself away from the moment and once again tended to the meal she was preparing.

Mother and I sat down to enjoy the food she'd made. There were boiled roots and fresh herbs, some type of meat I assumed was wild rabbit, and potatoes. I could see a broken loaf of bread sitting on the kitchen counter that mother had perhaps forgotten to plate—or perhaps had set aside for the Den's upcoming celebration—but I didn't dare ask for it. I didn't know the reason behind this feast; it could've been because of my birthday, or it could've been for the sacrificial celebration portion of our ceremonies. In the Den, when you came into a good meal, you didn't ask questions; you just ate and said thank you.

The meal may not have seemed like much, but for my mother and me at that moment, it was the best meal we'd had for weeks. While we sat enjoying it, I thought about my father and how much he was missing. I hoped that, wherever he was, he was eating just as well as we were. And then I remembered.

"Where's Josephine?"

My mother stopped eating and put her fork down. She wiped her mouth and cleared her throat. "Finish your meal, Stanton."

"Where is Josephine?" I asked again a bit louder.

My mother stood up from the table, took my plate to the stove, and put seconds on it. Seconds didn't happen in our house. She was stalling the only way she could. She set my plate on the table before me, and without looking back, she walked out the front door.

***

I stared down at my empty plate. The second helping my mother had given me wasn't enough to calm the unsettled feeling in the pit of my stomach. Where was

Josephine? I looked beyond the kitchen stove to the closed door that led to our bedroom. I knew where she was. I knew why she was waiting. The thought of opening that bedroom door threatened everything I had just eaten, and there was no way I was going to waste a good meal. I looked at the mirror still propped against the wall.

I asked my reflection, "What would you do?"

"You know they'll find out if you don't," it said.

"She's my sister."

"You know that's not true," my reflection responded.

"I can't. I won't. She's innocent."

"No one is innocent," said my reflection.

"She can be. We can fight."

"If you fight, you have to fight like them. Otherwise, you'll never win," said my reflection.

My throat burned as I struggled to keep my dinner down.

"What is it you want?" asked my reflection.

"To break the Den," I said.

"How do you break something that is bulletproof?" asked my reflection.

I responded, "Disarm it."

"And how can that be accomplished?"

"By letting them believe they are the only threat," I said. I turned away from my reflection and stood up from my chair. I knew what I had to do.

70

Without faltering, I brought my plate over to the wash basin. I cleaned it thoroughly so as not to leave more work for Mother. I dried my wet hands by running them through my coarse, dark hair, cooling my scalp. I made purposeful steps toward the bedroom, not caring if I was breathing or not, focusing only on getting through the motions. My hand reached for the doorhandle of the bedroom where Jo was undoubtably waiting. I wondered how long she had known about this, how long Mother and she hid the truth about her becoming a woman, because we all knew what that meant. I suppose Mother would rather it be me than someone else, but anyway you dissect it, none of it was Jo's choice, nor mine. It was law.

On a man's eighteenth birthday, the Procreates matched him with a child-bearer. He didn't know who. He only knew when. Failure to comply was promised to be far more painful than any form of violence that could be taken against him, even more than what the isolation chambers were rumored to do to an individual. To that day, no one had defied the Procreates, and no one had found out what would happen if someone didn't comply with their eighteenth-year duties as a citizen of the Den.

On the other side of the door, Jo was sitting on the edge of the bed. She was thirteen, but she had an old soul. The coffin-dodgers often used humor with a ridiculing temperature towards the young to exert their dominance, but their ill-humored ridicule revealed their insecurities. Most of the young in the Den dismissed the coffin-dodgers without thinking twice about it but not Josephine. She sat with them. She talked with them and empathized with them. She smiled when they reminisced, and she respected the moments of silence between herself and them when they didn't want to remember. She was special.

She was smiling even then, sitting there on the bed, knowing what was expected. She still smiled as if to tell me that she understood. I sat down next to her, and she looked at me, unafraid of what was expected of us. She understood things were the way they were. I looked at her eyes, big and dark brown, just like Mother's and Father's.

She looked at my eyes. *Blue like the ocean,* she always said, which I found wistful since she had never seen the ocean in person. She put her head on my shoulder; I leaned my head on hers and closed my eyes.

"Jo," I said.

Without lifting her head or saying a word, she put her soft hand up to my mouth. She was brave and loyal to the Den to a fault, but her emotions gave her away.

"It's okay, Stanton. It's time." Her voice wavered as warm teardrops fell on the back of my hand.

I lifted my head off hers and took her small face in my hands. I wiped her cheeks dry and told her to hold her head high. There was not going to be any eighteenth-year duty carried out. Not in that house.

"This will be our secret. Nobody has to know."

"But it's our duty. They'll know." She looked at me with fear. "They'll find out."

I shook my head and held her close. "I'll take care of it, Jo. We need to keep our stories straight, though," I said, looking at her. "Do you think you can do that?"

"Lie?" she asked. The shame of asking her to lie trumped the shame she'd feel if we complied with the Den's egregious laws of procreation.

There was no question who was the driving decider in the Den's constitution; among the Procreates, the alpha dominated. The bestial and barbaric style of procreation laid out in the Den's law was beyond unorthodox, to say the least. Whether a citizen was born a Den baby or born in the old world, the fundamentals of right and wrong still existed, but the Procreates enjoyed blurring that line and blurring it often. So yes, I asked my innocent sister to lie, for her sake and for mine. I nodded my head in a simple response, and she nodded back. We spent the rest of the night figuring out how to buy ourselves more time as we both knew the inevitable was going to happen soon enough.

The truth. The Procreates would find out at some point that we defied their law, which meant that my plan to break the Den would need to be put into motion sooner than I had planned.

The Journal

I decided to take a different route today. I decided to walk underneath the bridge. People like me don't walk under the bridge, but today felt like a good day to be defiant. I knew what I was going to see, and I wanted to see it. Why else would I go down there? Under the bridge, the light is sucked out. It's dark, and damp, and quiet, and lonely. It's not so bad when you know you have something better to return to. I guess that's why I liked going down there. I like seeing how the other half lives; it makes my blood move.

The water flows constantly down there, but none of it is usable for anything life-sustaining, for a human that is. The tunnels under the bridge primarily function as sanitation overflow, rendering it entirely useless. I've been down there once or twice and seen a facedown body floating along carelessly. Maybe they got thirsty and figured it was a legal way to quench their thirst. Nobody knows for sure because nobody respectable comes down here. A body sweep is conducted monthly, followed by a half-decent effort to correlate cause of death. I always make it a point to clear my schedule for those days.

Today the smell was particularly putrid. I gather it was from the near-dead form lying up against the far wall. I waited for a while to see if the person was moving; they weren't. I made my way over. The stench became so strong that I began to worry it was sinking into my clothes. I walked up close enough that if this person opened their eyes they'd be able to recognize me. By looking at the condition this person was in, it was highly unlikely they were going to have the energy to open their eyes let alone speak about what they'd seen to anyone. Even still, the thought of being caught by this person turned my lips up.

His skin was covered in bloody lesions oozing clear signs of infection as young larvae stalked each wound, waiting for their turn. He had been stripped of his shoes and socks, leaving his feet and toes exposed to the elements. His fingertips were raw, his nails tinged a deep purple and blue. I leaned over and put my ear close to his emaciated face so that I could hear each slow, gurgling breath. Then I sat by his side and watched his chest rise and fall until it stopped moving altogether.

Liv

There is no way my body will sit and wait for Hannah to make a move. I can't even believe she'll come, not until I see her with my own two eyes. I think about my options. My hands are leaving sweat prints all over the kitchen counter.

Prints, I think to myself. *Evidence*. My mind goes back to the report in her email.

I reopen the mail icon and tap on the new email in Dani's account from 24andMORE. Just as I'm about to open the email, I notice it's greyed out.

"Son of a bitch," I say out loud.

I waited too long. I shouldn't have waited. I think quickly: either Dani just accessed this from somewhere, or Pete has found it. But what if it is Dani? My leg jumps on its own again, and I feel myself holding my breath.

"Fuck," I say. I grab my cell and force myself to call Pete. It rings twice before he picks up.

"Pete Ryan."

"Pete, it's Liv." I hear rounds being fired off in the background. It's mandated that officers still engage in weekly firearm testing, always preparing for an outbreak. It takes every part of me not to reprimand him for answering his mobile during an active weaponry session, but I need Pete on my side unagitated. The line goes silent; he muted himself five seconds too late.

"Yeah, Liv, what do you got?" he asks in a low voice.

In a matter of seconds, I run multiple scenarios through my mind and end on this one. "I wanted to say thanks for the burger you brought over." I wait.

Pete pauses as well, his mind sorting out the code. "Yeah, no problem. How was it? Did I get it right?" he asks.

"Down to the condiments," I say, pausing and waiting.

"Great. Glad you got it all. I realized I had your fries on the way back to squad. Sorry. Had no opportunity to turn around."

"Yeah? Well, did you and the guys enjoy them?"

"No, they were too good to share," Pete says.

My breath releases. "Well, I think you owe me one and I you."

"You got anything on Dani?" Pete asks in a louder voice. I hear other voices in the background.

I clear my throat. "Still going through her room. Come over after shift if I don't call back by then." I hang up.

I put my head between my knees and let my phone drop to the floor. I run my fingers through my hair and gently massage the back of my head. The tension creeps in even as it releases.

"Relax," Steve would always say. That was something he was always a little too good at. Steven and I were never wired together right. That's probably why we knew we weren't going to work out. I never really had the time to have his back, and he had no problem stabbing me in mine.

My mind digresses. I snap my thoughts back to the fact that Pete hasn't given me away, not yet at least. I know neither of us has much time, but I need the hard drive he took to destroy all the evidence before it gets out of his hands. I have no doubt Pete and I are on the same page, but it's a matter of him being able to wipe it before someone else gets to him. No one can be trusted anymore. It doesn't matter if it's the captain or a rookie or a veteran: everyone is out for themselves, and everyone is committed to our pledge to prevent another outbreak at any cost. Pete is always being watched. I am always being watched. Now, I'm chained to my four walls until I hear from Pete. I can't chance leaving and missing him. I know Pete will clean up the evidence. I know it.

I hold the open tablet rods in my hands and read the two reports from 24andMORE until I can recite what each report says line-by-line in its entirety. Then, I wipe Dani's tablet.

"One down; one more to go," I say. "C'mon, Pete."

The room dims, and without looking at my cell, I know it's around 7 p.m. Since the Superstorm, the days and nights have never quite synced back up. Nor have the seasons. I took for granted a lifetime of reliable changing seasons and long summer days filled with warmth and sunshine. People say they went to sleep and woke up in a different world the day after the Superstorm, but that's just not true.

The days got longer, hotter. The sun and heat more persistent. It was a slow change, but no one took notice while it was happening. Then, the day after the Great Superstorm, the rain just stopped, and it has never returned, not even a drop. The heat is unforgiving and has only intensified as our days continue to stretch on. Dehydration and insomnia are real, everyday obstacles for us all, and daylight grows longer with each passing year.

When the night eventually comes, I find myself begging for the darkness, and my fear is I'm not the only one. But people have stopped paying attention to the trends because everyone has become so prosperous. Same dance, different song. The only thing anyone has ever really cared about is money. Now we have more of it than our city ever had, and with infection rates zeroing out, everyone has become ignorantly complacent. But there is another storm coming. It's been building up strength all these years. I can feel it in my bones. I can see it in the faces that tense up when they don't think they're being watched. I can see it in the way people ball up their fists in frustration with no outlet to release it. I can see it in all the things we aren't allowed to see anymore.

Local government has held firm on convincing our city that without acting on our urges, the infection will never take a hold of us again. The infection that is the very violence we have eradicated has somehow morphed into a representation of everything we are. You're either with us or you're against us. So, people stifle their urges. We all do it. For the greater good. To prevent another outbreak. But it's inevitable: I don't know when, but I know it's near. Another rolling blackout like the last one and global warming will be the least of our concerns. What the government hasn't realized is that all the emotions that go into creating the violence we eradicated haven't gone away. You can't take the violence out of people. It may not be active, it may lie dormant for however long it must, but just like the storm, it is coming.

They'll never accept it though, the government; therefore, the people won't either. They will never believe it, and yet every year we find ourselves holding our breath. We have forgotten what it means to speak our minds and fight for what we want. We have forgotten how to feel like our own selves.

Teddy Goodbread was the last person who questioned the government's processes and procedures in reinforcing the eradication of violence infections. Teddy was a good cop. He wasn't infected. I never once saw him draw his weapon, even before infection rates dropped. He just wanted to know the same thing the rest of us did. How can we expect to stop an infection that is in people's minds? Goodbread was a good seed, married with a little girl. Then one day, he was gone. Just gone. Disappeared. There are only so many places you can go within the fault lines, and even if you're able to cross them, no one knows what lies beyond. No one could carry enough provisions to find out. So where did Teddy go? That's something Pete and I would've looked into fifteen years ago.

Times are different now. In the early days of eradication, we had our wall of missing persons, and as infection rates went down, our wall became busier, cluttered to the point that even if the government hadn't told us to keep our noses out, we wouldn't have been able to make heads or tails of all the missing persons.

People naturally asked questions. They looked for their missing friend, husband, mother, wife, sister, brother, daughter, son, grandfather, or grandmother, and every one of them eventually reached the fault lines, empty-handed, frustrated, and forced to either ignore their urges or face treason charges. When those who searched came to us, our rehearsed response was always the same: *I'm sorry for your loss. The storm must have claimed your XYZ.*

That's what we have become: Xs, Ys, and Zs. Our explanation wasn't good enough for a lot of people, and who could blame them? So, they took to the streets. Not in a rioting sense; no, they wouldn't dare. But flyers were put out in designated places the government knew were low-traffic areas that wouldn't cause any public disruptions. So, after Teddy's disappearance, his wife did what all the others did. She went to the edge of the fault lines and found nothing. She came to us and found more of the same. Now his face litters our streets along with all the other missing, and I'll be fucking damned if my daughter's face will be found on our streets or on our wall.

My forbidden feelings boil my insides, and I let out the loudest scream my body can muster straight into my couch cushion. I strike the arm of the couch like a punching bag. I repeat this until my face turns red, saliva runs down my chin, a vein bulges out of my neck, and my hair goes wild. I stop beating my couch before any bruising starts appearing on my fists. I feel better. Not a lot better, but good enough to get back to work.

What did I miss? I ask myself as I get up off the couch.

I pace the living room in long strides while taking deep breaths until my heartrate slows down. I review everything I have so far that could lead me to Dani. It's hardly anything, just the reports. That's all I have. I must have missed something. I go back to her room.

Ever since I started working graveyard shifts, I've become used to moving around in the darkness. I have to remind myself to flip on the lights in Dani's room.

The stark light tickles my nose, like the feeling I used to get when I looked at the sun right before I sneezed. I close my eyes, shaking off the impending sneeze, but then I keep them closed. Things seem clearer to me when my eyes are closed.

I walk her room like a blind person feeling my way along new territory for the first time. I stretch my arms out, telling myself to ignore the feelings of familiarity, and search for anything that seems out of place. I walk the room with my fingers and toes leading the way. First is her tall dresser to the left. I run my fingers over all six drawers and each rounded knob; then, I reach up to the top and brush my hand across it and down the side. Nothing out of the ordinary there.

I shuffle my feet along the area between her dresser and the adjoining wall where her desk is. Her desk is small and low to the ground. I run my fingers along the empty top and bump into the small vase. Pollen from the dead flowers dusts the tops of my hands as crunchy leaves tumble to her desktop. Next, my hands find the small hutch that sits above her desk with three little cubbies. I stick my hand in the first cubby and feel only the smooth woodgrain beneath my fingertips. In the second cubby, I feel more of the same. There's one last cubby in the hutch, and I think I feel only the same wood again but—wait, what's that? There's a break in the woodgrain. This is different; something's here.

I press all around the inside of the cubby, and the

woodgrain gently pushes back on my fingertips. I open my eyes, and there in the last cubby is a door, a small, hidden door that pops open when I push down on it. It flips open like a tiny trapdoor. I quickly take my hand out and blink over and over again. I can't believe what my eyes are seeing. Dani is not a secret door type of kid, or perhaps I really, really don't have a fucking clue who my kid is. Dani knows she doesn't need to hide anything from me, not only because I've never gone looking before, but because I'm not that sort of mother.

I've been a cop for nearly twenty years, a detective for more than half of them. I've seen the things that nightmares are afraid of, and never once have I ever been afraid. Right now, here, in my daughter's room, staring at a trapdoor the size of my palm, I stand frozen in absolute terror. There's not a whole lot of things you can fit in a space that small, and yet there are many things that small that could be in there. I know before knowing what's in that tiny trapdoor that its contents are going to change everything.

"Fuck it," I say out loud and reach inside the tiny door.

I instantly pull my fingers back. I don't retract my hand from pain but from surprise. What I feel is familiar but forgotten; I haven't felt something like this since I was a kid. A sudden wave of nostalgia hits: *I'm on a white beach with my parents and sister and our dog. My mother and I are holding bags and walking*

before the sunset with our feet and fingers searching
through warm sand, collecting beach treasures.

I want to be sure before I take it out; I don't want to be disappointed if I'm wrong. I feel tiny ribs protruding. I run my fingers over the ridges, back and forth along the length of each small rib, scraping my nail between each ridge. I feel the scalloped edges where the ribs end and the tiny, ear-like protrusions begin. I flip it over and put my thumb in the small divot on its smooth underside. I stand on my tippy-toes and peer in the tiny door to see what my fingers felt, but it's too dark. I take my last breath, knowing once I lay eyes on what's inside, there's no unseeing it. With that breath, I let go of all reason and take the small object out. My fingers close around it, and I slowly open my fist one finger at a time. There in my hand lies a perfect, purple, patterned Atlantic calico shell.

Stanton

It was unusual for Mother to be gone so long. Even though this was no ordinary day, being well into the evening, there was nowhere my mother could go that the Procreates would allow. I supposed today was an exception. Even though it was my birthday, it was still also the eve of the Den's sacrificial three-day ceremony. Typically, curfew was pushed back for all on celebration evening, but this year's annual celebration was already getting off to an untraditional start. Either way, allowing Mother to break curfew was the least they could do for matching me with my sister. This wouldn't be the first time the Procreates made special allocations for Mother or Father.

Jo and I decided on a plan moving forward as people would have certain expectations of how we would behave and feel after completing our duties. In order for our plan to be believable, we had to put on the façade of having gone ahead with what the Procreates expected. It would wear quickly, though; that was our fear. How much time would we have before the truth exposed us? We tore apart the room but then put it back together. It wouldn't be like us to be disrespectful and leave the house a mess. When the room was tidy, we decided to go our separate ways. It seemed more believable if we weren't found together. Jo left to find Mother, which I assumed Mother would've wanted. I stayed and practiced pacing around the house to imply wrongdoing.

Pacing around the house, I realized why Mother had demanded I leave the filthy water from our makeshift bathtub. It was for when we were done. *Wash away the sin,* I could hear Mother saying.

If I wanted the lie to be believable, I had to do all the things they would expect me to do. So, I took off my clothes and sank into the murky water. It was freezing, and the dirt from my first bath swirled around my limbs as I settled into the tub. I let the icy water cover my body inch by inch, waking up every nerve ending until my skin was covered in small bumps.

I let out a breath of relief and watched the water rise above my eyes as I sank deeper. Its icy fingers tingled their way across my scalp. I lay still with my eyes open, staring up through the layer of grime, watching the images the swirls of dirt made in the water. My chest tightened as a sensation of fire began to build up in me and the swirls started forming pictures. My chest burned as an invisible pressure bore down on me, but I couldn't take my eyes off the disjointed, cloudy compositions just inches above my head. The images moved freely while pins and needles set into my body. I watched more intently as the images started moving towards each other, forming whole pictures like puzzle pieces finding each other. My head and body felt lighter the more in focus the water's images came, and I ignored the convulsions my body was beginning to make. My body shook underneath the frigid waters, but I ignored it even as cold water invaded my lungs. I didn't need my lungs under here; the pain didn't matter. The images were nearly in focus. A white light numbed my limbs. I could see it, I could see the image; my body shook violently, sending small waves through the makeshift tub. The image…it was a house. A brown house surrounded by green woods. Could this be the house John told me about? I saw a door. A golden knob. I reached my hand out to turn it and felt someone I couldn't see grab my arm.

"Stanton! Stanton! Come on, come on, come on," a voice wailed.

Something stomped on my bare chest, *stomp, stomp, stomp*. Warm lips covered my mouth, followed by more chest stomps.

"Wake up! Wake up! Stanton!" the wailing voice sounded closer with every shout.

My body ejected a stream of filthy water, and I gasped in moist air. I was freezing and naked on the floor with Father kneeling next to me. Father ripped his shirt off and wrapped it around me. I didn't move. I just lay there, watching Father rush to collect all the blankets and clothes he could find. Father covered me; he picked up my head and held it in his lap, just like he did when I was a young boy, bundled up in his arms. For a minute, I was just his son, and he was just my

Father, and he had saved my life. Again.

"Dad," I said quietly through my sore throat.

My father looked down at me, still holding my head in his hands. He looked surprised; I don't think either of us could remember the last time I called him anything but Father.

"I saw you," I said.

"Stanton, quiet. We can talk tomorrow when you've had time to rest," he said, soft but stern.

"I saw you—"

He gently pressed his hand to my chest. "Your mother is going to kill us both. No more talking tonight." He slowly sat me up and looked around, but it was just the two of us. "Let's get you dressed and in bed before your mother gets back."

I was freezing and exhausted, but I wasn't in shock. I couldn't shake the feeling, despite nearly drowning in our bathtub, that Father was being dismissive. Too dismissive. He was avoiding something. He didn't want to talk about what just happened, and he didn't want to hear what I had to say.

I often overhear Father tell his men that the less they know the better off they are. Thinking about it now in this circumstance, it painted Father in a new light, a light I'd never pictured him in before: suspicion.

"Where's Jo?" I asked. I would have asked it anyway to feed into our plan of deceit, but I felt a pang of fear for Jo. This compounded my shame at letting

Father believe I had defiled her, at allowing myself to be of the Den. He would know the truth soon enough, though, like everyone else. Hopes of redemption helped keep the lie alive.

"With your mother," he said. "They'll be back any minute. Come on now, Stanton." Lifting me with his strong arms, he helped me get dressed, and when we finished, Father cleaned the bathtub. I watched as he worked quickly to empty out the soiled water that had tried to make a ghost of me.

With his back turned, he said, "We don't say a word of this to your mother. Agreed?"

I thought about his question, knowing there was only one acceptable answer. "Agreed, Father."

Liv

I can't focus. None of this makes any sense. The warming nostalgia and momentary awe cuts short as suspicion creeps in. I try to look at the situation like I would if this were a case I was working, but it's not the same. It hasn't been the same since before the infection stopped. The fact that this involves my daughter makes it even more difficult to wrap my head around. People have always been simple for me to figure out, and evidence just makes sense to me. But my kid is an enigma. It's at times like this I wish I was a better mother. I feel fucking helpless.

I stare at this beautiful purple shell in my hand. It's actually in my hand, actually real. I had many just like this once when I was a child. Once, the Atlantic calico was a common saltwater scallop, but today, nothing about it is common. I haven't seen one of these in over fifteen years. There's no way to access these anymore. We hadn't smelled, tasted, swum in, or even seen a body of saltwater for years before the Superstorm. The storm surges leading up to the Superstorm halted travel and tourism for years even before it hit, crippling any opportunity of leaving or entering the state. Travel bans were placed on each state that limited who could travel where until eventually only those with authorized travel clearance were permitted to cross state lines. Soon after that, all interstate travel was banned no matter who you were, and when that happened you were stuck wherever you were. The last time I saw anywhere other than here was when I went home to say goodbye to Sasha. After the Superstorm, all items that weren't locally sourced, personal or public, were seized and destroyed. I would know: I led the remnant raids. If anything had been left behind, I'd know about it.

Where did Dani find this? I turn the small purple shell over and over in my hands. I notice a small hole bored through the top of it. It's odd to me for some reason. I can't figure out why the hole is calling attention to itself.

I let out a slight gasp. *Is this…?* Staring at the small hole bored through the shell, I touch my chest at the same place a shell just like it used to sit.

I jump from an unexpected vibration on my hip. "Jones," I answer.

It's the concierge. "Yes, Ms. Jones, Detective Ryan is here for you. Can I send him up?"

"Yeah, go ahead," I say.

I don't have time to figure out what to say to Pete about what I found in Dani's desk. It seems like he's at my door before I even end the call. The problem with having a partner you're so close with is that they know you too well. He'll call me on my bullshit.

"Fuck," I say through my teeth.

He already knows about the reports. He doesn't know what they all mean exactly, but he knows about them. It's just a matter of time before he puts it all together.

I'll just come clean, I say to myself. *I'll come clean.* I repeat it like a mantra.

I open the door for Pete to come in. Right away he knows what I'm looking for.

"I don't have it, Liv," he says with his hands up. "But I took care of it."

I close the door, resting my head on it as I lock the bolt. I turn around, leaning my back on the door. "Did you see the pictures?"

"What fucking pictures? Jesus Christ, Liv. When were you going to tell me?" Pete asks, a thin gleam of sweat spreading across his forehead.

I nod, acknowledging that I know he put the pieces together but relieved that he doesn't seem to know about the photos on Dani's tablet. "Let's just focus on Dani," I say, trying to steer the conversation.

"No," Pete demands. "Cut the shit, Liv. I want answers. Tell the truth."

I fix my posture and clear my throat, walking by him as though he isn't there.

"This is bullshit, Liv. How long have we been partners?"

"I know, Pete. I know."

"Why would you keep this from me?"

"Because what does it matter to you?"

He pauses. I can see his mind working to make sense

of this while trying to not overstep. He knows once I shut down it isn't easy for me to come around.

"Listen, I know this isn't how you would've wanted me to find out, but you don't think this explains a lot?"

"It explains nothing about Dani," I say.

"Not about Dani. About you, Liv. About you. Why would she have these reports, Liv?" Pete talks to me from the next room. I stand motionless in the middle of my kitchen. It's easier to forget about someone when you don't have to talk about them, when no one asks about them because no one knows about them. Michael is always with me, but until now I've been able to hide him away in the back of my mind.

"Pete, please…"

His voice is closer now. "Liv, it's me. Just look at me."

I draw in a long, heavy, deep breath and turn to face Pete. "She found out, Pete. I'm certain of it. That's why she has these reports. I don't know how she could've known." A strange sense of relief responds to the deep sadness that flows through me. For eighteen years I was able to keep Michael all to myself. Eighteen years. Pete stands next to me, quiet for a while. We both stand with our backs against the kitchen counter, thinking about what to say next.

"Well, I can't say I'm surprised," he starts with a small smile. "She's your kid. She was bound to follow in your footsteps at some point." He keeps quiet when I don't respond. "Is he...?" Pete looks at me.

"No, Pete. He's not yours."

He just looks away and nods in silence.

"It happened before you and I met," I say, looking at the same faraway distance as Pete.

"Who was it?" Pete asks.

"Jesus, Pete. Now? Really?"

Pete holds his hands up peaceably, but he isn't surrendering. "What happened?"

I shake my head, trying to shake away the early memories of Michael so that I won't have to explain myself. It doesn't work.

"Listen, I know you don't want to talk about it. I get it. But if you want to find Dani, and you think this has anything to do with where she is, then you know we need to talk about this. All the details. I need to know, Liv."

I immediately regret involving Pete because I know he's right. If there's any way we're going to find Dani, we have to explore all the possibilities, probable or not, even the ones I don't want to consider. That means I can't cover up my lies anymore. "Maybe Dani went to the fault lines," I say, knowing that isn't where we're going to find her. She knows trying to cross the fault lines is a waste of time.

Pete's strong grip on my shoulders shakes me back and forth. "Liv, snap out of it," he yells at me, startling me out of my thoughts. "I can help you, Liv. I can help you if you just tell me the truth. Otherwise, you're on your own." He releases his grip on my shoulders.

I watch Pete walk to the door. Just as he's about to leave, I call out to him.

"He's dead!" I yell it across the room, over and over, falling to the floor and burying my head in my hands. "He's dead."

I feel Pete's presence as he kneels beside me, his hand on my shoulder again, not shaking me this time but steadying me. My skin is hot and damp as I struggle to level off my emotions. I've had eighteen years to come to terms with my decisions, but there will never be enough time. Pete wraps his arms around me, and I scream into his chest until my blood cools. I lift my head, smooth down my hair, and wipe my face dry. I tell him everything, and with each word, I relive the traumatic memories of my son like a silent horror film in slow motion.

I was an arm's length away from making detective, in my mid-twenties, and finally coming to terms with the ceaseless disappoint my parents felt for me. I was never good enough for them. I made the choice to have a career in law enforcement instead of finishing college, and they made the choice of viewing me only as a blue-collar cop. They never shied away from an opportunity to remind me. So, I stayed away. Far away.

I went to Old Chicago when I was young with no plans of looking back. But then I got a call. My best friend from childhood had gone missing. I looked into it unofficially. It didn't take long before people I had no intention of seeing started seeking me out. There was a guy I knew growing up. We had a past. One thing led to another, and about eight weeks later, I found out I was pregnant. I was already back home in Old Chicago and had left everything from my childhood where it was supposed to be, in the past. But when I found out I was pregnant, I made the decision to keep the baby.

Then the world started to go fucking crazy. The storm surges before the Great Superstorm came one right after the other, each one stronger and more destructive. Infection rates were at their peak, and the world was not an accepting place, but I still wanted my baby.

He wasn't supposed to come for another twelve weeks. The storm surges wreaked havoc on the hospital systems. Logistics were all over the place, resources were scarce, and hospitals were shuttered due to insufficient staffing. Hospitals across the state, and particularly in the city, were stripped of staff as a result of the twenty-fourth gene's discovery. No one was safe from becoming a target for eradication, and the government wasn't taking any chances, no matter who you were. I was lucky I even had access to regular prenatal visits.

A routine appointment revealed the baby's heartrate had increased to a point of concern and continued to climb, so they rushed me to the hospital. Because of the lack of resources and medical personnel, my doctor took me in her own car while her nurse put an IV in me in the backseat. Next thing I knew, I was in the OR. I couldn't hear everything the doctor and the others were saying, just bits and pieces. They gave me something through the IV that made me foggy, and the OR lights kept flickering from the storm. I remember that vividly. I remember hearing them say something about an emergency c-section, followed by comments about not having all the supplies.

My doctor told me she needed to get the baby out right away. They had me hunch over and gave me a spinal block; before I lay back down, my legs were numb, followed by my waist and up through my chest. I was paralyzed from the chest down before my head hit the table. The nurse holding my hand whispered she was sorry there was no oxygen available. It didn't matter because there were no machines available for taking my vitals. Everything was a literal shot in the dark. I don't think they were even sure they had enough anesthesia to make it through the procedure. Everything was silent, and they worked fast.

Minutes later, my doctor said I was going to feel pressure. What she should've told me was that it would feel like a five-hundred-pound man was bearing down on my chest with all his strength and breaking my ribs. I didn't care about the pain, though, because he was almost here. I lay in anticipation, counting the threads that divided me and my baby, waiting through the silence to hear my baby's first cry. But I heard nothing.

There was more whispering, words I couldn't make out, but no sounds of a crying baby. I didn't need a monitor to know my heart rate was off the charts. Someone said something about the baby's heart, and I heard them counting out compressions, followed by silence. My sight blurred; I struggled to breathe, and that was the last moment I recall before I lost consciousness.

I awoke in a shared hospital room connected to a machine that sounded like a broken locomotive. A long red tube connected it to the IV in my arm. When my doctor stopped in, she told me I had hemorrhaged during surgery and had since undergone multiple transfusions of both cryoprecipitate and blood. She told me I was one of the lucky ones; the blood bank had been generous. She warned that while the pain may not be extreme at the moment, soon the surgical anesthesia and pain medication would wear off, and there would be no more pain relief because none was available. I didn't care about the pain, not in that moment at least. When I asked where my baby was, the doctor took a deep breath. Having been raised by a doctor, I knew that a deep breath was rarely followed by good news.

She told me the baby was stillborn, that they had tried to resuscitate him, but after multiple failed attempts, they called his death. Then, a miracle happened. Just after they called his death, the baby started breathing shallowly. Knowing the baby had heart issues in utero, they rushed him into surgery. With no pediatric surgeon on site and limited resources, they performed open-heart surgery on my undead, premature son, and he survived. It was a medical miracle, the doctor said.

When my nurse asked if I wanted to see him, of course I said yes. What sort of monster says they don't want to see their undead, newborn, miracle baby? The nurse taking care of me had dozens of other patients. Some patients were from the maternity ward, some were from ICU, some were from trauma...we were all just mixed up amongst each other, and this one nurse, this one human being, was doing anything she could to help us despite knowing she wasn't enough. It was commendable but too chaotic for me to handle. As I observed this nurse desperately trying to be enough, my anxiety started creeping in, and as my anesthesia began to wear off, the pain carved out its path.

The nurse prepped me to see my son for the first time. I held onto the bathroom sink, naked, staring at my reflection in the mirror as this stranger sponged me down. Shaking from nerves and pain, blood running down my legs, I saw my reflection in the mirror and couldn't recognize myself.

After the nurse cleaned me as well as my dignity

100

would allow, I reassured her it was enough and that I was ready. No wheelchairs were available, but I would have chosen to walk to the NICU anyway. I wanted to prove I was strong enough for what was ahead of me. When I got there, all it took was one look at my son to know I could never be the mother to him that he needed. I watched in sorrow and amazement as the NICU nurses worked in symphony, fearlessly navigating all the wires, reacting to every sound and siren in harmony, easing emergency situations with a calm that made my world seem even more rough and hectic. It was second nature to them. My nightmare was their everyday world.

My son: so tiny, so fragile. A thick layer of bandages and stitches covered his tiny chest, yet he just lay there, sleeping peacefully. I watched him for hours. I watched his tiny chest rise and fall in rhythm with the ventilator that covered most of his face. I listened to every sound, every beep, every alert. There were so many wires, machines, needles, and meticulous, around-the-clock wound care routines. He had a serious, inherited heart disease and needed a transplant yesterday. He'd require long-term therapy if he even made it past his first few months, and there weren't nearly enough medical professionals or resources to keep up with all the care he'd need. I did the only thing I could. I sang to him a song my mother sang to me when I was a child. The lyrics went 'Aba daba daba daba daba daba dab, said the chimpie to the monk; Baba daba daba daba daba daba dab, said the monkey to the chimp.' It was the only song I could remember. We were always separated by his isolette incubator, but at least he heard the sound of my voice. I never even got to hold him.

He did open his eyes once. Blue like the ocean, I thought. He just stared at the shell dangling from my neck. How in the world was I supposed to care for him? And alone? I convinced myself that he deserved better than what I could give him.

I was discharged the day after giving birth, which I understood was not the traditional best practice, but the doctor insisted it was safer for me to be in my own home. The hallways were lined with unattended patients, which made me question whether they were discharging me early for my own good or for theirs. Either way, I was too tired and in too much pain to argue.

The baby had a long road ahead. He needed an additional surgery to put in a pacemaker, and that was all they could do while waiting for a heart donor. Knowing he wouldn't be able to come home and that I wasn't allowed to stay with him, the least I could do was give him a name before I left. His little ankle bracelet just said Baby Jones on it. I thought about his name like it was the last decision I was ever going to make. Afterall, it would end up being all I was going to *be able to give him. My father would have rolled over in his grave if his grandson wasn't named after him. So, his first name was Michael. I wanted him to have a piece of me, so I gave him my childhood best friend's name for his middle name, Sasha. For his last name, I figured it was only right to let him have his father's family name, Stanton. My son's name was Michael Sasha Stanton.*

Stanton

I didn't wait for Mother and Jo to get back. I didn't want to risk them seeing the truth, not yet. The less Mother and Father knew about our lie, the better; they couldn't be implicated in something they didn't know about. I didn't think Mother would be too eager to see me again tonight anyway.

It was now past the extended curfew, but Father gave me the green light to leave post-curfew. Father had a special arrangement with Lester. As the head of the militia, and the strongest of them all, Father was an asset to Lester but also a clear risk if he were to turn. So, Lester and Father kept close tabs on each other, but it was understood that my father ran the Den on the ground and Lester from above. So, if Father said it was okay, it was safe to assume he was right. With all things considered, it seemed appropriate to take advantage of that tonight.

My father didn't speak to me after he finished cleaning the bath. Once he knew I was okay, he just went into the bedroom and closed the door. I assumed he went in there to burn the sheets, but Father has always been an enigma. I think that was where I got my introversions from. Another reason I was grateful to spend most of my time with the dead. I didn't have to speak with them unless I wanted to, most of the time at least. It took me years to control blocking out the voices or letting them in, but even still, the strong-souled ones could never truly be silenced.

Despite everything that had happened that night, the only thing I could think of was what I'd found in John's pocket: the journal. Melanie would have taken it only one place; only one place would have been safe enough: the shores. The shoreline was forbidden, but that was what made it safe. No one would be there to look, let alone find what we had.

The militia didn't watch the shoreline in the evening for a few reasons. One was that all militiamen had normal day jobs in the Den. Their role in the militia was in addition to their regular duties. Everyone needed to rest at some point. The other was that Father said it wasn't necessary to guard the shoreline in the evening because of the curfew, and even if someone were to break curfew and go to the shoreline, most people in the Den couldn't swim. If you couldn't swim, and no one was there to save you, that left little reason for anyone to go there. Aside from these reasons, it took energy to get to the shores. Energy was not something the people of the Den had in abundancy. Nobody was interested in wasting it to go somewhere that couldn't get them anywhere.

What Father didn't know was that when Jo and I were young, every month when he left with his men for days, Mother took us to the shore in the moonlight and taught us how to swim. Jo and I never asked why Father never took us, and we never asked why we went only at night, because we knew. We all knew why.

The shore became the perfect place for Melanie and me. I taught her how to swim, and she in turn kept all my secrets.

There was no right or wrong way to get to the shoreline. If you cut through the valley and walked far enough through the hollows, you always ended up at the shore. The land constantly shifted because of the rain, and that changed the terrain, so it felt like you never took the same path, but if you had the patience to make your own path and walk the distance, you'd get there. Most people in the Den did everything they could to prevent having to go into the valley. Most people thought it was beneath them, figuratively and literally. Most thought there was nothing down there except the overgrown forest and the holding cells, neither of which appealed to most. They didn't want to risk injury or damage to their worn soles only to find places they couldn't or didn't want to enter. So, most people stayed up above.

I remembered the first time I took Mel down to the shore. I didn't need to explain where we were going or why. She let me take her hand, and she trusted me. Maybe it didn't even matter to her where we were going; maybe she just wanted to go somewhere she'd never been, somewhere she could put everything in her short life behind her, even if just for a short while. Mel had a complicated past, one that I didn't really understand. She told me only bits and pieces. I figure she'd tell me her entire story at her own pace, but I found that down at the shoreline, she was different. There was a spark to her I didn't see when we were up above. The way she looked across the water reminded me of the way I felt when I connected with a lost soul: hopeful. Hopeful for the truth, for something better, for release and peace. Hopeful that the end didn't have to be your end. Being alive didn't necessarily mean you weren't dead. The moment you stopped searching for the unknown was the day your world stopped. Somewhere, there was more; there must be.

The clearing was just ahead. She was already there. From the looks of it, she had been there for a while. She sat with her arms resting on her legs, looking out across the water as she always did. The moon was high on the horizon, and the rain and soft wind moved the water just enough that its reflection looked like it was dancing in time.

Mel made no move to turn around when she heard me. I walked softly in the wet sand and sat next to her without a word. I took my worn, dirty shoes off, put them next to hers, and dug my toes into the cool sand. It was worth the blisters we were bound to get on our walk back. The sand felt like cold silk wrapping around my feet. The water came up around our ankles and took the sand that covered our feet back out with it. We dug our toes in again and again until they turned into prunes.

A cluster of dense forest arms lined the beach. It waited patiently for us as we let the rain wash every last grain of sand from our feet. We took our shirts off, wrung out all the water we could, and sat close together under the thick branches, drying off the best we could before making our next move. Watching from under lowered eyelids as Mel put her shirt back on, I noticed she wasn't wearing her necklace.

"Where is it?" I asked.

I wasn't sure at what point in our lives the shore became her territory, but ignoring my question, she took my hand and led the way. I trusted her as blindly as she'd trusted me that first time I'd brought her there. We walked for a long time. Long enough that the moon, straight overhead when we started walking, was now behind us, and there was a faint light in the distance ahead. She led us south along the treelined shore to a part of the beach I had never been to. In the eighteen years of my life, I was certain I'd walked every inch of our shoreline, but this area didn't look like any part I'd walked. The sand sloped down, so we walked down a fairly steep hill. The rain slicked up the sand, and Mel caught me once or twice as I tried sorting out where she was taking us. The farther downhill we walked, the more the ground beneath us changed. The sand slowly turned to fine gravel, then to rock, and eventually to concrete.

"Where are we?" I asked with no response as my pulse picked up in excitement.

The concrete turned into a road, and at the bottom of that long, alien hill, I saw a structure. Though difficult to make out from our distance through the rain, it looked like a house. It *was* a house! A brown house. It looked like the house from my vision underwater, but there was no way. How could it be? I lost grip of Melanie's hand; either the rain or my sweat let her slip away, but she grabbed my hand again tighter to make sure we didn't break contact. I must have stopped at some point because I felt her tugging on my arm.

Suddenly, there we were. My breath escaped my body, and the same burning sensation I'd felt under the murky bathwater returned. It was the house from my vision. Right there in front of us at the foot of the long driveway. Thick, wooded forest surrounded the big, beautiful house. It was untarnished. I stared with my jaw open in absolute disbelief. Underneath the surface of the soiled water in my bathtub, I didn't try to make sense of what I saw. But here and now, awake with no visions, I couldn't make sense of what was right in front of me. I had so many questions. How could this be? Where did this come from? How had I never found this? Or seen this? Who else knew this was here? What was inside? Questions raced through my mind as I worked to sort out these impossibilities.

Mel grabbed my face with her warm hands and stared into my eyes; in a wave of flashes, I saw two young girls with dark hair laughing and dancing, chasing each other inside a house, this house. She lifted her hands from my face, and the rain cascaded down our cheeks. I stared at Mel, just as confused by our inexplicable connection as I was by the images she'd shown me.

"Mel," I said, but she turned away from me, grabbing my hand and leading me to the front of the house. We stood before the garage. She reached for the handle, and I followed her lead. We pulled up, opening the giant garage door.

A faint odor inside smelled similar to the fuel we put in our boats. It had to be car fuel or oil. I saw its stains on the floor. Mel grabbed my hand and walked us up a set of short, carpeted stairs, and there it was, the same brown door with the golden knob from my shaky image. Looking at the blurred versions of ourselves in its reflection, Mel reached out for the doorknob.

Everything went dark.

***

I woke to a feeling that could only be described as déjà vu. My father was sitting hunched over me again, my head in his lap, as if I'd never left the house that evening. The only differences were that I was dressed, drenched but clothed, and I could see Mother and Jo in the background.

I remembered Father's words to me earlier: *We don't say a word of this to your mother.*

I kept my mouth shut and slowly sat up. My hair was damp, and I smelled like I'd slept in the forest for days. I looked around the room at Father, Mother, and Jo; each looked as concerned as the next. Mother and Father were having another one of their telepathic conversations, and my mother's crinkled brow and narrowed eyes exposed her deep level of concern. She had much to be concerned about. I couldn't make eye contact with Jo. Mother and Father clearly felt the same discomfort at the situation, and still no one spoke.

I broke the silence. "What happened?" I asked, testing the waters.

Mother and Father looked across the room at each other again. Father spoke first. "You passed out, Stanton. By the edge of the valley."

No, no, no. I wasn't by the valley, I thought.

"What?" I questioned.

"You left last night after…" Father looked at Jo and immediately away again. "I shouldn't have let you go. It's my fault. Where were you going, Stanton?"

Mother still hadn't said a word or moved an inch; she studied me.

"How long was I out?" I asked, trying to evade Father's question.

Father nodded toward the cloud-covered light coming through the window. It was morning already.

"We don't know, but a while. It took a long time for your mother and me to find you."

"I was alone?"

"Who would be with you?" asked Mother.

The sound of her voice pierced the room. It was like I hadn't heard her voice in ages even though it had been just hours. I reached my arm over Father's shoulder and hoisted myself up. The three of them looked at me.

"No one was with me. You're right, I was by myself. I'm lucky you found me first, Father. Thank you." Father stood and exchanged another look of concern with Mother. "I should probably get some rest," I said, turning to head to the bedroom.

"Wait a minute," Mother said. She had something in her hand, something small, wrapped in cloth.

John's journal. I jumped inside my skin, working overtime to contain my reaction. Relief quickly turned to suspicion. Where had Mother gotten this? Mel hadn't given it to me before...

Mel. Where was she? I didn't want her involved in my mess, so I was careful not to mention her in any way. But knowing Mother and Father already suspected I hadn't been alone made this transaction more uncomfortable. We all knew we were each hiding something. I calmly reached my hand out as mother crossed the room, her fingers on the small journal and her eyes on me. She handed it over without hesitation.

"Where...where did you find this?" I asked.

"It was in your pocket."

We both knew that was a lie. That was the difficult part with Mother. I never could quite tell when she was being honest or not. Lies are not necessarily harmful, although I preferred the truth. With her, though, it was a coin toss. Most people have a tell, but one thing Mother and I had in common was we both committed to the lies we told as much as we committed to our truths, which made it difficult to tell which one was which sometimes. Eventually people stopped questioning. This time, though, we both knew neither of us was being truthful. That journal wasn't on me when they found me. I didn't even have pockets in my pants.

"I thought I'd lost it," I said, riffling the damp edges of the journal with my thumb.

"Must've been with you the entire time. You must've forgotten you had it," she said, turning away.

"I guess I must have," I said, opening the door to the bedroom. I turned to enter but not before asking one last question. "Trojans. Does that mean anything to either of you?"

Mother and Father looked at each other with genuine expressions of confusion. I could tell by their faces they had no idea what I was asking about.

Father answered, "What does it mean to you?"

"Nothing. Just curious. I think I should lie down for a short while. The Procreates will be expecting me this morning, and I have more work to do. I don't want to be a zombie all day."

"Leave the door cracked. I'll leave your meal by the door so that I don't wake you if you're sleeping," Mother said, not bothering to snicker at my wit. So much for reducing the tension. We both knew I wouldn't be sleeping. She wanted to make sure she could hear me if I tried to sneak out the window.

"Yes, Mother," I said, pulling the door shut to all but a crack.

My head spun, but I couldn't tell if it was from lack of sleep or from the excitement of having John's journal back in my hands. In a way, I was relieved that I didn't have to hide the journal from Mother and Father. On the other hand, I knew this wasn't the end of it, and they were sorting out how to handle this new piece of evidence.

Evidence, I thought to myself. "The Procreates," I said out loud.

They would already have been here had Mother or Father told them about the journal. I questioned why they didn't tell them. If Lester found out I was hiding something that could be useful to him, forget about it having anything to do with John, he'd have had me for treason for withholding information. The Procreates would also have Mother and Father for treason simply for knowing the journal existed and not turning it over to them.

My thoughts multiplied as I tried to make sense of

the situation. I retraced my steps from last night to that moment, but it still didn't make any sense. I left the house to meet Mel. We sat in the rain on the shoreline. She and I then found the house. Wait, we didn't find the house. She already knew where it was. She didn't falter one step, I remembered that. She knew exactly where she was taking us. How did she know where to take us? How long had she known about the house and the secret path before taking me? Why did she wait to show me? I continued to question every thought that came.

We found the house, and right before going inside, I blacked out. But then where did Mel go and how did I get all the way back to the edge of the valley? Surely she wouldn't have just left me passed out alone. Without a search party, it would've taken Mother and Father days to find me, and that's if they got lucky. Something wasn't right. Something was off, very off. One of them knew something I didn't. Or both.

I thought through it over and over and played every scenario in my mind to get it all to make sense. None of the scenarios made sense, but that didn't mean they weren't possible. Where were Mother and Jo? Mother never told me where she was going. Jo had left the house, and Father said she and Mother were together. Was it possible Mother and Jo found me? Followed me? Then went back to get Father to help carry me home? Physically, neither Mother nor Jo could have carried me through the hollows on her own. Mother was smart enough that she could have figured out a way to get me back without anyone knowing, but she still wasn't strong enough, not all that way by herself. I would have had multiple injuries from being dragged, and I didn't have a scratch on me. I was carried. I must have been carried. Where was Mel during all of this? Where was she right now? I needed to find her.

I changed out of my damp, dirty clothes and put on a dry set so that I wouldn't ruin the newly-made bed. Looking at the fresh bedsheets reminded me that Father and Mother still didn't know the truth about what happened between Jo and me. *It's still too soon to tell them,* I thought.

I placed the partially-wrapped journal in the middle of the bed and paced, deciding whether or not to read it. This was different than speaking with John. He allowed me to have the short conversations with him I'd had. This felt like a direct invasion of privacy, but his journal could contain imperative information about who he was and where he came from, and I needed more answers. There had to be a reason John had this on him. He wanted me to read it. He was trying to tell me more. A part of me knew this journal would change everything. Maybe that was exactly what we needed.

He wants me to read it, I convinced myself.

I gently peeled back the cloth I had wrapped around the wet journal. It was a bit drier but still in a delicate state. In the dark of the holding cells, when I'd found it, the magnitude of this small notebook hadn't quite hit me. There in broad daylight with it laid on the bed in our house, it seemed so much larger than itself.

I inspected the cover, both front and back, for any discernable markings but found nothing. I carefully opened the notebook. There were three markings on the inside cover's bottom left corner, initials most likely, but the water had smudged away any legibility. I feared it was too late and the rest of the journal would be the same. I was wrong. It was immaculate. The rest of the journal was entirely legible through and through. I sat on the bed with the journal in my hand and started from the beginning.

There are dark corners in everyone's mind.

The Journal

Have you ever seen the streets run red? Today, I saw blood spilled onto the concrete. It spread thick and quick like a knocked over pail of paint. Of course, it was an accident. Suicide is illegal. Evidently, someone fell from the top of a midrise building, a maintenance worker. It was hard to tell from where I was standing if it was a man or a woman. Hard to tell because their head was cracked open face down and covered with blood.

They wore a plain blue colored jumpsuit giving no indication whether they were a male or female. The blood sprawled out eagerly in any direction it wanted, it was free. Thinned out by the searing heat from the pavement made it spread even more freely. I watched the retrievers try to remove the body out of site as quick as possible. It was a rehearsed routine, like a dance.

The retrievers wore white outfits that covered them head to toe much like hazmat suits, which seemed funny knowing how difficult it is to get red stains out. Whoever made their uniforms was either a stupid optimist or a masochistic genius. The uniform conundrum brought a cornered smile to my face.

I stayed in the distance under the willow trees. I continued to watch long after others left. After they vacated the body the more difficult task of cleaning the blood laid before them. The retrievers repeatedly slipped in the shiny puddle of blood, and each time they fell, I covered my mouth with both my hands to stifle my laughter.

Liv

For a while, Pete sits in the quiet darkness with me. We sit for so long we almost fall asleep on my kitchen floor. I'm starting to think I'm only going to have to explain part of the story, but that's wishful thinking.

At the end of a deep yawn, Pete says, "What about the gene reports?" He says it as casually as asking someone what they want for breakfast.

God damnit. There's no way out of this one. He's all in now. I hope he hasn't read the entire report, but I know he's a better detective than that. I'd be asking him to commit treason if we find Dani and he doesn't turn her in. The reports not only prove Dani's bloodlines but also expose that she has the twenty-fourth gene. Which she undoubtably inherited from me.

Whether violence is a product of nature or nurture has always been a button-pushing topic. Up until infection rates peaked, it was just that, something that lit a fire under people's asses. But everyone was able to sleep at night because the answer wasn't provable, which meant people still believed they had a chance of controlling the outcome.

An enormous amount of energy and resources went into trying to find a scientific way to determine whether violence is inherited. To everyone's surprise, after centuries of debate, Novyx scientists found an answer: they discovered the twenty-fourth gene. The twenty-fourth gene is responsible for indicating if an individual has an inherited predisposition for violence. It was groundbreaking, and it was all based on Novyx's award winning research into epigenetics. Once Novyx announced they had reliable data ensuring unmistakable positive identification of the twenty-fourth gene, it was game over. Novyx seemed to have found the answer to everyone's fears, and they made promises to take away those fears.

All the twenty-fourth gene is to me is a fucking scapegoat, a parcel of peace for a country in peril. Novyx came out with their data at just the right moment, yet no one questioned the timing of their discovery. Everyone was just happy something was finally in their control, but it never was really in the people's hands. I can't blame the public, though. I really can't. It was the answer to a lot of people's questions. For everyone else, it was a solution to the most pressing obstacle we faced: eradicating violence.

The Superstorm didn't drown out the infection. It just amped it up even higher. People who had little before the Superstorm survived with nothing, and those who had nothing before the Superstorm had a newfound sense of entitlement after it had ravaged the prosperous. For the first time in our city's history, we were all equal. From an economical stance, at least. The government was the only protected entity, but even its stockpiles were limited, and it was desperate to find a way to bring back means. After the Superstorm, the first task was the eradication of violence. An infection, Novyx had labeled it, and the best way to rid the city of infection was by targeting those identified as having the twenty-fourth gene.

Government officials had multiple ideas on how best to do that. The first was obvious: go loud and go hard, using force and fear. They quickly realized that would have the opposite effect of what they were trying to accomplish, and they were already facing an uphill battle.

They brought Pete and me in to consult, one of our first jobs as partners. We advised they do the opposite of their original plan. We advised they move quietly. Initially, our recommendations weren't received well, but we reassured the higher-ups that *quietly* didn't necessarily mean *slowly*. Quiet would lead to less resistance, which would ultimately speed up the process. A single blood bank somehow had gone unharmed during the Superstorm. We started there. We analyzed blood samples from individuals we already had access to, and if a sample tested positive for the twenty-fourth gene, we observed them for signs that the gene was manifesting violent behavior. It was quiet and peaceful and effective, but it wasn't quick enough for the government leaders. They demanded that we seize any individual who tested positive without observation or question. Pete and our team were ordered to go door to door, removing people from their own homes or their places of business by whatever means necessary.

Pete and I opposed the orders, but we were young cops with detective promotions within reach, and we'd already seen the administration make people who opposed them disappear. We have always been simply trying to survive. So, against our own natures, we followed orders. We knocked down doors. We chased people through the streets. We dragged people from their homes. We seized the so-called infected from their work desks. We held people down and used every scare tactic in the book. However, the results were inarguable. There was an immediate downward trend in violence. We had found a way to slow the infection.

We were making an impact on the rise of violence, and hope was reborn. It was the first semblance of hope we had seen since the infection's peak. It gave us a high that was indescribable. We weren't vigilantes; we were vindicators. We had ourselves convinced. It seemed we traded one addiction for another, which prompted the question whether one was truly better than the other.

To answer Pete's question about Dani and the gene, I have no response that won't implicate him in treason, and he knows it. Just the fact of him knowing what the reports contain and not acting instantly is treason. For better or worse, Pete is all in, whether or not that's what either of us wants. He meets my unresponsive silence with an approving nod, but we both know that if we started this day thinking we still had time, we were wrong. We have to make moves now, or Dani will be better off if we don't find her.

It wouldn't be Pete if he didn't have one more question before leaving. "So, whatever became of Michael?

I allow myself one last, sorrowful sigh and let it all go. "Michael. Michael is what I called him. He died a day after I left the hospital. I never got to say goodbye."

Pete knows I'm not one for sympathy, and this is all more than I'd ever planned on sharing with anyone, so this will conclude Pete's questions, for now. I send him away, demanding that he rest, even if only for a few hours, so that he can refocus, but I really just need to get rid of him so that I can get my head right. I need to be focused. I tell him to wait for my call and remind him we still have the parade ahead of us. We both have more on our plates than we have room or time for, yet that's when we both perform at our best. I have another hurtle I need to surmount if we're going to have any chance of saving my daughter. That hurtle is Hannah.

She likes to work on her own agenda. I don't know if she's actually going to show, and if she does follow through, it'll be on her time, regardless of what I ask of her. That's how it's always been with us.

We were Irish twins, a surprise to both our parents. They never openly admitted to us that I was unplanned, but it was evident in the way they raised us. In the way they favored Hannah. It was no secret she was the favorite. I didn't resent Hannah for it, but I'd be lying if I said I didn't resent our parents. It wasn't Hannah's fault I always got the short end of the stick. At least, to me, that's the way it seemed. Of course, Hannah would say I'm crazy and would roll her eyes in the same way our mother would when I used to ask the same question too many times. One of us was bound to become one of them.

Hannah has never been a patient person. One could argue that I'm rather impatient as well, but there's a distinct difference between being impatient and being resistant to bullshit. Hannah is impatient; I'm bullshit-resistant. She'll never admit it gave me a leg up, and it made for a tumultuous childhood for the two of us.

We had some good moments. Some memories are worth remembering, but as we grew up and apart, those moments and memories became more seldom. Hannah excelled in all the areas I did not, and so ensued an unintentional competition that would last our entire lives. Her accomplishments were praised as mine were cast in the shadows. Even then, I didn't blame her, but I had to be better than her. We were integral to each other's growth and success, but Hannah would never see it like that. She just kept topping off the top.

She's had me under her thumb for a long time. As our city's leader, she has reached the ultimate status amongst our family members and our peers. She now reigns supreme; it's what she's always wanted. She played the long game well and now holds all the keys and makes all the calls, including mine. Even still, she'll never admit to such smugness; it would be unbecoming. She has bigger fish to fry than sorting pettily through a complex sibling rivalry, that's how she'd explain it. I pity her, though, and she knows it. Despite all her success, she's never had as much as I've had, even with all my losses and shitty decisions. She is alone. She has always been alone. The one person she did have, she gave up on long ago.

***

It's not even 6 a.m., but sunlight spills into the kitchen, bouncing off the stainless-steel appliances, threatening to blind my tired eyes. My cell chirps from the other room. Low battery. I go to retrieve it to set it on the charging pad and hear another phone ringing in the distance. *My burner?* I question.

No one has the number to my burner; that's the entire point of having it. I walk suspiciously toward the ringing sound and lift up the couch cushion the phone has been crammed under. I don't recognize the number. I slide up the green phone symbol, and her voice comes through the other line.

"It's me." Her voice is calm and quiet.

Frozen midstance, I lower myself onto the couch for stability. "Dani? Sweetheart?"

"Did you find it, Olivia?"

It kills me when she calls me that. I bite my lip and fight the urge to release my usual response. "Baby, where are you? Are you okay? Can you tell me where you are?"

There's a knock on my door. *Fuck,* I think to myself.

"Is she there?" Dani asks.

"Who, Dani? Where are you? Tell me what you see. I'm coming to find you. Are you okay?"

"Not her. Don't let her in," Dani says.

The knocking is louder and less patient. It's Hannah. I feel it. How the hell does Dani know? There's no way she can possibly know who's at the door. I hold the burner to my ear and run to the door, trying not to lose them both.

"Talk to me, Dani! Talk to me. Tell me where you are. I'm coming…"

I reach for the deadbolt, and as I turn the doorknob to open the door, Dani says, "Come home, Olivia."

The line goes dead as the door opens. There on my threshold is my sister. I quickly slide the burner in my back pocket as Hannah pushes her way through the door.

"I said 7 a.m.," I say, standing with the door still wide open.

"Let's get to it," Hannah rushes.

It's been a few years, but she hasn't changed one bit. Her perfectly-styled, shoulder-length, brown hair brushes by me as she intentionally nudges me to the side with her shoulder. Despite heatwave temperatures, she's covered shoulder to shins like a new age nun. I sometimes wonder, between her heart and her head, if she's even human.

With the door still open, I grab my micro ID tablet. "I agree." I leave the door open as I walk out.

Hannah will have to follow. She showed up; that means she's going to see this through. Her type A personality won't allow her not to see something through. I can't risk wasting time after talking to Dani.

Come home. I play her words over and over in my head.

They make me wince as I struggle to keep memories of my past shoved down. It's that much more difficult with my sister so close that I could slap her. I hit the elevator button with my elbow, Hannah just a few steps behind. The elevator reads floor four and doesn't budge.

"God damnit," I say. "What's the fucking point of these fucking bullet elevators if they don't fucking move?" I head toward the stairwell.

"Liv," Hannah says behind me. "I can't go in there." She stops before the stairwell entrance.

I call over my shoulder, "Don't worry, sis. I'm not going to push you down."

I hear her muttering something behind me, but hearing her means she's following me. I know why she doesn't want to come in here. She's not supposed to be out of her security detail's eyesight. Even in the age of zero violence that I helped create, I, her sister, am still considered a threat to her. Although many silently scrutinize Hannah's revolutionary way of ruling, that's how she describes it. So in a way, I don't blame her security for acting like she carries a bullseye on her back.

*If people could have their way...*I find myself saying in my head. Choppers chatter right outside the thick brick walls.

"Way to be inconspicuous," I say aloud. If she doesn't want anyone to know she's here, she sure as shit fucked that up. Typical, though: she never missed an opportunity to make an entrance.

"You have until the bottom of the stairs to tell me what this is all about," Hannah clamors behind me. She's trying to remind me that, at the moment, her security service has no eyes on her. We have privacy. Why would she help? She showed up, but did she come only because she's afraid for Dani? There's always a hidden agenda with her. I run these questions through my mind and take advantage of what may be the only chance I have. I flip open my micro ID tablet to an image of a baby, my niece, and hold it up inches from Hannah's face. She stares hard and then slaps me in the face.

"Always beating me to the punch, sis," I say as the warmth of her hand spreads through my cheek.

She's never seen this picture, but speaking firsthand as a mother who's lost a child, you never forget the face of your baby.

"How dare you," Hannah spits out. She had never raised a hand to me, not out of compassion or self-restraint, but rather because of her own laws. I see the anger in her eyes. I've lit the fire, and she feels its burn.

Still holding the picture up to her face, I step in closer. "How fucking dare *you*."

"You shouldn't have done it if you couldn't see it through," Hannah sneers.

"Easy for you to say. You weren't the one who had to do it. You wouldn't be who you are if I hadn't seen it though," I say through my teeth. "You. Owe. Me. Hannah. You're going to call off your men, and you're going to get in my fucking car."

She scoffs in my face.

"Dani knows. She's missing, and she knows, Hannah. She knows. If you don't help me, I swear to God, I will ruin you. You may have given up your daughter, but I'm not giving up mine."

Stanton

By the time I finished reading the journal, the pages were dry, and the meal mother had left by the door was frigid. I must have read John's journal cover to cover twenty times to try making sense of it all. It didn't make sense, though. It was the ramblings of a madman, but there had to be a reason he carried it with him all this way, from wherever he came from. Pages in the back had been ripped from the binding, and it drove me crazy not knowing if those pages held anything of significance. Part of me wished the missing pages were the key to unlocking the nonsense in the rest of it, but the other part of me wished it was meaningless; either way, I'd have an answer just good enough to lay John to rest.

I had to find Mel. She'd know what to do with this. She'd always been able to make sense out of the things I couldn't.

I felt underwhelmed by the information I had read and frankly a little guilty for placing the urgency of finding Mel secondary to the disappointing and anticlimactic content of John's journal. I made quick movements to make up for the time spent on reading and not searching. While there were still the questions of where John came from, how he got here, and what was on the missing pages of his journal, I had forgotten what my purpose was to begin with: I still had to give the Procreates an update. Once I found Mel, we'd have time to talk about the house again. If it was real, and not just a vision in my head, then it'd still be there when I found Mel.

I thought getting dressed and acting as though the disappointment I felt was just temporary would ease my distress, but the more I tried to block out my frustration the stronger its presence grew. I had spent my entire life acting, pretending, in order to avoid calling attention to myself or my family. But if what was written in John's journal was true, if his world was as oppressive as ours, and if people there were just living a mirrored life of ours, then what was the god damned point of living anywhere at all? John's journal made it evident that everything I had held out for here had no chance: every hope for a better life, every hope for something new, every hope for the truth. What would be the point of breaking the Den if it just led us to another one? I was angry at John. Angry at him for sending me down a rabbit hole with no way out. Angry at him for giving me hope that didn't exist. I was angry at myself for believing what he said meant more than just the words he spoke. Nothing John told me made any sense. It had no purpose; it meant nothing. All had been for nothing. The anger swelled from my stomach to my lungs and through my chest. It spread warmth through my body and out through my head, and I felt myself perspire as my body flared from the inside out. My hands tensed into tight fists.

Mother was waiting for me at the table when I opened the bedroom door, the plate in my hand still untouched. She looked at me disapprovingly, and I set the plate down.

"I'm sorry, Mother. I'm just not hungry," I snapped at her.

"I don't care if you're hungry, Stanton. You need to eat." She pushed the chair out with the tip of her foot.

Mother's sternness was always well-intentioned. I knew she appreciated that Jo and I had been easy children for her to raise. We didn't argue, we followed the rules for the most part, and we didn't stir the pot. It made for quite a boring household, though, and life, for that matter. I felt more alive with the dead. Just the thought of possibly discovering something unknown gave me a reason to keep going, to keep waking up every day. To keep following the Den's relentless oppressiveness. To allow myself and the ones I loved to live a life of constant degradation. It made it all worth it, the chance that there was something more. But there wasn't. Not according to John's journal. Part of me felt mocked.

I stared at the chair Mother had pushed out. The chair and my mother both waited for me to take my appointed seat. Mother and I locked eyes, and her vision shifted as she recognized the precipice of oncoming defiance. Clearly, she already knew what was going to happen and seemingly welcomed it.

Was that a smile? I thought to myself.

I slammed the full plate down on the ground where it shattered, spraying bits of gruel back up onto my face.

"I won't goddamn sit down, Mother!" I yelled, terrified by the sound of my own raised voice. My eyes widened, sweat beaded on my forehead, and my pulse raced, but my mother's disposition remained unchanged. She simply uncrossed and recrossed her legs. "You're just going to sit there?" I screamed. "Why aren't you stopping me?"

I grabbed chunks of congealed gruel off the floor and threw them around the room. Her expression didn't change. She sat in the same composed, legs-crossed position and watched me go from zero to sixty. She just let me, and with that I became unhinged.

I stormed into the bedroom and ripped the sheets off the bed, tearing them with my teeth until the shreds couldn't be torn anymore and my jaws ached. I grabbed a pen off the small nightstand and stabbed the mattress again and again, lifting my arm up high and jamming it back down into the soft mattress until the pen broke in half.

I wrapped the shreds from the torn sheets around my hands and punched the wall over and over until my fists went straight through. My arm viciously swiped everything off the large dresser in the room, and I ripped out a drawer and tried to break it over my leg, cutting my thigh open. My blood oozed out slowly, and the rage continued to flow along with it.

Back in the kitchen, I emptied every cabinet, smashing anything breakable I could find. I picked up the entire ice box and threw it with all my strength, spilling its contents out over the floor. I turned around, a red-faced madman; my chest burned through my clothes, and blood trickled down my leg. I walked across the shiny, gruel-coated floor, leaving a trail of red behind me. Picking up a piece of jagged, broken dish I'd shattered, I stood up slowly and saw my mother through the red. She still did nothing. I ran my finger over the sharp, broken edge of the shard. I pressed it into my fingertip until a small pool of red blood collected in my hand. Looking at my mother, I brought the edge of the shard up to my throat and held it there while she just stared.

"Go ahead. Do it," she said in a calm voice, raising her eyebrows.

"What?" I said in confusion. My ears rang in disbelief. My hand held the makeshift knife at my own throat even tighter, and I felt a warm trickle down my arm as the room began to spin.

"If that's what you want, Stanton, I'm not going to stop you."

In a last fit of rage, I swung the sharp blade around me, blindly slicing through the air above, below, and beside me. The newly-familiar feeling of my chest readying itself to explode was overcome as my throat started closing, and the air was sucked right out of my lungs. I dropped the broken dish and crumpled to the cold, bloody floor. I rolled over, face up, and a vision flashed like a bolt of lightning across sky: unspeakable violence and dead, bloodied bodies everywhere, and there in the heap lay Jo…

***

I awoke lying flat out on my back. When I opened my eyes, the nightmare before my blackout remained. I looked around the demolished room and down at my hands and legs, which were covered in blood. The taste of metal coated my dry, chapped mouth as I tried to pry it open to speak. My lips split, coating my mouth with a fresh layer of warm blood.

Too soon to speak, I said to myself. I tried to sit up, and the unforgiving, self-inflicted vertigo fought my body back to the ground. It was too soon for that, too. I looked at Mother, lying on the floor next to me, her face towards mine, her eyes wide open.

"There's something we need to talk about," she said calmly. Her soothing voice settled me like it had when I was a child. The power of a mother's voice is undeniable. I turned to my side, lay my head on Mother's stomach, and listened to her speak.

"You remember your father and me as we have painted ourselves to be remembered. But your father and I, we are imposters. We are very different than who

136

you know us to be, and it's time you start learning who we really are."

Liv

"They're going to come for us Liv," Hannah says.

"Jesus, Hannah. It's not like I'm kidnapping you."

"That's not what they think," she responds, looking up at the helicopter that has followed us since we exited the side door of my building.

My fingers tap anxiously on the steering wheel. "Call them off. I told you already."

She shakes her head. "You know I can't do that."

"Well, what the fuck, Hannah?"

"It will implicate you even more," she says snidely, looking down at her smashed mini microphone.

"It had to be done. You know it."

"We can still stop. We can stop, and I'll explain to them that you were just a little too excited to reunite. I won't charge you—"

I push my foot down harder on the gas. "When have I ever been excited to see you, Hannah? They'll know you're lying right away. Go ahead, charge me with whatever the fuck you want. I'm not afraid of you." Hannah always tries to set the pulse of a conversation, like she does everything else, but she isn't going to control me this time. This time, I'm in the driver's seat. "I have some questions for you, too, while we're at it," I demand.

She just stares out the window, watching as her concrete jungle of a city flies by us. Fifteen years with no rain has wreaked havoc on the city's foundation. Things can't grow without water, and anything that could have has cracked and crumbled in the brutal, incessant heat. Our resources are limited, and they all go toward furbishing the city. Appearances have to be kept up, very in line with Hannah Jones.

The farther we move from the city, the less aesthetic our surroundings are and the coarser the roads become. As I drive, the streets become riddled with lesions, and only the city's fuel fog remains in our rearview.

"What's beyond the fault lines?"

Nothing but silence, so I push down harder on the gas.

"What's beyond the fault lines, Hannah?" I weave between potholes that she's chosen to ignore and that are now coming to haunt her.

She covers her mouth, trying to keep her shame buried down deep. Come hell or high water, I'm going to get the truth out of her. I continue to swerve at suicide speeds until she vomits out the window. She doesn't quite make it all the way out, and some of it flies back onto her perfectly made-up face and her neatly-pressed white pants. I'm not even bothered by the stench of it all; just seeing her a mess for once makes me smile. She catches a glimpse of my enjoyment and continues the silent treatment while scraping her own vomit out of the tangled strands of her hair.

"What do I need to do to get you to turn that goddamn helicopter around?"

"I'm not playing your games, Liv. I should've never come."

"Why did you come then, Hannah? I mean, what did you think this was going to be? A happy reunion? When's the last time either of us reached out unless we needed something?" I pause, but she has nothing to say. "You remember the last time I saw you?" No response. "You were being sworn in and—"

"I remember," she says, grinding her teeth. She spits vomit along the dashboard. Wiping a stray strand of saliva from her mouth, she sneers, "What gives you the right, Liv? You have no right to call me out here, to take me against my will with no explanation. I'm not just going to sit here and take your shit!"

"Let it out!" I yell with eyes wide open, pressing down harder on the gas.

"You're crazy, Liv. You're goddamn crazy."

"If I'm crazy, then what does that make you?" I laugh while bobbing back and forth again between giant potholes. Hannah grabs for the door's armrest to stabilize herself, so I swerve a little harder to the left and tap her head on the window.

"You fucking crazy bitch!" she screams. I swerve again and her head taps a little harder. "I'll fucking kill you!"

"There she is! There's my sister!" I yell with glee.

She throws heavy punches at my arm and claws at my neck and face. I press both feet down hard on the brakes, sending the car into a three-sixty. We both grab the 'oh shit' handles as we spin out in the middle of the concrete jungle, just the two of us and her helicopter. We're both out of breath when the car finally comes to a screeching halt. The smell of burnt rubber stings our nostrils. We're one, just for a moment, in fear. The sound of the chopper straight above pulls us out of the moment. Hannah looks at me with wild hair, makeup running down her face, and vomit on her clothes. I haven't seen her look this real in a lifetime. Unsure what she's going to do next, I have no choice at this point but to let her make her own decision. We both knew I wasn't going to be able to outrun the chopper.

Without a word she opens the passenger door and climbs out with purpose. She strides without faltering to the front of the car. My foot rests lightly on the gas pedal. She waves her arms up above her head, and I'm not sure what signal she gives, but the chopper lingers for only a minute before backing off. She watches from outside the car; I watch from the driver's seat. We both stay where we are until the chopper is out of sight.

She looks at me through the windshield and then walks up to the driver's side. "I'm driving."

I unbuckle my seatbelt and shift over to the passenger seat. She gets in without readjusting anything. I point to the gearshift. "You have to press the clutch and—"

She peels the tires on the pavement and the car jolts backward, sending me flying into the vomit-covered dash. I struggle to get my seatbelt on. I can tell she's pleased with herself.

Smiling, she says, "I got it."

She drives faster than I did, which surprises me. Hannah has always been the slow and steady type. When Dad was teaching her how to drive, and I was forced to go along because Mom needed 'mom time,' it was me in the backseat listening to our dad berate her for not being able to park right the first time, every time. I learned from the backseat how to drive even before having to endure those lessons with Dad. Just because Hannah was the favored child doesn't mean it was always sunshine and rainbows for her. Being the favorite wasn't always what she wanted, and I could understand that. Who wants to feel like they need to be perfect just to be loved? Hannah shouldn't take all the blame for how she turned out.

"Where are you going?" I ask her.

Her eyes are set on the horizon, and I can tell her gears are grinding away. "You want to go to the house, right?"

Confused I say, "Yeah, but..." I look behind us. "The house is that way," I point through the back window.

She doesn't take her eyes off the horizon. "No, it's

not."

Now more confused, I turn around to look behind us again. "No, Hannah, we aren't going the right way. We have to take 88 to get there."

"I know where 88 is," she snaps and then pauses. I can tell she's having some sort of internal debate. "It's not there anymore."

"What?" Shaking my head, the frustration creeps in. "What do you mean?"

"You asked about the fault lines?"

"Yeah?" I look out the window and realize I don't recognize the surroundings. It still looks like the same concrete jungle, but it isn't.

"They move," she says, unsure if she's making the right decision in telling me.

"What moves? The fault lines?"

"Yes, Liv. How else do you want me to explain it to you? They move, they fucking move, and they move everything with them." Her fists wrapped tightly around the steering wheel. I hear the leather stretching under her grip.

I shake my head. It's not possible. "No, that can't be right. I've been there. You know that. What aren't you telling me, Hannah?"

"I'm telling you the truth, Liv. We found out the fault lines aren't fixed. They shift. They move. They grow. When we completed our early expeditions, we set markers to map out the new terrain. The Superstorm had shifted the land, and we came upon the fault lines by accident when we were re-mapping. So, we marked them and went back to the city. Didn't think twice about it. But the next time the expedition team went back to remeasure, none of the markers were there, and the atmospheric readings were completely different."

"But you said the fault lines were walked end to end."

She takes her eyes off the road intentionally. "I lied. It's physically impossible to go end to end. We followed the fault lines from what we thought was start to finish, but every time we went back the design had changed, expanded, and things that weren't there before were there and then gone the next time. It just keeps changing. Every time we go back."

"How long have you known this? How long have you kept this from me?"

"I didn't know what it meant. I still don't know what it means."

"Well, how can you say that now? How could you do this, Hannah? All those missing people? How could you do this? Take me there, now."

"That's where we're going. That's where the house is, so that's where we're going."

The magnitude of what Hannah has just told me isn't quite registering. I keep seeing the faces of missing people flashing through my mind. All the missing persons photos littering the tunnels. All the lies we told about not finding anything or anyone at the fault lines. We never found anything because we didn't bother to look. We trusted Hannah's expedition teams to report any missing persons, dead or alive. Our missing persons board, neglected, layers upon layers of pictures of the missing…not a single one has been found. Not one.

What the hell happened to me? I ask myself. *I never would've given up so easily back in the day.* I can't breathe; it feels like invisible hands are wrapped around my neck. I open the window, but the stifling heat makes me feel queasier. *No,* I say to myself and swallow my vomit along with my fear of acceptance.

"Tell me more," I say through my clenched jaw.

"What do you want to know?" Hannah asks.

"Other than the house, what else has moved?"

She sighs. "We aren't sure about that either. We have expedition teams out regularly to investigate any changes or shifts in pattern. I really don't know, Liv. The university said the logical assumption is that when the Superstorm uprooted structures, it took whatever was in its path, and whatever wasn't taken by the waters or swallowed by the earth settled wherever it lay when the storm cleared. So far, every structure standing has been accounted for in its proper place, except for the house. The Superstorm must have taken it out, and it must've settled right by the fault lines. But since the fault lines shift, the house is never in the same place. We're working on finding out how it all makes sense and how the fault lines work."

"Are you fucking telling me that the fault lines are crossable? All these years, Hannah…"

"Not really."

"What? What does that mean? Well, why the fuck haven't you taken your choppers out there to find a way through?"

"We have. We've tried everything. We can't get more than a few miles past the fault lines before everything shuts down. Nothing can hold power past the first few miles, and the difference in temperature is extreme. It's well below freezing, and we don't have the necessary means or resources to survive on foot. I've lost five choppers, eighty trucks, fifty fuel tanks, months of provisions, and all the men that went along with the expedition parties. Before you accuse me of anything, they all volunteered. They knew what they were risking, and they still volunteered."

"Jesus Christ, Hannah. Jesus Christ. Where are the reports? What happened to their families?" My mind searches to make sense of all this new information. "What did you do, Hannah? What did you do to those people?"

"I told you, they volunteered. They knew there was a possibility they wouldn't return."

"Where are their bodies? What did you tell their families?"

She doesn't respond.

"What did you do, Hannah? Where are their families? Their spouses? Their children? What did you do with them? You got rid of them all, didn't you? So they wouldn't ask questions? So they wouldn't spread the word that you don't know what the fuck is going on?"

Still no response.

"Why was I never told any of this information? My men and I should've been part of the expedition teams. We have agreements in place, Hannah, agreements that you mandated." I pause, realizing the agreements with the remaining authorities were made with only one side in mind. Hannah set us up, and we all took the bait. Embarrassed, insulted, and downright horrified, I murmur, "After everything I've done for you..."

With her nose and chin turned up, she replies, "You were kept out of this for the same reason you've never been able to keep yourself out of trouble. You're too impulsive, which makes you a liability."

"A liability? Like your daughter?"

"Let's talk about why we're really here, Liv," she says, settling back into herself.

"Turn around, Hannah," I say, realizing the terror of the situation I've put myself in. I anxiously look around us as Hannah speeds up. The surroundings whip past us as I reach for the door handle. She speeds up even more.

"Uh-uh, I wouldn't do that if I were you. Not unless

you want your body ripped to shreds by the pavement."

"You're fucking crazy."

She's enjoying herself. She's enjoying watching me realize this was exactly what she had hoped would happen.

"You said something about Dani earlier…"

"Don't you say her name," I threaten.

"You said Dani knows. I believe your exact words were, *she's missing, and she knows*."

The only way to beat Hannah is to stoop to her level. To disarm her. The rage wells inside me, but I can't let her see it. I have to control myself for Dani. I realize now how much danger Dani is in.

"Why are you asking so much about Dani? I can count on one hand the number of times you've asked how your niece is doing."

"Isn't that why you called me? Because you want my help to find your daughter? So, let's find her. She has something of mine. I need it back."

"I never said Dani was missing until after you showed up this morning." I try to divert the conversation.

"I have news for you, sis. You're not as good a detective as you think you are. I already knew long before you called me that Dani was missing. Longer than you've known, apparently. Some mother you are.

"Some mother I am? Some. Mother. *I*. Am?" My control is slipping. I clench my fists and bury my nails

148

in my palms until I feel them break the skin. "What about you, Hannah? There isn't enough brainwashing technology in this world to make you forget."

She's silent. The slightest downshift in speed follows the familiar sound of her hand wrought tight around the leather steering wheel.

"Oh, wait. That's right. Nobody knows. No one is supposed to know. Is that still the story? That no one is supposed to know about your bastard child that you abandoned and had me pay off Sasha to take care of? To cover up for you for years so you could win, so you could be the best? How would your confidants feel knowing they swore in a fraud? How would your citizens feel realizing they've been blindly following a hypocritical monster? A monster who has gone against everything we've preached for the last fifteen years. Everything we have hidden from the public. You had a chance to redeem yourself, Hannah. You had a chance. When Sasha died, you could've made everything right. Melanie was still young enough that she wouldn't have remembered anything. People would've forgiven you for lying to them. They would've understood." I look at her stone-cold face. "But you couldn't bring yourself to do it. I don't know what's worse: you spending a lifetime convinced you did the right thing or me helping to cover up a lifetime of your mistakes." I rest my tired head in my hands, defeated. "I mean Jesus Christ, Hannah. We sent her to be slaughtered."

"The Den isn't a slaughterhouse," she responds.

"It may as well be. You know you never had any intention of bringing anyone back from there. Is that where you sent all those missing people? All those people who couldn't find you the answers you were looking for? All those people who asked the wrong questions?"

She smiles coyly to herself. She has the look of the evil in her eyes. "I don't know about all those missing people, Olivia, but maybe there's a reunion over there for you yet."

"What are you trying to say?"

To my horror she replies, "Are you sure your son died all those years ago?"

Stanton

The curve of my spine cried out for a good stretch. I sat up against my body's will but made it to a seated position. I stretched my arms up toward our low ceiling and latched my hands behind my neck, pushing my elbows as far back as they would go. My spine let out an audible crack, thanking me for the much-needed movement, which wasn't going to last long.

"Get comfortable, Stanton."

"Mother, I need to find Mel."

She looked at me. "You need to apologize, Stanton."

"I'm sorry, Mother," I said, lying back down on the floor next to her. I really meant it. In my fit of fury, I had been...out-of-body was the only way I could describe it. I'd seen red and nothing else. I was ashamed, but at the same time I felt a strange sense of satisfaction. My mind went back to the questions I'd had before reading John's journal. So many things didn't make sense.

Mother hadn't moved from her spot on the ground. She was still, and her eyes were wide open as though she was searching for a deeper level of relaxation.

"What did you see, Mother?" I asked.

"What do you mean?"

"Just now."

She paused thoughtfully and replied, "I saw you, baby. I saw you."

She had never called me anything other than my name. I looked at her, my face cocked in a confused distortion. "Mother, I'm not a baby."

She gave a little laugh. "I know, Stanton. It's just a saying." Her eyes fixated on me. She took a long gaze at me, and I couldn't understand why she wasn't blinking, like she was afraid to close her eyes. She had stared at me long and listlessly before, but this was a different sort of stare. It felt different. It felt like she was remembering something and saying goodbye at the same time. It reminded me of the open eyes of the dead, longing to reveal themselves while leaving their last looks behind. When I spoke with them in my mind, like when I spoke with John, the dead still felt alive. So much so that sometimes I couldn't tell the difference.

"Mother," I said, looking at her, unsure of what was happening. "I really need to find Mel. And I need to see the Procreates; they're expecting me."

"They can all wait. You listen to your mother now. If there's anything you hold onto, just remember this: you are our son. Your father and I love you. Everything we have done has been to protect you. It always has been and always will be to protect you."

I knew little about who Mother and Father were before the Den and even less about who they were in the Den. Who they became wasn't who they were before, and I thought a part of her already knew I'd been expecting this conversation or at the very least been waiting for an explanation for why I was the way I was.

"I know," I said taking her hand in mine. And with that, she took me into her world.

***

The day Stanton was born, my life and Lyman's life changed forever. The Superstorm was growing; he was born just a few weeks before it hit. I was a nurse, a special kind of nurse. A NICU nurse was what I was called. I worked with newborn babies who were born before their time, premature babies.

When Lyman and I met, he was a private investigator, but before that he had been a police officer in Old Chicago for many years. Police officers where we were from were like Lyman and the militia here in the Den, except where we came from, the cops were more organized and functional with access to resources necessary to do their jobs. When he was a police officer in Old Chicago, he had a partner he was very close with. She had no interest in smalltime crooks, and Lyman was drawn to that. He'd never been a small potatoes sort of man. They both had things they needed to prove to themselves. She found an ally in Lyman, which made their partnership effective and long-lasting. They worked together for many years.

Over time, though, his partner became more aggressive and extreme in the tactics she used to capture criminals, and it deteriorated their relationship. She became more violent, more manipulative.

She convinced Lyman that the best way for him to contribute to their partnership was to be the brute force. They committed crimes in order to solve crimes. When Lyman realized how corrupt his partner had become, it was too late for her, and he was too involved. In the middle of their last case together, his partner left, which was very unusual. He described her work ethic as a fault in her character. She was obsessed with her work, so for her to leave mid-case was a red flag. He tailed her to a small town in Connecticut where he found out she was involved in something darker than he could have ever imagined.

He uncovered that she was there because a childhood friend of hers had been murdered. That wasn't the worst of it: the murdered woman had a child who was missing, but he found out the missing child never belonged to the dead woman. After searching for answers about the missing child, Lyman realized his partner was part of a cover up that, if revealed, would cause Old Chicago's downfall.

***

I let go of Mother's hand. I knew what she was getting to, but she was still holding something back.

She answered the question I was thinking. "What do you remember about Mel?"

My own breath must have gone unnoticed because

when I went to speak, it was as though the air had been taken from my lungs. I took a cleansing breath and answered, "I remember when she and I were children."

"How young, Stanton, do you remember? What was your first memory with Melanie?"

I answered easily, "When her mother died. And you gave me the shell to give to her."

"That would have made you five years old, and Melanie would've been six. How much do you know about Melanie? Have you ever wondered why you have no memory of her before you were five?"

Mother was right. I tried to think of an earlier memory of Mel, but I couldn't. I had memories well before age five, but Mel wasn't in them. "I always sensed she was different, like me. But she couldn't speak with the dead; she would've told me. I always thought she would tell me her story when she was ready."

Mother replied, "You're right, Stanton. She can't speak with the dead, but she is different like you because she's one of the only children here who wasn't born in the Den." She stopped to let this sink in.

What mother was telling me didn't make any sense. "So, she was in the library with us then?" I asked, trying to convince myself.

Unblinking, Mother said, "We weren't the first ones here. There were others already here, in the Den, when we arrived. We just didn't realize it at first. To be honest, it was so chaotic when everything happened, we didn't really know who went down there with us and who came out after, let alone who belonged and who didn't. We did the best we could with what we had in the mayhem we were tossed into. We took record of every person we could find who survived the transition to the Den. Stanton, you were the only child who survived."

"Which means Melanie was already here. That doesn't make any sense. How is that possible?" My voice was rising.

"I'm trying to explain," she said slowly, trying to keep me calm. "Please try to stay calm. We don't want you to…" she stopped mid-sentence.

"Black out?" I asked.

She just stared at me. "We don't have all the answers, Stanton. We've been searching ever since we transitioned here for answers. But you had to have known, Stanton. You never stopped to ask yourself as we grew our civilization where all the people came from? Think about how many people are here now. There's no way we all came from that basement. There are people here unaccounted for from day one who are older than the amount of time we've spent here. How did they get here? Just by numbers alone, only so many bodies can fit into that basement. Some people ended up here in ways we don't know about. And that's what we've been trying to find out. For eighteen years, your father and I have been working in secret to find the answers. You're incredibly smart; this much you must have figured out. Where do you think Father goes every month for days at a time? Yes, some months he goes with his militiamen and sweeps the Den for new resources or terrain changes, but they don't go every month. Between those times, your Father searches for answers to the unknown. It's in his blood, and yours, too."

Answers were beginning to form. "Mrs. Rappaport wasn't Melanie's mother, was she? What exactly have you and Father been searching for?"

"No, she wasn't her mom. And your Father and I, for the last eighteen years, have been looking for a way to get out of the Den. The Procreates keep the count system for more than just tallying people. They do it because they know there has to be a way in, which means there must be a way out. They've been lying to us all this time. I know you know this. Back in Old Chicago, your father found out that the missing child of his partner's childhood friend was Melanie, and Melanie was his partner's niece. Melanie's biological mother didn't want her, so your father's partner paid another woman to pretend she was Melanie's mom. Your father says he never thought his partner would've done it had she not believed she could get away with it. The woman pretending to be Melanie's mother was murdered at a time in our world when violence was out of control. Melanie's biological mother refused to reunite with her, and your father's partner feared the worst for her niece if she stayed in our world. There was only one option for her, your dad said."

"She sent her here," I said. "But how? When? The Den wasn't created until we arrived." Her gaze appeared now to look through me. "Mother, what else aren't you telling me?"

"I told myself you were ready," I heard her say quietly to herself.

I held her hand again to remind her that I was still there with her. As we held hands, sorrow connected us.

"Your dad." I'd never heard her call my father *dad* so much. "He didn't stop tailing her from that moment on. He felt a deep distrust and betrayal, but even more so, he felt his partner had to be taken off her pedestal, and he couldn't do it under her eye. He believed that if she was capable of something like that, what else was she capable of? She had become a monster in his eyes, and he became invested in keeping her from any further violation of life. He gave up his career with the police force so that he could solely focus on the crimes of his partner. His instincts told him there was much more to her than he knew and that she was a danger to the city."

She took a long pause. I could tell the more she divulged the more she questioned if she was doing the right thing. I reassured her that she was. "Please, Mother, I can take it." The truth was so close I could taste it. What I'd been waiting to hear my entire life was resting on the tip of her tongue, and I might never get this opportunity again.

"That investment turned into a vow when you were born. You were so mighty. All two and half pounds of you. You were perfect in every way. You tried to leave us multiple times, but you fought your way back every time."

I touched my chest and felt my scar through my shirt.

"The world was not a good place when you were born. We had to do what we could with what we had, and it wasn't much. You were born twelve weeks early. There are so many complications that can happen that early on. It was a miracle you survived birth, let alone all the things that immediately followed. You were born sleeping. We spent an hour trying to resuscitate you. We were calling your death when you opened your eyes ever so slightly and started breathing. Your breaths were short and shallow, but you were alive. You had come back from the dead. But you were sick. Very sick. You were born with a disease called familial dilated cardio—"

"Myopathy," Mother and I said together.

"How did you…?"

"Keep going," I nodded.

Mother was distracted by my surprise knowledge, but she continued. "You needed open-heart surgery immediately. You needed a pacemaker to help keep you alive, and there was a high risk you wouldn't even make it through the procedure. Afterwards, the doctors said that with extensive medical treatment you might see your first year of life at most."

She had to stop to collect herself. In my eighteen years of life, I'd never once seen my mother shed a tear. I could see she wasn't going to let this moment be any different.

"You spent the first few hours of your life fighting harder to live than anyone I have ever known. There was no giving up in you, and there never has been. If anyone deserved every opportunity to live, it was you. I watched you every day. I watched you change and grow stronger. You defied every medical expectation given your condition, but the threat was still present since you also had a condition called tachycardia."

"Explains the blackouts, "I said.

"Yes," she responded.

"And here I thought it was because I just had too many feelings." I tried to force a smile, but we both recognized that wasn't going to change the course of the conversation.

Her expression didn't change. "Your pacemaker was only a temporary solution; you needed a heart transplant. The doctor's original approximation of your life expectancy was a generous prediction, and it was made before your tachycardia was officially diagnosed.

Your end of life was approaching. You had just a few weeks at most without a heart transplant, and it needed to be successful to give you a fighting chance of survival. I felt defeated when I heard the news. After everything you had gone through and everything we had done, you still faced the same odds. Death was your destiny. All we could do at that point was make you feel as comfortable as possible."

I looked down at her. "Why do you keep saying *we*."

Caught off guard, she asked, "What do you mean?"

"You keep saying *we*, Mother, but I haven't heard you say one thing about Father being there in the hospital when I was born."

She fought to keep her eyes open. "He was there. Not the entire time, Stanton. I think you know where this story is heading." Her voice asked for mercy and forgiveness before even admitting the truth. I always knew we were different; I just never got one piece to fit into the other because too many pieces were missing. But the puzzle was coming together now.

"Tell me, Mother. The truth. We all deserve it."

"How long have you known?"

"Your eyes are brown. Father's eyes are brown. Josephine's eyes, they're brown too." She gave no sign of being surprised by my revelation; we both knew she shouldn't have been. "Mother, it's scientifically impossible for you and Father to have created a blue-eyed child. I mean, not entirely impossible, nothing ever is, but impossible enough."

A small smile crept across her face, but it was like a micro-expression; I couldn't even be certain I'd really seen it. "How do you know so much about that? I never taught you that."

"Believe it or not, Mother, you're not the only one around here with secrets." We were slipping away from the course I wanted to stay on, the course my mother had set out on. I circled us back. I needed to know the rest of her story as much as she needed to tell the truth. "Please, keep going." I needed to hear her say it.

Her eyes stayed open in a seemingly-permanent meditative state. We both knew this next part wasn't going to be easy for her. "Once I realized the situation, I knew I needed to give your…"

She paused for a moment, and I said, "I need to hear you say it."

"I needed to give your biological mother the opportunity to spend time with you to say goodbye."

I watched as eighteen years of lies released from her body. The blinds finally lifted. It was like watching magic happen. In just one moment, my mother gained back eighteen years of her life, and for the first time in our lives, she allowed herself to be free. She finally rid herself of burdens she'd kept buried for too long, freeing herself from the shame she'd felt for lying for so many years and forgiving herself for the relationship we could've had that she never gave a chance.

To be the sort of mother she was isn't for the faint of heart. How does one love a child just enough to not love them too much? She walked a very clear line, until that moment. Maybe she was tired of all the lies and cover-ups. Maybe she just wanted an opportunity to have a normal relationship with two children she loved. Or maybe it was something else entirely. Either way, I knew I should be angry with her, disappointed in her and my father for lying to me my entire life. Under normal circumstances, what they'd done would have been unforgivable. But I wasn't normal. I never had been. And our lives had been anything other than ordinary. Who was to say that, despite the chaos of the situation, I didn't deserve the best? I was certain she and Father were just that for me when I needed it. As for the truth, it can be subjective at times, like love.

"You and Father are not my blood," I said.

"He is your father, and I'm your mother. There are times, Stanton, when blood is not the only thing that binds you to someone." A few large teardrops rolled down her temples. I lifted my mother's head as though she were a child.

I held her limp, tear-stained face in my hands and said, "Mother, I've known for a long time." Her glassy eyes searched my face for hope that I wouldn't let her go. Her face had an expression of surrender. "But I've been waiting a lifetime for you to tell me. So, thank you. I needed to hear it from your mouth." Loss spread across her face. "You are, and always have been, my mother." I looked at her with a wide, reassuring smile. "There's nothing you could do that would make me love you less. I am eternally grateful for you. You saved my life. Twice from the sounds of it," I said smiling. "I have been owed this explanation, but you have also been owed the freedom to unburden yourself."

She took peace in letting me take care of her, for once. Her head lay heavy in my lap, the rest of her body uncharacteristically slumped over. I unwrapped a shred of bloodied bedsheet from around my wounded hand and wiped her face clean as best I could. She let the emotions drain from her body and stared at me. "I am still your mother."

"Damn right you are," I said.

"Do me a favor, Stanton? Call me mom."

"Okay, Mom." I had many more questions she knew she'd have to answer. But there was a burning question I had to get off my chest first. "Does Jo know?"

"She doesn't know, Stanton."

"What are we going to do about that?" I asked with sincerity.

"What do you think we should do?"

I didn't quite know how to respond. Mother always called the shots, and it seemed she always knew exactly what to do. Jo and I never played a part in decision-making. In our family, the decisions were always made for us.

"Perhaps it's best we don't say anything to her yet?"

Mom's stillness answered. "I think you're right."

Having never had an opportunity to make choices, I wondered if it was as oddly freeing for someone like my mother to be released from the weight of always making them, right or wrong.

Needing the confirmation, I asked, "And Jo is…?"

"She is not your sister by blood," Mother said.

She must have noticed my relief at her confirmation. I thought now would be as good a time as any to impart the truth. "Nothing happened, Mom," I said.

"What?" She asked, too shocked to move.

"Nothing happened with Jo and me. I told her it was never going to happen under our roof. You didn't really think I'd ever go along with those morbid procreation policies?"

She was speechless. To say she was relieved to hear Jo and I never completed my eighteenth-year requirements wouldn't suffice.

I thought I saw a glimmer in her eye when she said, "I knew it. I knew my babies would never…" She couldn't finish her thought, but we both knew what she would've said.

"We lied, Mom. I'm sorry. It was the only way to buy more time from the Procreates. We didn't want you and Father to be implicated for breaking the law." She didn't respond. "You're not angry with us are you,

Mother?

"No, Stanton. We all did what we had to do to play our parts in making the right decisions."

I knew she understood the reason for our deceit. The feeling of shame had been lifted for both of us with these new confessions. I was expecting more release from her, but she still appeared to be holding something back.

"What is it, Mother?"

She took a few moments to gather her thoughts. "There's something else I haven't been truthful with you about. For your own protection."

"You can tell me."

"You're different, Stanton."

"That's not news to me, Mother."

Her expression didn't change. "I mean you're different as in you're changing."

"Changing? What do you mean?"

"When you were a baby and nearing your death, I was getting ready to call your biological mother to come be with you, but then your father showed up. That's when your father told me about what she did to Melanie. I couldn't allow her to bring you any harm. She wasn't well, Stanton. She struggled through your birth and afterwards, mentally. She wasn't right in her mind. Knowing she was already unstable on top of learning what she did to an innocent child, I couldn't...I couldn't condone this woman having anything to do with you. She didn't deserve you."

"That wasn't your decision to make, Mother."

"I stand by it, Stanton. I'm so sorry for everything. But I stand by my decisions." She stared at me, trying to figure out what I was feeling.

"You and Father have both been in on this then."

"None of us would've survived this long without him."

That was answer enough. I couldn't fathom the number of lies my mother and father had developed and kept between the two of them for all these years and how isolating that must have been. The more I thought about it, the more impressed I became by how they carried on all this time so seamlessly without anyone seeing through their façade. They were genuine deceivers.

Mother continued, "Even still, Stanton, despite what your father told me, I still called your biological mother. I expected her to come say her goodbyes in person. I was prepared for you and her to be face to face. But she never came."

Silence passed between us. I felt her sorrow as a mother; not being able to say goodbye to a child is one thing, but choosing not to is another. I was beginning to understand why Mother's definition of good and bad wasn't always textbook. I pondered whether what she and my father had done was truly bad if it was for the good of an innocent soul? Was what my biological mother did all that bad? Leaving me because she felt unfit to be a mother? Would it have been better had she been able to take me home and raise me? Or was being condemned to the Den perhaps a blessing in disguise? For everyone? If good and bad can be subjective, maybe the same goes for heaven and hell. Maybe what everyone believes to be hell may in fact not even be close to what hell truly is.

"I understand, Mother," I said, taking her hand once again. "I really do." I meant it. I was old enough and intelligent enough to see why she made the choices she did. I didn't resent my parents. I didn't resent my biological mother. I'd be lying, though, if I said I didn't resent time. Time is fickle: it can be both beautiful and merciful, or it can be volatile and unpredictable. All it takes, sometimes, is one decision to determine the rest of your life. I think that was what upset me about the entire situation, that my life was decided before I had any chance to decide for myself. Confirmation that my family wasn't my blood was just that, confirmation of something I already suspected. But all the things I didn't know, all the things that I couldn't go back in time to know…well, those were just going to follow me to my grave.

She asked, "What are you thinking?"

"A mother would know." Hurt, she let her hand drop from mine. "I'm sorry, Mother. I didn't mean that. I'm just…"

"I know," she said. "It'll take time."

"No, it's not that. I was just thinking about something you said. What did you mean when you said I was changing?"

She didn't respond right away, fighting with the words that needed to come out. Then, she said with grave concern, "You're dying, Stanton."

Liv

It no longer feels like we're in a moving car. It feels like we're sitting still and the earth is moving under us. None of our surroundings is recognizable, but there isn't anything anyone could hold onto either. It's like driving through the desert: there's a destination, but the entire way there is filled with similar nothingness. In my situation, there is nothingness, and there is Hannah. It's a terrible combination that yields the unforgiving and the intolerable. Yet, I have no choice. She holds all the keys, and she's just opened a door I never knew existed. And I thought I knew every in and out.

I'm not sure how to respond to her comment about Michael, but I don't think it had the effect Hannah was aiming for. Amongst the craziness of our joyride turned bad, it gives me pause. Nothing matters but what she's said: *Are you sure your son died all those years ago?* I'm sure. That's the truth. I allowed myself to believe there could have been no other ending for him because that's what I was told. I think that's what part of me wanted to believe, regardless of the truth. I believed he was destined for death, whether with me or with someone else, and there aren't enough horrors in the world to prepare someone to watch their baby die. So, I chose not to, and I've never been able to forgive myself. It's the one thing in my life I let lie. Even when I was a child, an answer was never enough. I needed to know how and why and who was involved and what was involved. All the details, I needed to know them. But with Michael, all it took was one phone call from a nurse, and I said okay, and that was it. I never investigated it. I never even said goodbye. I just accepted it, no questions asked.

Hannah is not an honest person, nor does she have the accompanying honorable qualities, but she is my sister, and I still believe there is meaning in that. I'm not sure why now, though. Why tell me about Michael now? If I know Hannah, there's a reason she's chosen now. She needs me. I don't know what for, but there's no way she'd up our current charade unless she's getting something out of it. *Disarm,* I say to myself. *Disarm.* I think and choose my next words carefully.

"How long have you known?" I ask calmly.

Hannah's head tilts slightly, and I can't tell if she's surprised by my reaction or disappointed. I know it's not what she expected, and I need that for this to work in my favor. I see the tension begin to slip away from her. Her shoulders rest and her hands drop to the bottom of the steering wheel.

"Eighteen years," she says, avoiding my eyes.

I nod in silence. "Why tell me now?" She's slowing the car down finally. I make out a fork up ahead in the distance. It's the first break in the dull surroundings. I wonder which path leads where; we're about to find out where one leads, at least. It can't be much farther now.

She tries to stifle a deep sigh and says, "I thought I was doing you a favor. I thought that's what you wanted." I hear the first inflection of empathy in her voice ever. Maybe Hannah is human after all.

The fork in the road nears, and I feel a warm current ripple through my body. We're getting closer to the house and to Dani. I feel it in my bones.

"How did you find him? They told me he was dying."

She looks straight ahead, tightening her grip on the wheel once again. "I didn't know he had been taken."

"Taken?" That comment throws me.

"Whether you believe me or not, it wasn't my idea for Michael to be taken to the Den. It just happened. The Superstorm…"

She trails off as the fork in the road gets closer. It's now or never. She wants to tell me something, and if she doesn't get it out now, she may never. Every nerve in my body wants to scream at her at the top of my lungs. My insides burn right up through my throat. I fight every urge to rip her hair out to compel her to tell me what I want to know. But that's what she expects. That's what she wants. If there's one thing I've learned from being a cop for so long, it's if you pursue someone, they will run. Guilty or not. I figure most of the time people want to be truthful. To free themselves. They just need a reason to; everyone's reason is different, but people are the same. Secrecy was always

Hannah's way of self-preservation. She learned early how to harness that into power over others, but nobody can live with the number of secrets this woman has. No matter what, we are all simply human.

"I forgive you," I say.

Her face changes to crimson, and for a moment I think I've played this right. I hear the leather crying under her white knuckles, and the ground moves faster beneath us.

But I'm wrong. Hannah isn't seeking forgiveness.

She slams down on the gas just as we're approaching the fork in the road. I see a massive tree between the two roads. The tree manifested out of nowhere. For miles nothing, and now seemingly out of thin air is this bare, hulking tree, and we're barreling right towards it. She makes no attempt to move in either direction; she just races at top speed straight toward the massive, lone tree.

Hannah puts her nose to the steering wheel just as I did when I was a child on my family friend's lap, barreling down Sturgess Drive at warp speed. It isn't nearly as fun when I'm not in the driver's seat. In my memory, I see Hannah in the backseat in the review mirror. In this moment, I feel sorrow for Hannah, and it all makes sense. Hannah finally makes sense to me. I think I understand why she hates me so much. It isn't hatred, though. It's jealousy. It all falls into place: the lifetime of competition and her over-eagerness to be better than me.

Hannah wasn't the favorite. I was. I was just too prissy to have realized.

Our parents praised her more often, but dissecting our childhood at lightning speed, it's evident that our parents put much more time and energy into raising me. Maybe it was because Hannah was just an easier child: she didn't need as much attention or coddling, so she never asked for it. Despite the constant praise, she really didn't get much else from our parents. I can understand how she felt dismissed and insignificant in her own way. I've been wrong all along. It's never been about her being a better version of herself; it's about her being better than me.

Her eyes are wide and wild as we speed through space towards the massive tree. I put my hand on her chest and yell for her to stop. Her eyes become wilder the louder I scream. I've seen the look many times. There's no turning back for her, not in this moment. I reach for her arms, trying to break them from the steering wheel. I try grabbing the wheel and steering us away from the tree, but she overpowers me with robot-like strength. The tree is right before us.

"Hannah! Hannah, don't! Stop! Don't do it!" I scream.

Moments before impact, she turns and stares right through me. "We're home," she says as we collide with the tree.

I close my eyes, partially from instinct but primarily because I don't want the last thing I see to be our grisly deaths. I hold my breath and tell Dani in my mind I love her with all my heart, and I wait for the impact's effects.

Nothing. I feel nothing. Time goes by in slow motion with no pain or sound.

It happened that fast? I think to myself. *Are we dead?*

My chest moves up and down, and I feel air moving in through my mouth and nose and down into my lungs. I feel the fingers of my right hand gripping the door handle, and I feel my left hand in someone else's. I'm afraid to open my eyes, unsure of what's less acceptable at this point: reality or death.

I slowly open my eyes. I don't know yet if I'm dead or alive, but I can tell I'm still in the car. Terrified at what I'm going to see, I don't dare look up. I let my eyes dart side to side, down at my chest and lap, and over to my left hand. It's in Hannah's hand. All I can do is stare at her pale, dainty, bony hand wrapped around my own slim-boned fingers. I see visions of us as children running wild through our house, holding hands with our hair streaming behind us, our laughter echoing.

She squeezes my hand. Unsure if this is reality yet, I want to stay here in this moment, just the two of us in a car holding hands, reminiscing about our childhood before the complicated memories began. I don't want to leave. I don't want to lose my sister.

Her voice breaks through the moment. "We're here," she says softly.

We release our hold. I draw my hand into my lap, covering it with my other hand to feel the fleeting warmth from my sister's palm before it dissipates. I'm not ready to accept reality yet.

Still unable to bring myself to raise my line of vision, I open the car door and climb out. Hannah and I walk around to the front of the car and together take in what's before us. I rub my eyes clear, and what I see in front of me is nothing short of a demented house written into a Stephen King horror novel from long ago.

The once beautiful, well-maintained, treelined lawn from my childhood has been turned into an extension of the driveway, just more concrete jungle. The trees have been ripped out haphazardly and concrete laid carelessly with patches of dead grass and weeds punching through the cracks. The heavy, roaring garage door is off its hinges, hanging on by its last rusty bolt, swinging like a shredded tin can in the wind.

There's no familiar smell of car oil. Just emptiness and death. I smell death in the air of this now dead house. I have a habit of walking away from things I should be walking towards and walking towards the things I should walk away from. So, despite the stench spilling out of this house, I find myself again on the short set of carpeted stairs, facing that same brown door with its golden knob. I don't need to turn the knob; the doorjamb is broken. It's basically a hunk of wood without a purpose. I press my foot against it as the door whines open.

Wrinkles form on my face as my body recoils from the sights and smells. The house has been stripped to its frame like a luxury car, lit on fire twice and shit on. There is literal shit spread across the floor, right where that timeless, red oriental rug once lay. Nonsense graffiti scrawls across the fireplace, which now resembles a toothless mouth.

No more sundrenched screened-in porch. It's been blocked off with a chipped, white-painted concrete wall that has been sledgehammered into graveled pulp. The busy kitchen with the sanitizing bright lights is now empty, dark, and filthy. No family dinners here. Not for a long time. I enter the small yet formal dining room, which is now the center of a makeshift garbage dump site. I walk into the family room, and I'm surprised to see a stained outline where our old antique dresser stood decades ago. It's difficult to imagine what this room was used for as the rest of the floor is ripped up, the walls are shredded down to their studs, and the windows have been taken out by their frames.

There's nothing left in this house but memories worse than the ones made here when it was actually a home. For the life of me, I can't figure out why Dani would come here. I leave the bones of the family room behind and walk across a dirt-covered floor where cracked mauve cobblestones used to be, making my way full circle. To my horror, as I stand in the middle of the shit-stained sitting room and look up, I see nothing but sky. This part of the roof has collapsed. The only things still standing in this decrepit, lifeless house are the crumbling walls.

Stifle the sound. Stifle the sights. Block the paths. Close the openings. Kill the joy.

This is not The Connecticut House I remember. No, I don't know why she would come here.

Stanton

Mother and I were startled by the sound of the front door. We both forgot we weren't the only people who lived there. I looked up from the floor at my father and Jo standing in the doorway. I started making movements to stand, but Dad put his hand up for me to stop.

"Stay, Stanton," Mother said to me from the floor.

Father immediately spun Jo around by the shoulders. He told her to go to our neighbor's house and not to leave until he came for her. He waited for Jo to be out of sight before closing the door behind her and turning back around. He stood with his back against the door for longer than seemed warranted.

"I'm sorry about the mess," I said to Father, looking around at the destruction that lay within our four walls.

He didn't respond, and he didn't take his eyes off Mother and me. It was as though he didn't even notice the house was torn apart and splattered with blood. He finally walked toward us, dragging the only untipped chair over from the table and sitting down with a grave look on his face. He let out a heavy sigh.

I searched for the same look of release in his face as Mother had. Did he know she'd told me the truth tonight? I looked for the weight of eighteen years to be lifted off his broad shoulders. I longed so badly for him to appear more human to me. I had always seen my father as a soldier: strong, sturdy, emotionless, obedient. He kept us safe and protected us, and I aspired to have many of his qualities, but his obvious obedience to the Procreates and the Den also made him appear weak to me. Strength showed itself in many forms; some were weaker the stronger they tried to appear. I hoped that, for the first time, he would allow me to see him for what he really was: a tired and worried father with no control, desperate to find a way to free himself of the burdens he carried. There must have been something liberating, no matter how weak it may appear, about finally shedding his imaginary armor and letting his walls down. To, in essence, let it all hang out. That was what we were all doing there anyway. But that look of freedom wasn't what I saw.

My father scratched the back of his head and rubbed the back of his neck. That was one of his tells when he was trying to self-soothe. He sat in a contemplative pose, looking back and forth between Mother and me before speaking.

"What did she tell you?" He had a strange look on his face. I couldn't tell if he was scared or confused. I imagined he was both, seeing as things weren't exactly business as usual in our home.

"That you aren't my parents. And that I'm dying," I said unflinchingly.

Father sat up even straighter, taken aback by my plunge-into-the-water response. "No beating around the bush from you, Stanton, huh?" He looked at my straightforward face and puffed his chest out just enough to remind me that he was the man of our house. "Okay," he said, nodding at nothing. "What did Mother tell you *exactly*?"

"How long have you known?" I asked. He raised a bewildered eyebrow. I knew this was just as difficult for him as it was for Mother, but he needed to warm up to the conversation.

"How long have *you* known?" he asked back. His look of concern quickly turned into a look of readying to go on the defensive.

"I...I..." Stuttering, I looked at Mother, who said nothing. I understood where my secrecy came from. We all kept our cards close to our vests, but evidently, they had many more years' experience than I did. Clearing any hesitation from my throat, I said, "You know that I've known now for a while. It's okay though, Mother, Father. My destiny has always been death, and here in the Den, that is a certainty."

My father stood with his arms up and then used them to cover his face as its color showed his true emotions. With a raised voice, he boomed, "Enough with this bullshit, Stanton!" He pointed a frustrated finger towards Mother. "Stop looking to your mother for answers. You're not a child anymore. You make up your own mind. Your mother and I have sat by idly for years, watching you deteriorate, watching you self-sabotage and sacrifice yourself and your childhood, and for what? So you can just take a back seat to your own life? You spend all your time in the holding cells with those dead bodies…" He looked away from Mother and continued, "You've convinced yourself you're destined for the same? I'll be fucking damned if my son dies here in this godforsaken place. So cut the crap, Stanton. It's okay not to be okay. It's okay to want to fight, especially for yourself. You don't have to be such a—"

"Calm down, Lyman." Mother's voice sounded off, though her face was still unflinchingly stern. "We are undoing his entire life. Just calm down." I heard her, but I wasn't sure Father was calm enough to. It was like he was just ignoring what she was saying.

Father continued to pace the destroyed room, back and forth. He looked back over his shoulder in our direction, wiping his mouth and pointing at Mother and me. He wanted to say something, get something off his chest, but he held himself back. I knew he wasn't going to be particularly enthusiastic about Mother telling me everything, but I supposed I was expecting, well… not this reaction from Father.

"Tell him to calm down, Stanton. Tell him he needs to take a seat," Mother said to me.

My legs were dead with pins and needles from sitting on the floor for so long, but at that moment, I didn't dare move. "I'm not sure that's such a good idea, Mother. I don't think he's going to listen to me."

Father turned around with the same mixed look of confusion, fright, and frustration. "What did you just say?" he asked, his eyes narrowing.

"Nothing. Mother just said…nothing, Father. I didn't say anything."

I didn't want to deter him from sharing more with me. I wanted him to pick up where Mother left off; I didn't want to get in the way of it. I was excited and anxious at the same time: excited to see this new version of my mother and father that I knew existed but doubted I'd ever witness, and anxious because everything I'd ever wondered about being real was suddenly possible.

Wanting something I thought was impossible created a safety net for me. It allowed me always to be right and forced everyone else to prove themselves. My secret made me special; it set me apart from everyone else in the Den. It allowed us small but significant leniencies that no one else got to have. My powers provided us with an extra layer of protection against Lester and the Procreates because I had something they needed. I was no help to them if I couldn't do my job, and my job requirements were fluid. That was the one thing they couldn't control. That was the one thing only I could control.

It was clear not all Mother's and Father's secrets were laid out on the table, not for me to see at least. I got the impression they were picking and choosing what they wanted to disclose. I wondered just how far down their well went.

I needed to do something to keep the momentum of Mother's conversation going. I offered to them both, "I've never seen my death, but I feel it. The same way you feel someone is watching you, and yet you're never able to see them. That's how it feels to me. I know it's coming. I just don't know how or when. Maybe if you tell me what you know, it could help me see." I looked up at my father. I knew I was reaching, but I was hedging my bets that he didn't have any option but to be forthcoming about my impending situation.

"Tell him, Lyman," Mother said, her unchanging gaze on me.

Father needed some time to collect himself; it was obvious. As I said, strength comes in many forms, but during times like this my mother was typically the one who yielded the most strength. But Mother insisted he speak his turn.

"I'm assuming your mother told you about your heart condition, then?" Father said, looking at the scar revealed by my bloody, torn shirt.

"She did," I replied. "But I already suspected."

Father again just nodded. "Your heart condition made for a short and bleak future for you. Your mother…" he looked down at her for the telepathic approval to continue. "Your mother and I were prepared to stay by your side until your last breath. You needed a donor heart, and with the state of persistent panic in Old Chicago, the chance of you receiving a heart transplant in time to save your life was zero. Your mother was by your bedside, and I was right outside the NICU doors when the sirens rang out. The Great Superstorm had made landfall."

I looked at Father empathetically and saw in the movement of his heaving shoulders that he was beginning to calm down. I was careful with my expression so as not to make him feel forced to continue at a pace he wasn't comfortable with. We waited a few minutes, and he continued.

"The hospital was right up against the old city's shoreline, and the water swelled with every wave, threatening to swallow the hospital whole. The rain was so heavy it sounded like the hospital was under Niagara Falls." He stopped, realizing I wouldn't know what Niagara Falls was, or so he thought.

"Got it, Father. Please keep going."

"Large areas of the hospital instantly flooded. Unable to withstand the Superstorm's assault, the hospital's power shut down. There was about a ten-second gap from when the power shut down to when the generator kicked in. It was the longest ten seconds of our lives. In those ten seconds, all life support for you and all the other sick babies in the NICU went down. Our ears rang with sirens, alerts, beeps, all signaling disaster. Ten seconds later, the lights went back up, the machines turned back on, and the hope of your last few days riding out as planned resumed.

"Once the backup generator kicked on, the hospital should've had at least three or four days of fuel resources to keep it running, but those resources had been looted days before, and no one had replaced the stolen fuel."

He paused, remembering all the details I was sure he'd struggled to forget.

"The fuel resources were scarce with the Superstorm giving us no way to retrieve more. The hospital had only enough fuel to get through the day, if that long. We listened to the news on my hand-cranked radio."

I saw the slightest semblance of a smile. "Your mother always made fun of me for keeping that radio around. She called it cranky."

I smiled but quickly stifled it when I saw the seriousness return to his face.

"There wasn't really news, though. There was broadcast hysteria. We listened as orders were called out for the infected to be captured. We prayed they wouldn't make it to the hospital in time to take us, but they were inside the hospital within minutes, searching for anyone infected. They were going to take us all; every one of us was in some way infected in their eyes. The NICU went on lockdown, and it was just us and two hospital security personnel guarding the nursery until the generator died. Your mother watched your life support stop with a cruel swiftness. There is no reasoning with machines."

Father looked at me with affection. "I wasn't going to spend your last moments of life not with you. I locked myself inside the nursery with you and your mother. We did our best to block out all sounds and light and focus every ounce of our energy on you. Watching you, smelling you, hearing only you. I rested my hand on top of your tiny chest," he said, patting his own chest. "It was covered with useless wires, and I felt your heart just beneath my hand. It was still beating. You were defying death. Amidst the anarchy, your mother and I locked eyes, and we knew we couldn't stay there. Mother freed you from all the wires and wrapped your tiny body up in what we could find. She put you inside of her shirt to conceal you as best we could, and I led us to the back emergency exit.

"When we got out of the hospital, the downpour was so heavy that we could see just a few feet in front of us. We walked away from the shoreline, and we saw people falling out of large shipping containers, climbing over each other, scrambling around in the mud to get to their feet so that they could escape, but there was nowhere to escape to. We saw some of them running toward the closest building, and we followed. It was the library. You were wrapped in your blanket underneath your mother's…"

He looked at my mother with the same affection

he'd just shown me. He quickly wiped his eyes and continued, "Your mother's scrubs. That was her work uniform. I peeked in to look at you, afraid you'd suffocated from being wrapped up in too much, but you were sleeping as though the world wasn't coming to an end. You were the peace, the calm through the storm. When I looked at you, everything began to fall back in order. The surroundings didn't seem so terrifying, the sounds became less deafening, the sights swirled all around your face; but your face was perfectly in focus. We found our way like the blind down into the basement of the library. I led your mother. She never took her eyes off you, not once. I wrapped you two up in my arms, and we sat in a small, musky, wet room, surrounded by strangers, but we had you. We were together, and we were alive. That was all that mattered. Through the scared cries and outbursts of agony, an ear-splitting clap ripped through the air, followed by a blinding light. The next time we opened our eyes we were here in the Den." He motioned around with his hands out.

"When we emerged, as you know, things were different. Somehow, though, you were still with us, entirely unaffected by everything that had occurred. We held you close and kept our distance from the others. We didn't know how much time we had left with you. We were prepared to go to any measures necessary to protect you. Hours turned into days and then into months. Years later, you're still alive. You don't seem to understand, Stanton. You're not supposed to be alive right now. You had only hours to live at most back where we came from, but ever since we've been here, in the Den, it's like you were never dying to begin with.

"Even still, every day with you has been a gift and a nightmare: knowing at any moment we could lose you but so grateful for every day you came home through that door. We are, eighteen years later, living on borrowed time with you. You've been symptom-free for years; it's a miracle. There's no reasonable explanation. You lived a normal and happy life here in the Den until you started seeing visions. Your heart disease symptoms started slowly returning the more and more you used your gift.

"Once Lester sank his claws into you, we started searching for a way out. We didn't know for sure what was happening, but we needed to be prepared. The Den healed you, but it can't save you. We need to get you real medical intervention, treatment, and resources we don't have here. Over the last few months, your symptoms have worsened exponentially. Your frequent blackouts..." he trailed off. "You're fading, Stanton. Which is why it's time. We need to get you out." He looked at Mother again. "I need to get you out."

Realizing that my purpose here in the Den and everything I thought made me special, everything I believed set me apart and protected me, was actually bringing me closer to my own death didn't matter much to me when I thought I was going to breathe my last breaths right here in the Den. Now that I knew there was a chance I may not have to, and it wasn't just a dream, I didn't know if I'd be able to escape death long enough to reach what was finally within my grasp. My father and mother had talked more and revealed more to me in those few moments than in my entire life. I wasn't sure if I should have been happy they were finally opening up or if I should have been angry they'd kept me in the dark all that time.

Nobody had anything to say, not right away at least. I needed a break. I needed some time to step away from it all. I had more questions than I could process.

I stretched my legs out and reached my arms over my head, feeling the muscles from my neck down to my sitz bone thank me for the attention. I looked around at the mess I had made. I gently raised Mother's head from my lap; Father watched intently as I stood up and shook out my sleeping legs. Without a word, I began to clean the room around me.

I saw my father in my periphery stand as well, but my mother stayed lying down. Perhaps this was all a bit too much for her; I wasn't about to press her to rush to her feet. I was about to make my way back over to help her up, but Father had already sat down by her. I watched them exchange affection in a way I'd never seen before. Father held her hand and cupped her face in his other hand. He then combed his fingers through her hair, brought his face down to hers, and whispered something in her ear. I looked away to give them privacy, but it made me happy knowing that this had brought us closer together and closer to the truth.

I kneeled, picking up the soggy remnants from the ice box. Father's shadow kneeled beside me. He put his warm and sturdy hand on my shoulder and hugged me the way only a loving father would hug his son. I could count on my two hands the number of times Mother and Father embraced me together. I could count on just one hand the number of times they said *I love you* to me. So each and every time was more meaningful than the last, especially knowing however few gestures of affection I received were all on borrowed time and I might never feel love again. I paid attention to all my father's angst, and love, and sorrow, and uncomfortable resentment, and I embraced it all because I knew it was genuine. The love in that house was real. We were all real, despite how unbelievable our story was.

During one of my secret library visits, I read a book by a man named Mark Twain. He wrote "Truth is stranger than fiction." While that may be provable, I'd like to believe that true life is better than fiction as well. I was always so certain of who I was and the life I'd led, but now I wondered if my life was ever really mine. In moments like those, there on the kitchen floor with my father hugging me, surrounded by destruction and uncertainty, I found my truth, whether in fiction or not. This was my life, and this was my family. My destiny changed once before, and I could do it again.

Right before he broke his embrace, he whispered in my ear, "I need to show you something."

The Journal

It was rare for me to be alone in the car. Today I was, what a special day it was. I've witnessed your regular fender bender and accidental red light runs and rolling stop accidents, nothing too serious. Nothing that ever stopped time. I must have gotten lucky today. I was on 88 coasting at normal speeds. The highway was relatively deserted. There weren't any cars in my direction in my eyesight and few cars blazing by me on the other side of the divider.

There was an onramp in the distance. One of those where you pray that you don't get side swiped when merging. I love those kinds of ramps. I sped up a bit to try and match the speed of the oncoming car, after all the rules of the road say match your traffic's speed, right? No harm done here. The onramp was approaching, and the other car was trying to figure out if I was going to let them in or if they were going to have to speed up to pass me. We played this game for a few seconds and they made their way safely onto the expressway.

Disappointed and a bit bored I figured I was going too fast after all. I lowered my speed and drifted into the other car's lane. They must have been speeding or not paying attention because when I moved over I heard tires squealing along the asphalt and the smell of burnt rubber lit up my nose.

The last thing I saw out of my rear-view window was that car from the onramp spiraling out of control. I watched from my rearview as the spinning car got smaller and smaller until I couldn't see it any longer. Later that day in breaking news was a fatal car wreck on 88. A car had spun out of control and smashed head on into the highway divider. No survivors, everyone in the car was dead upon arrival. I couldn't help but smile as I swiped to X out.

Liv

I run out of the house, violently ejecting everything from my stomach. My head spins. The heat feels like it's lighting my skin on fire, and the rubber on my shoes sticks to the steaming ground. Hannah and I are now both covered in our own filth. Quite the fucking pair we are. Hannah stands back and watches me empty out until I'm just spewing bile from my lips. She makes no movement to help me or comfort me, but I don't expect her to.

"Some mother you would've made," I say through gasps and spits.

"I can hear you," she says from a few inches away.

I slowly stand up, blinded by the unforgiving sun that's baking me like it baked this shit pie that sends out a stench worse than what just came out of my body. "How are we here? What the hell happened?"

Hannah saunters over like she's been waiting for this moment for a long time, as though this entire thing is an elaborate setup. It wouldn't surprise me. Just when I think we're getting somewhere. "Are you asking about the house? Or the tree?" she smiles.

"What the fuck is wrong with you? Why are you smiling?" I say, looking at her crooked, goofy-ass smile. For some reason, I hear laughter coming out of my mouth too. We're both standing there, covered in vomit, in front of our childhood home, which looks like the set of a horror film. I guess if you can't laugh at that then there's something wrong with you. We both laugh until our stomachs are about to burst. We cry-laugh and wipe our tears away and cough as saliva leaks from our mouths. Literal, knee-slapping, tear-ripping laughter. What a scene. Us laughing like two crazy lunatics.

Once we shake out all the years of repressed laughter, we wipe our faces and mouths dry with the backs of our hands, like we're mirrors of each other. In the horror of the moment, the insane laughter brings me back to her. Only for a moment, though.

Snapping out of it, I say, "Both. Tell me about both. Where are we? What happened?"

My clothes become a second skin. I struggle to find a place to sit on the hot asphalt that doesn't burn my ass. I sit on the edge of where the woods used to be, the toasted leaves crunching under my body. I'm hungry and thirsty and exhausted and convinced I've just lost my mind. I'm no closer to finding my daughter. In a place that for so long was a sanctum for me, I have no clue where I am.

I have a recurring dream about being in this house with my sister when we were small children, way before we knew all the complications and issues we were being groomed to encounter. In that dream, I'm always lost. Even though within my dream I know exactly where I am, it feels like I'm not supposed to be there. I feel the same way right now, in this moment, in

196

the oppressive heat with my equally oppressive sister, who is seemingly unaffected by our surroundings. Sitting outside an apocalyptic version of my childhood home, I still don't belong here. I am still lost.

"How many times have you been here?" I ask.

She saunters over and stands above me. She strokes her hair, trying to get the sticky edges to sit down properly, smoothing her fingers over her cheeks and under her eyes. She shakes out her pants and pats the filth off her shirt, not caring where the dried bits of vomit scatter. She puts her hands on her hips, and for once I'm grateful for her shadow blocking me. "I've been outside the house twice. Inside...?" She looks down at me. "Just this once."

To my surprise, she takes a seat on the earth right next to me. "Who else knows?"

She props her elbows on her bent knees. "Just us," she says with a soft smile.

A part of me wants to believe her. I want to trust her more than anything. That smile of hers always had a way of making me feel special. But I have to shake that off. I'm not here to fix us. I'm here to find Dani, and so far I've done nothing but waste time.

That's when I realize this was Hannah's plan all along. She's good at disarming me, and I walked right into it. Trying not to give myself away, I remind myself what I need to do to play at her level. I can't be like me; I have to be like her: conniving, deceitful. I can be as insincere as the best. I made an entire life out of it. With any luck, Hannah will have forgotten that blood holds similarities no matter how different one tries to be. I smile back at her and give her a little bump to her shoulder.

"Let's walk around the house." I hold my hand out to help her up, which she accepts. I'm getting back on track.

We walk around the exterior of the house. I don't think either of us has an immediate desire to go back inside, not yet anyhow. We walk down the small hill we sledded on as children, down around the first bend behind the house where there once was a fenced-in berry patch that she and I would wait all summer to pick clean, like survivors scavenging within the safe view of our own dwelling. We liked that then. We walk underneath the large back deck and count along ten wooden beams until we come to a small nail above our heads where we used to hide our spare key.

"Oh my god," I say, reaching up. "You can see where the key used to be."

The rusted outline of a key gives the illusion that one still hangs on the rusty nail. It seems paradoxical that in a place where nothing is left but a shell, here lies the key to its heart.

"Let me see that," Hannah snaps, pushing me aside to inspect the ghost key. She stares, outwardly unimpressed, but I can see she's envisioning the same apparition I am.

"Did you take it? When you were here before?"

"No," she says, still staring at the rust markings. "I didn't even come under here. There's no way it would still be here anyway." She marches out from underneath the deck, dismissing our conversation.

We emerge where the plush, green backyard used to be. Now, it just looks like an extension of the decrepit driveway. Concrete covers the space where grass and trees used to be. It stretches as far back as the demolished tennis court.

"You never answered my question," I say as we walk across the concrete backyard.

"You've asked a lot of questions, Liv. Be more specific."

I stop walking. "Drop the act, Hannah. I don't care if you want to talk to me, but you owe me. You owe me answers. For everything. Everything I've done for you. And all the things you've never done for me. Answer my questions."

She purses her lips and swallows hard. With resistance, she explains, "We are very much alive." She struggles to wiggle herself out of her long-sleeved cover-up, removing it with a sigh of triumph and slamming it on the ground. It makes a thud as the sweat she's been accumulating splatters in dark patterns on the pavement. "Give me that," she says, pulling my hair-tie from my hair. She whips her hair up into a top bun and then lifts her undershirt.

"Holy shit," I say in shock. "What the fuck is that?" There, under her shirt, is what I can only describe as a small x-ray screen implanted on her chest. It's imbedded, a part of her body. It allows for a complete view of her heart. Confused and astonished, I stand and watch my sister's actual heart beating through a screen on her chest. I have to say it to myself to put the words in an order that makes sense. "I can see your heart." I instinctively reach out to touch it. It feels like a soft silk screen right over her organ.

She pulls her shirt back down and closes my open mouth. "Do you believe me now?"

"Are you sick?" I ask, still in shock.

She scoffs. "Quite the opposite. But that's not what your original question was. You want to know how we got here, right?"

I just nod.

"The tree? It's a marker, but an illusion at the same time."

It doesn't make sense, but I nod again anyway.

"When we started mapping out the fault lines, I told you we left markers. But the markers move. Like the house. They are never in the same spot. So, we implanted invisible roots that react and appear only when authorized personnel are within the vicinity. Think of an infrared machine that reads your DNA. It works the same, but it's implanted in a person."

"Fake DNA?"

"Not exactly, but sort of. It's too complicated to explain." She sees she's insulted me. "Right now, I mean," she finishes. "But this machine…" she taps on her chest. "I don't need anything else. It's always active and will show me any invisible roots we have implanted to continuously track the fault lines. It's just another step we've taken to move toward finding a way to master the fault lines so that we may one day move beyond them."

"Who else has this?" I motion with my hands at her chest. "And why is that so important?"

She gives a smug smile. "As of now, I'm the only one who has this new device. And why is what so important? The fault lines?"

"Moving beyond them. That's the first time I've heard you talk about it like that." She slipped, and she knows it.

She leans her head back, looking to the heavens for help correcting her oversight. No matter how much she wants to be anything other than what she is, she will always be human. I don't care how many robotic implants she allows her scientists to test on her. She isn't going to find the answers up above; I don't believe in heaven. "My implant…it tracks more than just my heart rate. It tracks—"

"Location?"

She nods. "Yes, but for some reason it doesn't track

my location beyond the implanted roots. It's a learning process. Anytime I've ever crossed an implanted marker, my coordinates go unrecorded. I go dark. Everything does, every time."

I begin to wonder just what sort of intent Hannah really had in bringing me here. What started out so clear is now muddled and murky. "Where else do you have these invisible markers? And the house? Our house? No one knows about it? Where do they think you've gone?" I realize she's wanted to tell me. She wants to purge herself of herself, but she can't let anyone know. So, what does that mean for me?

Her voice picks up in speed and inflection. She's excited to finally tell the truth. Like I suspected, there are only so many secrets one person can hold. She shakes her head in off-putting excitement.

"They don't know about the house!" Her eyes are wild. "No one has any idea. We've set four implanted markers, one to denote each cardinal direction. Here's the thing, though: the implanted roots seem to remain intact, but their attached cardinal direction is constantly changing. That's how I know the house." She motions back towards the structure. "It's never in the same spot. We could come here tomorrow, and it could be gone. But I think..." she says, her eyes darting around. "I think I've figured out a sort of algorithm for how the coordinates shift in relation to their cardinal directions. That's how I was able to find the house today."

"So, it was a lucky guess?" I ask, a little disappointed.

"No," she says sharply. "I said there's an algorithm." She turns her nose up at me.

"No, I get it," I say, trying to keep her calm. "There's some sort of anomaly happening here. Like some sort of..." I search my mind for the right word. "Transient anomaly."

Hannah looks at me with surprise but quickly erases the look off her face. She takes pride in knowing she's the smartest person in her company. "Yes, just as I've said: an algorithm for this transient anomaly." She gestures towards me to let the record show I've been heard and that I'm correct.

She spent her entire life being watched, followed, surveyed, recorded. It was the main reason she gave up Melanie. She was always under someone's eye. They were always looking for a reason to disregard her, and she would never have herself be disregarded. That's just not in her nature. She sacrificed her own child only to live in purgatory. Is she finally beginning to regret her past and the decisions that reduced her to nothing more than a glorified pawn?

"In my field reports, I claim that the shifts in realty cause me to have retrograde amnesia, and they—"

"Can't trace it," I finish. She nods with a magnetic sparkle in her eyes. She's far more dangerous than I could've ever known. "What else does your implant track?"

"Changes in atmosphere, shifts in fixed cardinal direction, air pressure, oxygen levels in me and the surroundings along with other chemical elements and related levels. That's why we know the fault lines are uncrossable. Yet, we still waste resources trying to cross them."

"And again, why is it so important to you?"

"What?" she says, stalling.

"Whatever is beyond the fault lines?"

I see the wheels turning in her head. "We haven't had any communication for years."

"Who, you and I? Yeah, tell me something I don't know."

"We haven't had any communication," she stalls again.

"You've come this far, Hannah. Just let it out."

"We haven't had contact with anyone outside of New Chicago."

Pulling teeth, I ask, "What do you mean?"

"Since the Superstorm. All external communication..." She's still making up her mind. "All external communication has been down."

"What?" I say, genuinely confused. "You mean, like, with the Den?"

She shakes her head. "They're actually the only ones we have communication with."

I can't sort my thoughts. "Hold on, hold on." I shake

my head. "No, you said you have never had any way to communicate with the Den. That's why…" I step closer to Hannah and whisper, "That's why we sent Melanie there."

Mimicking my whisper, she responds, "How do you think I found out about Michael? Oh, yes, you've been so focused on Dani you completely forgot you have another child."

"Stop it," I say, backing away. "Shut up. Don't turn this around on me. You need to explain yourself."

"There's nothing more to explain, Liv," she says, spreading her arms out like wings and smiling widely. "I'm free. I've said it all. We can't cross the fault lines. Our society is dying. We haven't been able to communicate with the outside world in fifteen years. No communication. Zero. Every resource we've used has gone unreplaced. Here we are, fifteen years later, with a finite amount of resources and no way to replenish them and nowhere to go to find more. And the only ones who know are you and me." She's laughing hysterically again.

"You fucking monster," I say in terror.

"Am I? Am I!?" she cries out. She tears open her shirt. "See how much I fucking care, sister?" Her see-through heart is a solid, calm projection, not one beat skipped, not one beat over 60. "I tried, Liv. You can blame me all you want. You can hate me. I know you already do. But I tried, Liv. I tried for so long. For fifteen years. Longer than that! I gave up everything. Everything!"

Neither of us has noticed that during our conversation our feet have come to green- and red-colored rubble; the old tennis court has been beaten to a pulp. No poles, no net, no surprise. The woods are still here, but all the life is dead. The trees, once lush with greenery, are now all brown, revealing starving, shedding, emaciated branches. Breath evades me with every step. My heartrate picks up the way it used to when my instincts ran hot on a lead—or when my body would go into a full-blown panic attack. Right now, though, my body tells me we need to press forward, despite the wrenching feeling in my chest. The dead woods is where the rest of the answers are.

I turn to tell Hannah we need to keep going, but she isn't near me. I look across the concrete backyard, up to the back of the house where our father's study used to be. I've already accepted this may all be just a horrific nightmare. I've also accepted I may have gone insane. Given the distance and the heat, coupled with my exhaustion, it's entirely plausible I'm seeing things, but when I look up at that old study window, I see someone. Then, one blink and they're gone.

"Dani?" I say out loud. "Dani!" I yell as my legs turn and start moving me back toward the house. Hannah's voice stops me.

"Liv!" Hannah screams from behind me.

My long hair is matted to my sweaty forehead, and the ends flick sweat off as I whip my head back around and see Hannah's white pants and pale skin reflecting from the depths of the dead woods. I look back up at the distant, black study window and back at Hannah again. "Don't move! I see you, Hannah! Wait there! I'm coming!"

I run as fast as my legs can carry me to where Hannah has somehow transported herself. We both must have seen the same thing because it stops everything we were just talking about and doing.

We walk together right up to the edge of the well that, as it did in our childhood, sits deep in the now-dead woods. Finding the well still here holds little effect compared to what we see inside: water. This city hasn't had a drop of water in fifteen years, but here before us, at our childhood home, sits a well filled with clear water right up to the brim. We stare at each other's reflection in the well water's surface. This is impossible.

"Did you hear that?" Hannah says, instinctively crouching with nothing to hide her.

"Hear what?" I ask, unable to take my eyes off our reflection in the water.

"Shh!" There's the faint sound of twigs breaking nearby. "That," Hannah whispers.

I reach my hand out and let my fingertips hover right above the mystical water. It has to be an illusion. I'm just about to break the water's surface when I hear what Hannah heard. *Snap…crunch…crunch…snap.* Twigs and fallen leaves sound off nearby. My fingers recoil, and I too instinctively bend into a crouch and reach for my back. My fingers fumble around but find nothing. *God damnit.* I don't have my firearm. Why would I? I haven't needed it for years.

Hannah is a few paces away from me. She's crouched down low, but her white pants shine like a beacon against the dead woods in the bright broad daylight. If something's trying to hide from us, it's certainly easy for them to see us coming. Easy for them to hear us coming as well. It's been a long time since either of us had a reason to sneak around.

We both crouch a little lower with each snap and crunch we hear. I guess we're definitely sisters in the way we both walk towards things most people walk away from. Hannah points to a large, black tree trunk a few feet away. I see the mark she's pointing at. I signal for her to go one way and that I'll go the other way. We nod silently and walk as lightly across the dead ground as we can. The only sounds and movements now come from our own feet.

Rounding opposite sides of the giant tree trunk, we see her.

Her. She's a woman. Or a girl? It's hard to tell from her clothing and the amount of dirt on her body. It looks like she's army crawled through the dead woods on her elbows, belly, and knees, beginning to end, and came upon this tree trunk behind the dead house in the distance. She's soaking wet. How is she soaking wet? Her hair is long and tangled, partially covering her face and knotted down her back. She doesn't look injured. There's no blood. She looks unarmed. She's shoeless and sockless. The rest of her clothes look tattered and faded. She's alive, barely. Her chest moves up and down slowly, and her mouth is moving, but nothing audible comes out.

"Thirsty...water...?" I say out loud. I leap up faster than I've ever moved in my life, faster than my feet can carry me, faster than any machine. I don't breathe; I don't think. I just run. I rip my shirt off in front of the well, and without hesitation, I dunk my hands and shirt in the water. Shocked by the feeling of the cool, natural fluid covering my hands and arms, I feel a sort of frenzied euphoria. I try my best to create a makeshift cup with my shirt and my hands and run like lightning back to the stranger who is moments from failure. I drop to my knees, scoop the girl up in my arms and into my lap, and put the shirt filled with water up to her lips.

At first, there's nothing. No movement. I put my head down to her face and listen; I don't hear or feel any breath coming out. I lay her flat out on her back against the dead forest floor and kneel over her, wringing out every last drop of water onto her face, hoping to revive her. Nothing.

"Hannah? Hannah, come down here! I need your help."

Hannah is frozen. She stares down in horror, mystified at what she's witnessing.

"Fuck, Hannah, get down here!"

She moves down to the dead ground in a panic and looks to me for direction.

"Two breaths when I tell you. Cover her nose and give her two breaths."

She shakes her head, terror glossing over her expression. I've never seen her so scared in my life. I grab her face in my hands. "You're the fucking alpha, Hannah. You got this." She gives me a fierce nod, but there's insecurity behind her eyes.

I start compressions. One after the other, *push, push, push.* "Breathe!" Hannah breathes twice, her hand shaking as she clamps the stranger's nose shut. I repeat compressions. *Push, push, push, push.* "Breathe!" Two more breaths. I continue compressions. *Push, push, push, push, crack.* The sound of a rib breaking. *Push, push, push.* "Breathe!" Two more breaths and...nothing. I raise my fist in the air and pound with full extension on this person's tiny chest. I break her ribs trying to get through to her heart.

Between repeated contacts with my flailing fist, I see visions of my son, visions of my daughter, and visions of a life we never got to have. I find myself wailing on this stranger's body like a human punching bag. I feel a hard grasp from behind me. Hannah pulls me off the body and fights to keep me from abusing it any further.

I break away from her, screaming, "No! NO! NO! BREATHE! BREATHE! BREATHE!" Hannah struggles to keep up with me: more compressions, *push, push, push.* "Breathe!" Two more breaths.

The last breaths.

The girl's blue lips expel a river of fluid as she lets out a loud, choking gasp. I stumble backwards and wipe the sweat from my eyes. I can't believe what I'm seeing. "Water?" I say out loud. "But how?" None of this makes any sense. Nothing since the moment I got in the car with my sister has made sense.

I'm about to launch into a litany of defensive questions, but I stop. I looked over at the girl we just brought back to life being rocked back and forth in my sister's arms.

Is Hannah crying? I think, looking at her. I rub my eyes. *No,* I shake my head. *No, you're seeing things.* I stand up and walk closer, and I see tears streaking the dirt on my sister's face.

A deep chill runs up my spine as I realize who this person is. There's no way. It's entirely unexplainable. Impossible. But a mother never forgets. She never forgets the face of her child.

It's Melanie. It's my baby niece, all grown up. We've brought her back to life right here on the ground in these dead woods.

Stanton

I didn't want to call attention to the fact that Melanie was with me the night before, but I needed to find her. She and I were closer than I think either of us realized. My intention was never to obligate her to be a part of my plan, but now I had reason to believe she was, in fact, pivotal to my plan. She was the only other child who wasn't born in the Den. That must have meant something.

Once I cleaned up after myself and put a fresh, unbloodied set of clothes on, Father and I left the house. As he led us away from our home, he gave stern glances or reassuring waves to many neighbors of ours who stood on their front steps, clearly concerned by the commotion that had come from our house earlier. He waved, and they went away. It was that easy. It made me curious what else my father had the power to just wave away. How simple deceit was for him. I understood why he put on that act, but it was nonetheless unsettling.

"Father," I said, trying to gauge where his heart was at that moment.

"Not in public, Stanton." He was back to business as usual. My feelings weren't hurt, but it was a quick turnaround to say the least. I didn't realize how easy it was for him to turn it on and shut it off, but I guess I learned that from him, too.

"Father, where are we going?" I asked, holding his stride. He was several inches taller than me with legs to match. Holding his pace was a task in itself, but now that I was a man, I couldn't let him see my struggle to keep up. He held his silence as he continued to wave off faces.

Ever since John showed up, people had developed prying personalities that made everyone a little more uncomfortable than Father would like. When people pried, things got uncovered, and knowing now what Mother and Father told me, there was a lot they wanted to stay hidden. I began to deeply regret the fit of rage I'd unleashed on our house. Amid my explosive behavior, I hadn't stopped to think about the effect it would have on us once it was over.

One of Father's men approached us as we walked away from our housing circle. Militiamen's daily contributions had them looking like everyday citizens. They dressed just as we did: worn clothing, poorly-fitted shoes, and no socks. They carried on day in and day out with their daily routines and mundane jobs. It made sense why they agreed to take part in the militia: the militia was the one thing that set them apart from everyone else. It was what made them special.

I wouldn't even have known it was one of Father's militiamen without the patch adorning his sleeve, a simple black patch with a compass stitched in gold thread. I'd asked Father before what the symbolism was behind their insignia, to which he always responded, "To remind us where we are."

His man whispered something in his ear that I had little interest in hearing even if he'd chosen not to whisper. The sight of that patch had brought things to mind, and I was working on figuring out how to prioritize them.

My father waited until his man walked out of earshot; then, he looked down at me and said, "Meet me by the shoreline just after sunset." And with that he walked off.

The transaction wasn't any less normal than usual: someone delivering a quiet but cryptic earful to my father, and then him disappearing for hours or days at a time. Because I now knew what I did about him, it actually made more sense how easily he disengaged and jumped from task to task. It made the unknown seem a little less ominous. I always chalked it up to him just doing his job as Lester saw fit, when in reality—well, Father's other reality—he was accustomed to this same sort of profession. More and more pieces were falling into place as I figured out how Lester and the Procreates came to be and how they chose their higher-ups, like Father.

Lester and the Procreates…that was something I needed to get out of the way before I could do anything else. With their attention unfocused on me for a while, I could buy myself some time to straighten things out with Mel and to see John again. I suspected there was more than what he'd given me.

***

The boy soldier waved me into the library's familiar back entrance where another child soldier patted me down. I could only imagine it was to see if I was armed. That was new, which triggered an entirely new list of questions. The child soldier stood at his full height up to my rib cage. I bent over so he could use his tiny fingers to search through my hair and upper torso for any hidden objects. I deduced that this was a new tactic put in place by the Procreates to supply additional protection measures for them. It didn't surprise me that this new safety precaution followed immediately after pulling John out of our waters. So much had happened in just a short twenty-four hours. It was a cause for concern, however; if the Procreates felt finding John was anything other than a mere coincidence, then why add these additional safety measures? They felt compromised. John had shown everyone that the Den's walls were penetrable, and they, the Procreates, felt vulnerable.

I put my arms out straight for the boy and welcomed the new violation of privacy. Around here, any change is good, at least in my book. The soldier ran his small hands down each one of my arms and gave a good stare at the self-inflicted wounds on my arms and hands. He didn't ask, and I didn't offer any words. I was certain

I'd have to explain myself around the next corner anyhow.

Without a word the child soldier motioned for me to wait in the main floor foyer. No chairs, no couches, just stand still on your own two legs until the Procreates agreed to see you. The point of this was to make you uncomfortable. It was a disarming technique they used. Just another way to break us down and weaken us. I knew this, though; after countless visits, I'd learned their tactics. I always came prepared physically and mentally to stand fast with intent. There is much one can do to busy their mind, but I preferred to use moments like this to clear my mind out. It was quiet. I was alone. No one was trying to speak to me, dead or alive. I took some solace in the poorly-lit foyer of the same place that, according to my father's account, brought me here to the Den. How enigmatic and yet serendipitous.

All things considered, though, was life better lived knowing you essentially cheated death only to find yourself stuck in a state of perpetuity that even you cannot escape no matter how you long to? Or, was life better lived knowing you were due for an untimely death beyond your control but with complete autonomy over how you spent your short days until then?

My conversation with my mother and father had simultaneously confirmed and changed so much. I didn't need more time to digest it all, but I needed more time to adjust my plan. For as long as my memory served, all I'd ever wanted was to break the Den. To expose it for the monster it was. To offer its citizens a window to truth. To remind its people that there was more than what our eyes could see. To prove that a whole world existed outside of it. But now that I knew it was true, that there was more beyond the Den, I couldn't make the same mistake Lester and the Procreates had made. I couldn't lie to the citizens of the Den about what may lie beyond our walls. I needed to find out for myself.

Lying to Lester and Procreates, though…well, that was likely not only necessary, but it might very well have been the only way to break them, too. I needed to find out just what we the people of the Den would be exposing ourselves to if there was, in fact, a way out. Or a way in. I needed to prepare them. To do that, I needed to prepare myself. That was not something to take lightly. Like Mother had said, I'd be undoing everyone's lives. For some, their entire lives. So yes, I needed more time. The number of hours an average human has in their lifetime is 692,000. Some may have more. But for me, and many like me, there was much less, and the clock was always working. With or against us, it was always working. Even then, as I stood there waiting alone in the dark.

I heard a voice in the middle distance. It echoed through the empty, open levels within the library. "Step forward," it said.

The familiar manikins sat before me: Lester, the alpha, and the other Procreates. They made no effort to cover up their impatience or to welcome me. They avoided eye contact and muttered about the value of their wasted time.

"Look at what we have here," said Lester, lifting his lazy, bony finger toward me. "Have you decided to grace us with your presence? We were beginning to question your value, Stanton."

I hated the way he said my name. I envisioned ripping his sawing tongue from his disgusting, cavernous mouth. I envisioned silencing him so that he could never speak my name again. Every time he spoke, haughtiness saturated every word, and he knew it. He derived power from making others feel insecure and uncomfortable enough to question themselves. He stripped people of their confidence and struck when they were at their weakest.

"Speak up, boy! We don't have all day," he said, grabbing his genitals and looking at the female Procreate to his right; she responded with an air of indignity. Of course, the moment she realized she had shown her humiliation to me, she picked her chin right up and squinted her eyes at me in a look of disapproval that said *How dare you humiliate me*?

I looked away as quickly as she did. It wasn't my intent to make her feel even more objectified. Lester seemed to enjoy the exchange, which made it that much more shameful for the woman.

Lester licked his lips crassly as he eyed me up and down. Either he had no sexual preference, or he simply enjoyed passing off any behavior as acceptable because he answered to no one. The longer his eyes lingered, the more I fixated on his stare. He and his Procreates needed to know that Lester wasn't the only one who could make others feel uncomfortable. With my glance unwavering, Lester finally let up on his obvious taunts and discrimination, but then his clock started.

"Speak quick, boy. You hard of hearing?" he said, challenged by my stance. He looked at his female Procreate once again, tapping his leg in a clear message of impatience. I, as a person, felt horrible for what we all knew was coming for that poor woman. I did my best to draw out my visit, but I too had my own agenda I needed to stay focused on.

I stood before him with my head held high on my shoulders, my hands clasped behind my back. *Stand proper when you speak*, I heard Mother's voice say. *Let them know you're a man.*

"John—" I cleared my throat and started again. "Body 5468 has spoken his last words."

Lester lifted the left corner of his mouth in a slim grin. "Already? And here I thought we were all just waiting around for our leisure. You tell us what we need to know and get it out fast, boy."

I nodded. "Body 0155468 is of the male gender. He is mid-lifecycle, approximately forty-five years of age. His origin…" I paused just because I could.

Lester felt it, but there was nothing he could do about it, not at that juncture at least. His grey-tinged skin turned a slight pinkish hue; I imagined the sludge within his veins beginning to boil him from the inside out. He visibly bit one of his lips as he drew them together in a look of shrewd irritation. He raised his hand to call out to one of his child guards, certainly to remove me with physical vigor. "Get this boy—"

I intentionally cleared my throat once again. "His origin is not of the Den."

Audible gasps rang out around the room. It made sense, but at the same time, it was simply ludicrous. Yes, John was bloated and maimed beyond recognition, but there had been several signs from the moment we discovered him that he was not of the Den. Before we even found him, now that I think about it.

John's body was pulled out of one of our water channels, which were fed from open bodies of water at our shorelines. Our water channels act like canals or rivers from lakes. Father said that, where we're from, they used a lock system to control the flow of water coming in and out of the smaller canals so that boats could go in and out safely, without contaminating the great lakes and keeping water levels in flux. However, in the Den the locks didn't work, and the incessant rain would render them useless even if they functioned properly. The open waters from the shoreline were one of the only resources from which we could access natural wildlife for consumption. Our boats were deployed daily to troll for edible lake life or any other kind of resource we could use. Which calls into question how John's body made it all the way through the open waters to our channels. He should have washed ashore, or he should've been found by a routine resource search, and yet he wasn't. The waters from the shoreline would have had to somehow carry him into the smaller channels within the Den's structure unnoticed, but how?

Lester didn't flinch upon hearing that John hadn't come from the Den. He looked side to side at his colleagues, scorning them with his disapproving expression, shaming them into falsely composing themselves.

"What a thing to say," Lester said, rubbing his wiry lower lip with his equally wiry finger. "You sure you don't want to rethink what you've just said, boy? You're going to scare all these people with a silly lie."

"It's not a lie, Lester."

His eyes widened at hearing his own name from my mouth. "Then what is it?" he demanded, rising to his feet to project his full form upon me.

I immediately responded, "He is a message!" I said it louder than I'd intended but didn't regret it.

221

"A message?" he shrieked, looking around himself in disbelief. "A message!" He laughed alone as his Procreates tensely looked on.

My chest tightened as I fought my body's urges to shut down. I took three big stomach breaths and composed myself while Lester did the same.

He settled back to his seat and crossed one stick-figure leg over the other. He motioned at me with his palms down. "You should settle down, son, before people start to feel unsafe," he said, squinting at me. I felt the presence of his child soldiers gathering behind me. "What a thing to say."

"It is the truth. Accept it or don't. It won't change it."

Lester projected his usual slimy, smug smile. "I should've stuck you down in isolation the first time I met you. A lot of good you've done us." He sized me up again, up and down, but not sexually this time. This time, he was looking for something else.

"Where is isolation?" I promptly responded. The isolation chambers had long existed as a warning to those who didn't toe the line. I couldn't resist this opportunity to verify their existence.

He waved his fingertip at me. "What is that?"

I must have broken my stance. He was pointing at my cut-up arms, and I felt a warm trickle down my leg. We both looked down as a red tinge seeped through the front of my pantleg where I'd cut it open earlier.

Lester's head cocked to the side, intrigued and clearly pleased that the situation appeared to be turning in his favor.

I quickly clasped my hands back behind my back. As for my leg, well, there was nothing much that could be done about that at the moment. I was caught. I cleared my throat again, trying to cover up my nerves.

"I injured myself by accident. I was trying to build something for my mother." I immediately regretted dragging my mother into the situation, but it was too late.

"You understand we will need to corroborate your statement," Lester said, signaling his child soldiers to find my mother.

"Wait," I said. "There's more."

Lester waved off his soldiers for the moment. "Go on."

"I had a vision."

"What of?" he asked, genuinely intrigued.

"Bodies. Blood everywhere."

With a straight face, Lester said, "Where?"

"Here," I lied. The vision was true, but I had no idea whether it would even manifest or not, let alone where it would happen.

He was silent. It wasn't easy to silence Lester. In his silence, I saw his mind working, which meant he suspected part of my claim to be true. What did he know that I didn't?

I seized the moment of silent contemplation to clutch a stronger hold on his fragile state of indecisiveness. "I saw you." Another lie. "All of you." Lie again.

I looked at the Procreates' faces as the panic set in. Their expressions changed from ones of entitlement to self-preservation, and instead of eyeing me, they now eyed each other. It elated me to physically watch the tables turn before me. With that one lie, I had fractured the structure of their thrones, and it was exhilarating.

First step in breaking the Den: cast doubt. Check. And may the rest of the cards fall, I said to myself with a smile inside.

The Procreates had the exact response I'd hoped they'd have. The commotion was overriding Lester's beckon to calm down. I took advantage of that.

"I can help, though."

At once, the room fell silent, and all eyes were once again on me. "I need more information. I have a plan, but I need time and resources to research it."

Lester was like a dog, and I knew he was trying to sniff out which parts of my claims were true and which were lies.

He said, "The nerve you have, boy. To come into my house, *my house!*" He struck his concave chest. "And spread this malarkey—"

"You will die first." It was another lie, but it was worth the risk. This was the most vulnerable Lester had ever been. At my words, he sucked in his breath, and his rib cage showed through his shirt. His eyes looked like they were about to pop right out of his bony skull. I gave him no opportunity to respond. "I need documentation of aerial plans of Old Chicago before the Great Superstorm. I need blueprints of all commercial, industrial, and residential structures in existence immediately prior to the Great Superstorm. I also need—"

"And what the hell do you need all this for?"

I held my finger up to Lester. "I'm not finished. I also need a complete compilation of all the surrounding bodies of water, including all marine charts. Please be sure those materials reflect charts that hold depth soundings and bed rock measurements. And lastly, I need any available texts that cover the topography of Old Chicago before the Great Superstorm in addition to the same documents that pertain to the Den."

The once-luminous room of the library sat dim and silent as the Procreates held their collective breath awaiting their alpha's next move. The silence made me think of how a space such as this should sound: silent and peaceful.

Lester's slow, cynical snicker permeated my reverie. His subtle yet mocking laughter erupted into a full-voiced, belly-bursting howl as he snorted at my requests. I didn't know if he objected more to my wanting access to those books or to me believing I was intelligent enough to absorb the topics. Certainly, if an idea didn't come from Lester, then it was no idea worth pursuing.

"You." He pointed at me, laughing between words, saliva dribbling from his unclosed mouth. "You want what?" he exclaimed, slapping his knee. The other Procreates uncomfortably looked around at one another, unsure how Lester wanted them to react. They had turned being a fly on a wall into an art form.

I stood my ground, waiting for Lester to stop seizing from laughter. I had never felt sorrier for him or his peers than at that moment. What an absolute embarrassment this man was who represented us and all that we stood for. It was beyond me how he came to be in power in such a powerless place. I could only imagine what he was trying to make up for in his previous life. It filled me with a sadness that I couldn't explain. I pitied Lester.

He worked himself into a coughing spell as a result of his infantile outburst. He reached out his hand as the Procreate to his right handed him a clean handkerchief to clean himself up with. Then he threw the soiled linen back into her lap. He nodded his head at a spot behind me where child soldiers still waited in the wings for their orders. The soldiers left promptly, presumably to fetch my mother.

She's going to have some words for me when I see her, I thought. *But she'll also be proud.* I grinned internally.

"You'll get nothing," Lester said, staring at me, trying his best to intimidate me. "You know the rules, Stanton. There are no books without proof of your visions. And seeing as I'm safe and sound here," he looked around him at the eyes trying to avoid his stare. "I don't think your…vision is accurate. I think, Stanton, your purpose here may need to be reassessed."

I cringed deeply at the words that darted off his tongue. "Yes. You're right. There are rules. But my vision this time…well, I just don't see any way we're going to be able to verify it beyond a shadow of doubt unless we wait until it's too late." I paused and looked around the room. "Are you all willing to do that?" I extended my hand to Lester. "My vision shows you first, Lester. Are you and your peers willing to wait and see what happens? Or do you all want to trust me as you always have since I have always proven accurate and allow me access to these books so that I can arrange a plan to save your lives?"

Silence fell over the room once more. Lester readied to speak, but the female Procreate next to him spoke first.

"Allow us two hours to compile the materials you requested." Her voice pierced the room in a surprising and pleasant way. It was quite a change of pace from Lester's loud, long-winded, wheezy tone. It was rare to hear any of the other Procreates speak. I tried to recall another time when I'd heard that Procreate's voice, but none came to mind. Lester gritted his teeth with a face full of contempt.

That poor woman, I thought to myself again. I wanted to thank her for having the gall to speak before Lester and against him. But she and I both knew what she was getting herself into by speaking up. What reason did she have? I let suspicion settle my sympathies for the female Procreate, nodded, and stepped back, signaling that I was ready to be dismissed.

"You can demand no such thing," Lester sneered at her and me.

"You're right, Lester," she said, holding her head high on her shoulders. "But together we can." She looked to her three peers.

"This is not a democracy," mocked Lester.

"It is not. Of course, it's not. This is the Den. And we adhere to the rigid set of guidelines that you put in place, Lester, so that we may provide ourselves with the odds of the best outcome every time. It has always worked in our favor. Why stray now?"

Lester had no response.

"Then let majority speak, non-democratically, of course," she said, looking toward Lester. "Who wishes to wait and see if Stanton's visions are true prophecy?"

Lester wormed around uncomfortably in his cushioned, oversized chair. Even he, though, did not lift his hand.

"Who wishes to grant Stanton access to the materials he has requested, which could potentially provide us with the only answers available to save our lives?"

Everyone slowly raised their arms. Lester still made no movement, but apparently it didn't matter.

"Let it be heard for all: four Procreate votes have been counted. That is more than enough to push this request forward. Stanton, you'll have two hours only to view the materials you've requested." She nodded her head at me. Lester stood up from his throne and turned to face her. He crinkled his fists into tight balls.

We saw what his idle hands were doing, and he felt all eyes on him. He instantly released his white knuckles and, staring down at his female counterpart, said, "Stanton, if you are even one second late, the request is off the table. And you," he said, pointing down at the seated woman. "You are summoned to my chambers immediately."

***

No matter how sick of the rain I got, it was always a welcome refreshment when I came out of the Procreates' headquarters. I felt alive. I had, for the first time in my life, finally stood up to Lester, and it felt good. Things were falling into place. I had broken down my mother and father's long-standing barriers. I was now armed with new information that would help me move my plan forward. I was finally gaining allies among the Procreates.

But I needed to find Mel. I had two hours to find her, update her, and get back to the library.

I made my way back down to the housing circles and over to Melanie's house. Excited to see her and filled with a renewed sense of hope, I looked forward to getting her up to speed. I knocked on her door with high spirits. My knocks were met with silence, though. I knocked again. Nothing. I looked at the window next to the front door, but the blinds were drawn. The rain muffled the sounds around me. It was difficult to hear any movement inside the house. I tapped on the window and again, no response. I walked around to the back of the house. There was an egress around back that Mel used when she didn't want her guardian to know she'd left, but seeing as their house was small, I always thought the veil of privacy was just that, a veil.

Melanie's guardian always felt Mel was much more fragile than she was. I thought Mel intentionally led her to think that; it made sense because naturally one would tend to go easier on a child who had lost what Mel had and witnessed what she'd witnessed at such a young age with Mrs. Rappaport. Mel was much smarter than me, much smarter than anyone I knew for that matter.

The back door was ajar, which was strange. I peered in through the open door and saw a shadow sitting on her bed.

The shadow spoke. "Come in, Stanton. Don't let the rain in."

I stepped inside with my heels right up against the inside of the door.

"Have you seen Melanie?" I could see clearly now; the shadow on Melanie's bed was her guardian. Although why she was sitting in Mel's room in the dark didn't make sense.

"I was going to…" I paused to consider her question. If Melanie were here, then why would she be asking me if I'd seen her? "I was going to ask you the same thing, actually," I lied.

Her guardian made no motion to stand up but nodded her head slowly. "She hasn't been home since yesterday evening."

"I'm sure she returned and maybe just left before you two had a chance to see each other. Is it possible you just missed each other this morning?" I felt guilty for lying to her. She was as worried as any parent would be. She didn't deserve to be kept in the dark, yet I didn't think she was ready for the truth either, and I wasn't entirely sure I knew any truth to share.

She looked past me and motioned with her head outside the door. "Do you see a set of prints other than your own?"

I glanced behind me at my tracks in the light layer of mud outside the backdoor, and I looked down at my muddy shoes. Mine were the only prints outside the door. I didn't know what to say, and I didn't want to lie to her any more than I already had.

"It's all right, Stanton. You're a good kid and a good friend to Melanie. I wouldn't expect you to go behind her back."

I was thrown off by what she said. While there was a curfew at night for citizens of the Den, during the daytime no curfew or check-ins were required unless it was part of your own household's routine. I knew for a fact it wasn't part of Mel's. The response her guardian gave didn't seem like a normal response from a person who suspected their child hadn't returned home, but Mel wasn't normal, and neither was her and her guardian's relationship. Mel always described her guardian to me as more of a friend than a mother, which had me wondering if she knew something I didn't. There were a lot of things to fear other than the threat of infection, and there were many ways to evoke fear. But she wasn't afraid; she was sad, like she knew Mel wasn't coming home and wasn't surprised by the possibility. It started to concern me, and I began to think maybe she was right.

I had one foot out the door when I said, "I'm sorry, I don't know where she is. I'm going to go look for her, though. You'll be the first one to hear anything."

"Here," she called out behind me. "Give her this if…when you find her. It doesn't belong to me, so it must be hers."

She came to the door and reached her hand out in the rain. I opened my hand, and she dropped a small, gold, oval-shaped piece of metal into it. The weight of it sat nicely in the center of my palm. I curled my fingers around it and tried to give her a reassuring look. I tried to be convincing, but I knew she could see right through it. I put the small metal object deep into my pocket. I didn't have time to inspect it.

It was imperative that I find Mel. I had to retrace our steps, and the clock was working against me; I couldn't be late getting back to the Procreates' headquarters. Lester was a liar but only when it worked to his advantage. If I wasn't there in two hours on the dot, I might never get to see another book in my lifetime. Worse, I might never have another opportunity to piece together my plan. Everything had to line up perfectly, but I had to make sense of all the pieces first.

Since citizens were not allowed to have everyday items like socks, we certainly were not privy to everyday devices like watches. Father taught Jo and me when we were young how to tell what time of day it was without a watch. The only problem was the cloud-covered sun didn't give us much help. As a result, I'd gotten very good at using my body's internal clock to navigate my daily twenty-four hours, and my body was telling me I had barely an hour to get to the shoreline and back to the library.

I ran over the slippery surface of the water-drenched grounds. My shoes were covered in mud, and water quickly found its way to my bare feet inside my shoes. I felt blisters form before I even reached the edge of the hollows.

When I reached the hollows, instead of carefully climbing my way down into the forest, I plunged into its depths by sliding down the clearest path I could find. I stood up in the depths of the hollows with fresh cuts that surely would need an explanation later, but there was no turning back at that point. I could see the shoreline straight ahead; I made it down there in record time. My lungs burned, along with my fresh, mud-rubbed cuts. I saw the forest overhang where Mel and I had been just the night before. I ran over, hoping I'd gain some sense of where Mel was. I thought of the house that she had led us to, the dark brown house with the long, winding driveway that seemed to rise up from the sand. I struggled, trying to sort out if any of it was just in my imagination. I knew it wasn't, and I knew in my gut that was where she was. I just needed to find it.

I walked south along the shoreline, what I remembered Mel and myself doing the previous night. In the distance, I heard a voice call my name. "Stanton? Stanton!"

I squinted my eyes to make out the figure walking toward me. "Father?" I called out. I picked up my pace to a full run.

As we approached each other, he said, "What are you doing here? You know you're not supposed to be here. I told you sundown for a reason."

What are you doing here? I wanted to ask him. "I'm..." I hesitated for a minute but finally just let it out. "I was with Mel last night. I can't find her, and I need to find her." I studied his expressionless face. "And I need to find her now because I made a deal with Lester that—"

"You made a deal with Lester?" he asked in an angry, panicked tone. "What deal, Stanton? Why are you making deals with him?"

"I really don't have time to explain." My own words surprised me, but I kept going. "I have to be back at the library in less than an hour; otherwise, the deal is off the table. I need to find Mel before that because she's imperative to my plan."

"What plan? Stanton, what are you talking about?" He stood in my way.

I grabbed him by the shoulders. "Father, listen to me! I have to find Melanie! I have to find her now! Are you going to help me or not?"

"She's not here, Stanton!" he yelled. "She's not here."

"How do you know? I lied to you and Mother. I was with her last night. You and Mother lied to me, too. You both had to have known I wasn't alone last night. Tell me the truth, Father. Where did you find me? How did you find me?"

Motioning with his hands for me to calm down, my father stepped closer to me. "Lower your voice," he said, looking around. "You are my son, and we no longer have any secrets. Melanie is not here, Stanton."

"What are you hiding from me, Father? No more secrets; no more lies."

My father looked around again before nudging me forwards. "You're never going to make it back to the library in time. Follow me," he said.

I followed him back west toward the tree line. "Father, no. I need to find Mel. There was a house." I pointed behind me in the distance. "That's the last place I saw her. I need to find the house."

"It's not there anymore," my father said.

I stopped walking. I was confused, bewildered, startled. I wasn't sure what Father meant. "You know? About the house? Why didn't you say anything? Why did you just let me think I was seeing things?"

He pleaded, "Please, Stanton, not now. I promise I will explain this all to you, just not right now. Let's get you back to the library. You made the mistake of making a deal with Lester, and you need to make good on it."

He turned his back to me because he knew I had no choice but to follow him. Back in the forest, I realized he was right: there wasn't enough time. I wasn't going to make it back before the two hours were up. We hadn't even begun to trek up the hollows yet. I picked up my pace and ran out in front of my father.

"There's a faster way," Father called out behind me.

I turned around; Father was waving me back to follow him. I looked up to the top of the hollows, but the distance seemed unreachable. I had no idea what my father was talking about, but at that point, I had to believe he wanted to help me and not hinder me.

I ran back down and followed him behind a large tree trunk, one nearly as wide as he was. When he stood behind it, I couldn't see him at all. I rounded the tree; my father was clearing loose forest debris from the ground. He was searching for something.

As Father moved dead branches, leaves, and layers of loose dirt, the sound of the rain changed. I heard water bouncing off something hard. There was an unmistakable *tink, tink* sound of water splashing against hollow metal.

I didn't know what the hell I was looking at. Underneath the layers of dead forest was a door, a grey, shiny, metal door.

Liv

I dig my heels and my hands down through the dead layers of leaves and dirt, searching and sifting until I feel cooler, even just a little. I close my eyes and for a minute imagine myself on a white sand beach, my toes and fingers buried beneath the hot sand, sunshine radiating through my body. With my eyes closed, I imagine Mom and Dad are there. I imagine Dani and Michael are there, too, and Hannah and Melanie. I imagine, just for a moment in the depths of my wishful fantasies, that we're a family.

I open my eyes and look over my shoulder. It's been quiet for a while. Hannah still holds this strange but familiar person in her arms. In a situation that makes no sense and seems entirely impossible, we're here together. I think for a minute that maybe my fantasy could come true. I hear movement coming from Hannah and the tired young woman she's holding onto. The earth makes sounds that bring us back from our haze. The heat presses down on us all, the thirst and hunger reminding our bodies we can't stay like this much longer. I take my hands and feet out of the earth, brush off my feet, and tie my shoes. My bones crack as I stand. A large bead of sweat trickles down the middle of my back.

I look at Hannah and the young woman in her arms. Hannah strokes her hair, which, now dry, shines in the sunlight with a mix of dark and golden brown. Her skin is very fair, as though she hasn't seen the sun in years. Her clothes, which were soaked through not long ago, are now as dry and crisp as the leaves crumpled under my shoes. It hasn't been long enough but too long at the same time. I need to find Dani. I know she's here somewhere. I can feel her.

I look at Hannah and speak a name so quietly I'm not sure it makes it past my lips. "Melanie?"

The girl looks at Hannah, who then looks at me with tears in her eyes. It's her. It's been easy for Hannah to lie all these years about how it felt to give up her child. It's easy to bury those emotions down deep when you aren't faced with the reality of it. I know; I've lived it also. Those tears she's showing have been years in the making.

Melanie's hand wraps around something hanging from Hannah's neck on a thin gold necklace. She tugs the necklace off Hannah's neck and wraps her hand tightly closed around it. Her eyes squint beneath the bright sun like she's been asleep in a dark room. Hannah and I look at each other as Melanie rises to stand between us. She has her eye on something by me. I look around but don't see what she's looking at. She shuffles her feet slowly along the dead forest floor, and her gaze goes from the ground to the well just beyond me.

Her pale, delicate hands tremble as she holds the

small, thin necklace. She stares at her closed hand intently. Her line of vision goes back and forth between what's in her hand and the water-filled well some distance behind me. Hannah and I share confused looks as we watch for what this girl is going to do next.

Her eyes lock onto the well. I step aside to see if that is in fact what she's looking at. She steps slowly in that direction. I offer my hand to her, but she just walks right by me. Hannah and I wait in stillness, but neither of us takes our eyes off her. She picks up her pace from a slow shuffle to a steady walk to a determined run. This girl, who was literally dead minutes ago, is now running toward what I assume was responsible for nearly killing her to begin with.

She is a Jones all right, I think to myself. *Always heading toward things we should be heading away from.*

Hannah, a few feet away from me, nods for me to keep close to Melanie. I follow her voiceless request, staying within an arm's length of her. At the well, she looks down at her reflection. I can't tell what she's feeling; I can't see her face, but it seems like she's at peace with whatever she sees. Then, in a sudden, swift movement, she flings Hannah's necklace into the well. We hear a single *plunk* sound as it drops into the water. My instinct wants me to plunge in after it, but Hannah doesn't seem disturbed by what's just happened. When I look back at her, she just sort of laughs.

"Was that your—"

"Locket," Hannah says. "Yeah." She's gazing at Melanie.

Melanie turns to look at me, and she appears to be smiling a little too. She looks past me at Hannah, who's standing, brushing dirt from her pants and trying to unstick her sweat-soaked shirt from her chest. She smooths down her hair and wipes her face. Melanie watches every movement her mother makes. She hasn't spoken a word yet, but her eyes speak all that's needed in this moment. She looks at Hannah with no rage, no anger or animosity. She looks at her as though she were an angel. She looks at her with wonder, and awe, and forgiveness. Melanie is a better person than Hannah or I. She finds forgiveness where it shouldn't be found and where it's not deserved. That says something about a person. It has me wondering that if what Hannah said about Michael is true, would he have it in him to forgive me?

"I'm going to see if there's anything in the car that can clean us up," Hannah offers.

"Wait for us," I say, but Hannah's back is already turned to us, and she has seemingly magically transported herself again to the tennis court rubble.

I hold out my hand to Melanie. I think I just want to feel her touch. It isn't even about helping her: I know she has the strength to do it all on her own. But it would solidify that she's real if I can just touch her.

She wraps her slender arm around mine. She looks at me, her eyes still adjusting to the bright light. Her eyes are a tranquil blue, like her mother's, and like mine. Like Michael's, too. I saw Michael's eyes briefly only once, but I could never forget them: blue like the ocean.

We take our time exiting the dead woods and crossing the green and red rubble. The slow walk across the paved, unshaded backyard feels akin to a death march through the Mojave, but Melanie doesn't seem to mind. I start archiving the questions I have for her in the back of my mind. I don't want to scare her off by asking her a million questions right away. The last thing I want is for her to feel like she's being interrogated, but she and I both know she's going to have to explain some things.

We have time, I think to myself. For once in her life, I just want to be her aunt.

We're coming up on where the wild berry patch used to be, and the driveway is straight ahead. Hannah is in the car with the engine on. I look at Melanie, smile, and point to her mother in the car, but when Hannah doesn't look back at us, the pit of my stomach turns on itself. What I should've expected her to do if something like this ever happened is coming true.

She's fucking running. Again. Fucking coward.

I drop Melanie's hand so that I can run to the car. "Hannah!" I yell. "Hannah!" As I sprint toward the car, she puts it in reverse. "Don't, Hannah! Please! Don't

242

fucking do this! Don't go! You don't have to do this!" I'm yelling and running, trying to reach her, yet she's unreachable. She turns the car around and idles, seemingly unsure of what she wants to do next. I put my hand out and plead with her through the open window, "Hannah, I know you're scared. I won't tell anyone." I lower my voice, looking behind me. "We can take care of it. Don't go."

She looks at me and then at Melanie, standing back in the distance. She mouths something to me through the window, but I can't make it out. It doesn't matter; whatever she has to say right now doesn't matter.

"God damnit, Hannah! Don't do this. Don't leave us here! Not again," I add weakly.

My car screams as she throws it into gear and slams on the gas. The tires burn on the pavement, and just as I'm about to reach the car through the cloud of tire smoke, she's gone. Gone. Hannah and the car just disappear.

I scream a litany of profanity and kick the tire tracks on the split concrete until my throat feels as torn up as the toes of my shoes. Then I remember this girl who looks like my niece back from the dead is watching me and surely thinking one of two things: who is this psycho? And am I in danger? Or maybe how do I protect myself from this psycho? I can't blame her for thinking any—or all—of this. I did, after all, make her disappear all those years ago as though she didn't matter. Why would she show me mercy now?

I turn around, aggressive and unabashed and ready to fire off questions, but she isn't behind me.

"Oh fuck," I say softly, realizing I've scared her off. "But there's nowhere to go…"

I see a flash of movement in my periphery in the direction of the garage. She's running into the house.

"God damnit." Going back into that house is the last thing I want to do, let alone have the time to do. I have little choice thanks to Hannah. Against all my reasoning, I go after my niece, back into the decrepit structure.

The putrid smell of death and shit shocks my senses once again. My eyes sting as they dart around the dilapidated house, and I see a flurry of brown hair flying up the staircase.

Damn, she's fast.

I run to the bottom of the grand staircase and see Melanie's foot disappear around the corner at the top of the stairs. A loud boom sounds in the room next to me as the kitchen ceiling crumbles. The house is collapsing with us in it. I eye the staircase that I ran up and down more times than I can count as a child; now, I stand at the bottom, unable to climb even one step.

"Melanie?" I call out. Then again, louder. Another portion of the kitchen ceiling threatens to collapse.

I look at the rickety staircase, unable to understand how she got up the stairs so quickly. Some treads are missing, and the ones that aren't sag so deeply I don't know how she could've climbed up without falling straight through. I ready myself, moving back and forth, trying to build up enough of whatever it is I'm going to need to propel myself up these stairs. Even if I make it up, I can't be sure the landing won't give out beneath me.

But then I hear a voice.

"Melanie?"

There it is again. A girl's voice.

"Melanie? Is that you?"

Then, two voices.

"Dani!? Dani!" I yell as I charge up the decayed stairs. "Dani!"

I look down and find myself at the top of the staircase, all trepidation forgotten. I turn left and run down the hallway. I fall to my knees when I come to the dead end where my old bedroom is. I hear two female voices whispering inside the room.

"Dani? Dani?"

I burst into the room. It's empty. "The closet," I say, turning around.

I swing the two old and battered closet doors open, nearly ripping them off their hinges, and there's Melanie, crouched down in a small ball inside my childhood closet. I look around the space as though Dani should be here too. As though she should just manifest out of thin air in the space of this closet.

"Where is she?"

Melanie just stares up at me. There's no fear in her eyes, no panic. It's like she expected all of this.

"Who were you talking to? Where is she?"

Melanie looks at me with an unapologetic expression as she shifts, revealing a clear message written on the wall in my daughter's handwriting: *DANI WAS HERE.*

My body falls heavily to the floor as I throw myself against the words my daughter scrawled across the wall. I run my fingers over the letters. I stare at her handwriting, imagining her hands writing this message. *Is it for me?* I think. It has to be. She had to have left this message for me. She was here. In this house. In this room, my room. *Where did she go?* I ask in my head. *Where are you, baby? Tell me where you are. Please, give me another sign.*

Like she's reading my mind, Melanie takes my hand from my daughter's inscription and places something in my palm. Papers. Small papers, like the kind from one of Dani's pocket journals. The edges are crumpled and jagged, like she ripped them out in a hurry. I look at Melanie, confused, as she nudges my hand to my face. She wants me to read the crinkled, loose papers she's just given me. I unfold the pages and smooth them out as best I can. I immediately recognized Dani's handwriting.

I finally found him. He's real.

Stanton

I'd thought just the day before that nothing in this life could surprise me. I was wrong. I stood with rain cascading down my back, my vision blurred, peering down at my father descending into the earth through a man-made hatch in the middle of the hollows. I heard his voice echo up through the dark hole.

"C'mon, Stanton. We don't have time to stand around. I told you I'd explain everything. Let's just get moving. Now."

I turned around and placed my foot on a hard metal rung. I didn't know why, but the sturdiness of it surprised me. It was clear that this, whatever this was, was created intentionally. I lowered myself into the same dark hole my father had climbed down. I looked up into the water free-falling on my face, and a figure disrupted the steady flow of water. The figure, one of the militiamen, I guessed, quickly slid the metal door shut above us, and darkness enveloped us. I listened in silence, trying to hear the figure up above.

"You ain't gonna hear anything, Stanton. It's soundproof," Father told me.

Ain't? I repeated to myself. My father had never used slang before. *C'mon* was a rare occurrence, but *ain't*? No, I'd never heard him say that before.

"Who are you?"

He laughed. "*Who are you?* That's what you want to

ask me right now? Not *where are we? What are we doing?* You really are something, kid."

Kid? Now I was certain this was a dream.

A light flipped on, but I couldn't figure out the source. My father held it in his hand. It wasn't a candle or a torch. It was a—

"It's called a flashlight," he said, handing me one with a smile. His smile faded. "Your mother isn't the only one who can teach you kids things."

Now, I decided, if it was a dream, I didn't want it to end. Down there, in the deep darkness of a secret, soundproofed tunnel in the earth, I was my father's kid, and he was talking to me like I was a person, not a machine or a baby he had to protect. We were two men finding our way together through the dark.

"I know it's hard to see in here but just stay close…"

"Father, I talk to the dead. The darkness doesn't scare me."

"Yeah, I don't think I'll ever get used to that," he said, nodding his head in the direction he wanted me to walk.

The fresh scent of earth mixed with the damp walls gave off a pleasant aroma. It wasn't a typical circumstance to feel contentment, but I very much preferred that dark, earthy dwelling over the crowded, exposed surfaces above us. The soil felt different down there. It wasn't rotted; it didn't smell spoiled. There was hope of life in the dirt walls that surrounded us, life

248

that hadn't been drowned by rain. As we walked through the long, dark tunnel, I wanted to ask my father so many questions, but I wanted to enjoy this experience more.

"Father?"

"Yes?" he said.

"There's something I need to get off my chest. About John."

"Don't stop walking, Stanton. We're almost there. Whatever you have to tell me is going to have to wait," he said, walking past me.

"It can, but not for long."

"Listen, Stanton. There's something I need to tell you. Something about…" He stopped, like something had caught in his throat. "Mother."

He picked up the pace, and in the dark, walking along the slippery insides of the earth, I struggled to keep up with him. "What about her?" I asked.

We saw a dim light ahead. "Hurry, Stanton. It's right there, straight ahead," he said, pointing.

It seemed that after just few quick, long strides, our secret walk had reached an end. The light from our flashlights bounced off another gleaming metal door above our heads. Father reached up, somehow unlatched the metal hatch, and shifted it over. The cloud-covered light hit our faces as though it was full sunshine. Just a few minutes in complete darkness made the sky seem brighter than it was, creating the illusion that it was actually sunny.

What a world that would be, I thought.

Father nodded for me to head up the metal rungs.

"You're not coming?" I asked, surprised.

"They're not waiting for me," he said.

"Where are we?"

"You'll recognize where you are when you're up above."

"What were you saying about Mother?"

Sorrow took over his face as he turned to use the darkness to hide his emotions. "Now is not the time."

"Okay, Father. I'll see you at sundown."

"Sundown," he repeated, taking the flashlight from me.

He stayed close behind as I climbed the metal rungs back toward the surface. Once I reached the top, he didn't hesitate to close the metal door behind me. I did as I presumed the figure from the hollows had done and replaced the loose dirt, leaves, and debris over the door to conceal it as best I could. I stood up and looked at my surroundings. Father was right: I knew exactly where I was. I was at the edge of the upper forest that sat adjacent to the library. I hadn't even realized we were going uphill in the underground tunnel. It cut the time from the hollows to the surface by more than half. The tunnel exited along the side embankment, which was clearly intentional and strategic as it was the least heavily guarded part of the library's grounds. Possibly no one would even see me coming. It made sense then how dad got around the Den so quickly, how his men seemed to show up out of nowhere.

I wanted to ask him how he built the tunnels or if he'd found them already built. I wondered who else knew about them. There was no way the Procreates knew; that was clear from the pronounced secrecy. It made me think what other 'networks' Father was privy to.

I walked stealthily through the forest to the nearest clearing and waited for the child soldier to turn the corner from the side of the library so that I wouldn't reveal where I'd come from. I moved quickly and quietly, bellycrawling under the barbwire and making my way to the guarded back entrance of the library. There, the polished Uzi swiftly waved me through to be once again patted down. The soldier gave me an up-and-down look as he patted my newly-muddy clothes, but he didn't ask any questions. Remembering the small metal object Melanie's guardian had given me, I acquiesced to the search so as not to make it seem like I was hiding anything. The child soldier waved me into the foyer, and I breathed a small sigh of relief. I had nearly forgotten I had the small pendant on me. I wouldn't be able to inspect it here. I couldn't risk it being confiscated.

Back in the cold, poorly-lit foyer, I waited. A soldier came to meet me. Wordless, he motioned for me to follow him as another soldier walked behind us. They led me down the corridor that circled the Great Room of the library's main floor and then took me up the back flight of stairs.

When we reached the second story, the child soldier tapped on the stairwell wall with his Uzi, and a door opened onto another hallway that was in a similar, circular structure. When I looked to my left, I could see straight down to the Great Room. I had never been on any level of the library other than the main floor. It was a new view of the library, a new view of the Procreates' grounds.

It was a message from Lester. He wanted to remind me that he still held all the keys to his house and only he could unlock the doors and allow people in.

But is it really his house if it never belonged to him to begin with? I asked myself.

The two child soldiers and I continued down a passage of doorways, their glass sidelights painted black. Anything that might have distinguished one room from the next had been stripped away or covered up. No numbers, no signs, no markings, just black door after black door. The lead soldier stopped abruptly in front of what I thought I'd counted as door eight. He pulled a key from his belt and slid it into the smudged doorknob. A lock released, and he pushed the door open with the tip of his boot. He motioned for me to enter, and the soldier at my back followed me into the dimly-lit room. One guard at the door and one inside the room with me.

I looked around. A plain wooden desk and a single wooden chair sat in the middle of the empty room. On the desk was a small lamp with a soft yellow light that illuminated the small stacks of books. I could tell by the lack of materials that the contents on the desk weren't what I had asked for, not all of it anyway. But that was why I'd requested more than I needed. It didn't take a genius to figure out two hours wasn't much time. It would be enough for me, though, to find the information I needed. It had to be. I wasn't going to have another chance. I was going to have to make do with what they gave me.

A low beep chimed behind me, the signal that my two hours had started. I sat down and looked at the short stack of books on the desk. My fingers slid over the bindings and titles: *Old Chicago Topography, The Great Lakes: Coast Guard Manual, Industrial Blueprints: Volumes I & II.*

I leaned over the small stack of books, opened the cover of the top book, put my nose between the pages, and drew in a long breath. The library might be Lester's house, but there was a warmth and intimacy here, just me and my books by a low light.

The child soldier peered over at me, clearly not understanding what I was doing. I doubted the child had ever even held a book in his short life let alone learned to read the words within its pages or appreciate its smell. I looked behind me and saw the second soldier standing by the open door. He checked a small timepiece on his wrist. Everyone was more on edge today than normal.

It made sense, though, given the events that took place under the bridge just yesterday with John and the omittance of our annual celebration, if that was what one could call it. Usually, on the day of the Den's violence-free anniversary, the Procreates pushed back curfew and played music from their old world over the Den's PA system. They turned on the electricity in every household that still had working wires and allowed for one hour of "twenty-first-century living," as they called it. The annual celebration tended to overshadow my birthday. I had hoped this year it would have come and gone unnoticed, but it was foolish for me to think for even a moment that the Procreates would completely abandon their code.

Jo, I thought to myself. The Procreates would be conducting their medical assessment on her any minute to confirm I'd completed my eighteenth-year duty. When they found out we'd defied them, I'd need to be ready for them because they would come for me. No act of treason went unanswered here.

The soldier kept looking at his watch; it reminded me of how little time I had in that room. I spread the books over the desk and started reading, sifting through the material between the pages. My father said there had to be a way out of the Den, and I was going to find it if it was the last thing I did. I was on the last book, *The Great Lakes: Coast Guard Manual*; I thumbed the pages, making a small fan movement. I liked the way the pages felt ruffling through my fingers. Something caught me off guard, though.

There was a gap between several pages. I picked the pages between my thumb and index finger again and riffled them. There it was again. A break in the ruffle. I did it slower this time and found the gap, but it wasn't a gap. There was something between the pages.

Careful not to call attention to myself, I kept my face and eyes down and made no sudden movements. I picked up the book slightly so that the soldier in front of me couldn't see what was between the pages. I tried to be gentle with the onionskin paper, which was so worn that it felt soft between my fingers. Clearly, the documents weren't supposed to be here, but someone thought they were important enough to keep in good shape to last through concealment.

I tried with all my focus to keep my eyes straight and down though they wanted to dart around the room to ensure no one saw what I'd found. I knew I wouldn't still be sitting there in the chair if either of the soldiers had any inkling I'd found something.

What is this? I asked myself.

The first loose piece of paper was a worn, greyish

color with black ink printing. It looked like a news article. The coffin-dodgers talked about the newspaper days in their previous lives and how the youth had turned technology against them, taking away small pleasures like going to the mailbox and finding their trusty newspapers with stories within their pages. They complained about being forced to learn and trust the new technology. Technology became a conflict for the coffin-dodgers in their old lives with its concepts becoming more elusive the more they aged.

They always said, "If you can't touch it, it ain't real."

I think I would've made a better old man than a young, sick man in their world. But I adapted. Their problem, though, was clear: they weren't able to embrace the change, so they cut themselves off from the power of knowledge and the power to adapt, which ultimately paved the way for the young to become champions of their minds, both in their old world and in ours now.

Adapt or be left behind, Lester preached. At his age, that was probably partly how he came to hold so much power in the Den.

I carefully unfolded the delicate, aged, soft newspaper clipping.

The 24th Gene is a Gamechanger but is it Provable?
By Steven Roberts

26 June: A dynamic duo is bringing to life new possibilities for tomorrow. Pictured here, Lester Angolore and Hannah Kerwin: the faces of Novyx and the parent company to 24andMORE claim they have identified a 24th gene. Can this marriage of law and science supersede all rationales of evolution? Law's most vicious yet effective foot soldier, Angolore, and the youngest Nobel laureate, famed scientist, and richest business tycoon under the age of 30, Kerwin, seem to believe it can, so much so that they've devoted their lives and their companies to the daunting task of discovering whether or not violence can be inherited, shattering decades-long debates and schools of thought on nature versus nurture. They claim that if violence is inherited, then the ability to eradicate it is within our reach. This raises the question we all find ourselves asking: If it's possible, how do we prove it? And what do we do once we have? Included here is an outline Angolore and Kerwin have provided to the public, comprising the bulk of their research, results, and plans to move forward in creating a state-within-a-state that is violence-free.

I couldn't stop staring at the photo of Lester and this woman, Hannah Kerwin. I couldn't believe what I was seeing. This article was almost two decades old, the photo perhaps even older, but I still couldn't believe what I was seeing. Lester, unmistakably. I'd studied many faces alive and dead in my life; I was good with faces. But even still, I couldn't believe this was Lester. It was flat-out surreal seeing him younger and in a different world, poised in a different light. It gave him context that I didn't want to associate with him: in another life, he had been human.

The photo was black and white, symbolically matching his actual gray-tinted skin. His smile even back then was wry and phony. In the photo, he stood with an overbearing hand on the shoulder of a woman, Hannah Kerwin. Certainly, these two did not appear to belong in the same world, yet not only did they co-exist but they were partners, the article claimed. The woman looked well-respected and well-maintained, completely opposite of Lester. The photo was only from the waist up, but I could tell by how she was dressed and the way her hair was neatly combed and sharply cut right at her shoulders that it had taken a lot to keep up her appearance. Such a far cry from Lester.

What were they doing together? I asked myself. *A twenty-fourth gene? Is that possible?*

The rest of the article had been conveniently torn off. I folded the thin paper as small as I could and slid it into my sleeve. Another piece of folded paper was with the newspaper clipping. It was a little sturdier and bulkier but still delicate. I carefully unfolded it. It had drawings on it. They weren't normal drawings, though; parts of them made sense, but other parts didn't. The drawings looked like blueprints, but portions looked like water table drawings. It didn't make any sense, like a partial blueprint above water mappings. My eyes studied the markings, the wavy lines, the numbers, dashes, and the beginning and ending of every line. There were no titles, no labels. There were no words. Just the drawings, like someone had made this with the intention that only they would be able to interpret it. I stared at the drawings until the lines started to blur and melt together.

And then I saw it.

The structures were drawn *into* the land, not on it, which was why the floating structures didn't make sense initially, and the water tables overlapped the land. It was the Den.

"Who made this?" I mouthed, silently. I heard an Uzi adjust, and I closed my mouth quickly to keep my thoughts from escaping my lips. *What is this?* I thought. *Water around us?* I traced the water table markings on the Den's drawing. *Water beneath us?* I traced my finger underneath the sunken structures, where there were more water table markings. *Underground water?*

The words sparked something I couldn't put my finger on. *How could there be water underneath us without us knowing?*

I grabbed *Old Chicago Topography* and flipped to an earmarked section. I remembered seeing similar designations of water underneath structures.

Underground lake, I read. A portion of the city had an untapped, underground lake. It had never been explored, at least not before the Great Superstorm. They must have found what was down there by now. Why would it matter here in the Den?

I realized someone wanted me to know this information. Why would someone want *me* to know about this? Who left these papers for me? The female Procreate? She had seemed overly eager to give me access to these books. Could it be Lester, trying to find a way out of the Den himself? No, it couldn't be Lester. There was no way he would risk letting anyone know there was a way out. No, it couldn't be him. What did I really know about the other Procreates? Who were they really? In their previous lives, like Lester, they were all someone else before they ended up here. They were the only ones with access to these books and to these rooms; it had to be one of them.

This meant they knew. Someone knew about my plan. Did they want in? Should I let them in? There were too many questions and not enough time to make sense of any of it. I folded the paper and noticed light blue lines on the other side I must've overlooked. I unfolded the paper and turned it over. It was a diagram of some sort, perhaps of a small machine. It wasn't quite round, but it wasn't any other shape either. It looked like a sketch of a small box with an oval ball inside; tubes extended from the ball and wrapped around the structure, each crisscrossed by smaller tubes that looked like small veins.

Wait...I looked at the diagram as a whole without dissecting each part. It was a heart. But not a human heart. It was a machine, a mechanical heart. This was a diagram of a mechanical heart. *Holy shit.*

I folded the drawing just like the newspaper clipping and stuffed it into my sleeve. The soldier guarding the door gave a sharp whistle, and the boy in the room with me quickly advanced toward me, motioning for me to stand. He pointed his Uzi at my chest, a silent demand I vacate the room. They led me back through the same dim path, down the dingy stairs, and back through the circled hallway on the main floor. On the way to the foyer, we passed the opening to the Great Room on the main floor where the Procreates sat centerstage, all eyes on me. In the split second I had to see their faces, I tried to sort out who, if any of them, could have slipped those documents to me and what their intentions could be.

Back in the foyer, I said, "I want to speak to them."

The child soldiers separated. One kept his Uzi aimed easily at my chest, and the other exited to the Great Room. He returned right away, obviously with an answer. The muzzle of his Uzi pushed me out the back door. The rain hit me with force. It was cold and harsh, unforgiving and unrelenting, not the welcome break I usually felt when leaving the Procreates' headquarters.

No, this time the rain was a stark reminder of why I wanted—needed—to find a way to break the Den. To break Lester. To get out of the Den. I touched my chest, and it pulsated in rhythm with the rain, fast and hard.

I needed to get out of the rain and get the documents somewhere dry so that I could inspect them. I reached into my pocket and felt cold metal touch my fingertips. I pulled the piece of metal out of my pocket; it looked like a small locket. I hadn't had time to inspect this either. Despite my heart's quick beats, I picked up the pace of my legs and ran from the library to my housing circle.

The atmosphere was particularly somber as I approached the housing circles. The militia was finalizing the stage where the sacrifice would be presented for all to see soon, but that didn't explain the morose feeling in the air. I looked around the grounds for my father, but I couldn't find him amongst his men. Something was off. Something wasn't right.

I ran toward our house, and I saw Jo in the distance. I yelled to her through the rain, waving my arms, but she didn't see me or hear me. I kept calling out to her, but she gave no response. She didn't even look in my direction. I squinted as I ran to get a better view of her through the rain. I got closer to our house and realized she was standing with her hands behind her back. Her clothes looked bloody.

Militiamen walked in and out of my house. Why

were they there? I ran faster, sliding on the loose gravel along the ground. Staying on my feet seemed more challenging with every step. I dug my heels into the thick mud and propelled myself forwards. But I stopped in my tracks when I saw my father emerge from our house.

"Everything is okay," I said, panting, spraying rainwater from my lips.

Two militiamen followed directly behind him, and they all walked over to Jo. My father put his strong hand on Jo's shoulder and led her away from the house as the militiamen followed.

Jo's hands were bound.

Bewildered by what I was seeing, I was about to approach them when I saw two more men follow behind them with a stretcher. Who was that? Who was on the board? I looked over at Father again. The rain was too thick, and I couldn't make out the expression on his face, but it felt as though he was intentionally avoiding my gaze. He walked slowly through the mud, guiding Jo along the way, deliberately moving slower than necessary. I stood with my feet stuck in the mud and watched this all unfold without a clue what was happening. Father and Jo, her tied hands behind her, walked toward me with militiamen close behind them. Everything slowed even more. When our paths crossed, I looked at my father, but I didn't know what to say or what to think. Whatever was happening had to be some sort of misunderstanding, and I didn't want to risk making it worse. I tried to speak to him telepathically like he and Mother did, but it didn't work when I tried. He wasn't responding to me. Or perhaps I couldn't hear him.

People from the housing circles had started to gather as the militia continued to march Jo away from our house. The neighbors loomed over the body on the stretcher, and a feeling of lead filled my stomach. Jo broke away from our father; I'm certain he didn't resist. His men immediately charged after her, but Father raised his arm, signaling his men to hold back. All eyes were on Jo as she ran through the thick mud. Her bare feet squelched over the rain-slicked terrain. It didn't offer her a friendly escape route, but that wasn't what she was trying to do. When she made it back to the front of the house, she threw herself on top of the body on the stretcher.

Everyone stood silent and still. Father and two militiamen made their way back over to Jo. They collected her and began the slow-motion march away from the house again. They were leading my sister toward the presentation stage. Why? What were they doing? What the hell was happening?

The men carting the body from my house moved in my direction. I stared at the ripped sheets that I knew came from our house and were now being used to cover the body that lay on the stretcher.

"No," I said. My shoes had sunk into the muddy ground, and I left them behind as I trudged, barefoot like my sister, through the ankle-deep mud toward the body on the board. "No," I said again.

"Stanton," one of the militiamen called out, shaking his head. "Don't."

I pulled the sheet back. Under it lay my mother, her eyes closed.

She's sleeping, I thought. And then again, *She's sleeping*. Her skin was pale blue. Her clothes were stained red. Her body made no movement. I stared at my mother, waiting for her to wake up.

"Go to John," she said with her mouth closed.

"She's awake!" I yelled. "Mother!"

I shook her body, and she slipped off the board, landing with a muted thud like John had when we'd pulled him out of the water and onto the boat's deck. I fell to the ground and pulled her from the muddy ground into my lap.

"Mother! Mom, it's me! I'm here. Wake up. I'm here. It's Stanton. Wake up, Mom." I wiped the constant flow of rain from her face. The men came for her, but I held on tighter the more they tried to take her from me.

"Stanton," I heard a soft voice say through the rain and felt a strong hand on the back of my head. "Let her go," said Father. "Let her go."

The men took my dead mother out of my hands.

Behind me, more men lifted my sister onto the sacrificial presentation stage. This was all wrong. I looked at my father.

"It was me," I said, looking at him. He just nodded his head in silence. I looked down at the fresh wounds up and down my arms. The cut on my leg throbbed in response to my confession. "It was an accident," I said, helpless and disbelieving. "I was just...so angry." I struggled to find the words because I didn't understand myself how it all happened.

"Not out loud, Stanton. Not here. Listen, son, I know you're confused right now. I need to be with your sister." Concern consumed his face. "But remember: meet me at the shoreline after sunset. Don't talk to anyone."

I watched, helpless, as Father blurred away in the distance. I looked at my sister, strung up for all to judge, to release their wrath upon, to unburden their minds against. She would be left up there in the cold, in the rain, and soon, in the dark. She was being presented as all that we were striving not to become. She was to be a representation of the monstrosities we'd vowed to eradicate. But it was wrong; this was all wrong. It made me question how many other times we'd been wrong. How many times had we condemned someone to death, believing what may not even have been true? Had we been monsters all this time?

The next day, we would each take turns binding her

with chains to anchor her to her final resting place, there in the same waters of the Den where John was reborn. I had to do something. I couldn't wait while my sister stood innocent, paying for my sins. I found myself heading for the holding cells.

***

The elevator was ready and waiting. I was alone again in the bullet train heading towards the brick wall. I reached into my pocket and pulled out the small metal locket. There were hinges on the side, which told me it opened. I pinched the small metal clasp between my fingers and carefully opened it. Inside were two pictures, one of a small baby and the other of a woman. The photos were small, but something about the woman looked familiar. The images were faded, but the woman clearly had dark, shoulder-length hair.

I reached back into my pocket and carefully took out the now-soggy, delicate newspaper clipping. The folded paper was stuck together. I slowly peeled each layer apart until the article was completely unfolded. I looked closely at the photo from the article and the small photo from the locket, back and forth between both pictures. I looked again closer, and again even closer.

Two old, worn items from the past, and both had the same photo of the same woman. In this reality, in my underground world called the Den, anything was possible. With that possibility came great uncertainty, but I'd never been more certain of anything. These were the same woman.

Which left me asking, *who was the child?*

An unsettling feeling crept into my body. A tiny corner had lifted out of the locket's small setting. With my fingertip, I pried back the part of the photo that stuck out, and the small photo popped out of the locket. It was folded in half. I unfolded the small photo, which revealed another woman. Who were these people? And why did Melanie have this locket with their photos?

The Journal

I finally found him. He's real. At first, I thought the reports had to be wrong. I thought, my mother is too busy to keep up such an elaborate lie for my entire life. I thought I was the best liar I knew. I was wrong, about so many things. I always suspected that I had a sibling, I was right about that. I have always been a little different and it didn't come from mom or dad, we are all so different. I wasn't sure where the report was going to lead me but when the shell found me my hopes had been confirmed. I had never seen anything like it in my life, it didn't belong here. I knew it wasn't from here. It just wasn't possible. It was a message, and it was only part of the message. That's when I began looking for the other parts.

I started with the usual suspects. Dad, but he was too busy chasing his own stories. Mom, but she was too busy chasing her own demons. Pete, but he was too busy chasing mom, and then there was Aunt Hannah. Naturally, she was the busiest and hardest to get to out of them all. I knew better than to try and get to her directly though. Even if I had, knowing her she would've sent me down a bigger rabbit hole just to get me out of her hair for as long as possible. But her idiot, blind followers didn't know any better. They knew who I was, and they gave me anything they could that wasn't tier one confidential in hopes that it would get them in better graces with their boss. It didn't, and it wouldn't have, but I saw a flaw in Aunt Hannah's system, and I'm not ashamed, I took full advantage of it. If it were her or mom in my shoes, they both would've done the same. I'm just following in their footsteps.

The report was easy to get. Once I had verification that Michael existed, I knew I had to go full press. I walked into Hannah's top-secret facilities like I owned the place. It was easy faking out her staff because the role was so simple. Be dominate. Be relentless. Be belligerent if need be, but always, always smile in the elevator. Because you never know who you're going to run into, and people tend to be more helpful towards pretty girls. It wasn't a coincidence. I ended up in an elevator with Hannah's VP of Novyx. He ran all of New Chicago's secret governmental departments. He didn't matter though, not to Aunt Hannah. He is just another one of her pawns. What mattered was what he had on him, a security identification card. With our developments I was disappointed in my Aunt. I thought it was going to be far more challenging to break in, and yet, all that stood between the truth and everything else was an old school security card. All it took was a casual yet suggestive rub of the arm, an accidental slip of my shoe, and a little sleight of hand and I had access to all of Hannah's secrets, all of them.

There was a secret floor. If you had the right card, which I did, and you held it to the elevator keypad longer than the first beep it would follow with a delayed second beep. The elevator would go all the way down to B and then down an unknown number of levels. I counted to ten before the elevator stopped with no indication of where I was and then the doors just opened.

There were several large laboratories and empty hallways filled with rows of rooms. I don't know what she had in all the rooms or what she was doing in all the laboratories but I suspected I didn't have much time before the dope in the elevator realized his card had been lifted. There were no personnel in the laboratories. Only machines. I walked around in plain sight watching mindless machines conducting complex experiments with no oversight. If I had more time, I'm sure there would've been significant scientific discoveries to uncover, but I was risking treason for one reason only. To find him.

Beyond the labs and beyond the row of rooms there was a large, dimly lit room at the end of a never-ending hallway. As I neared the dimly lit space a large, rectangular podium appeared in what looked like an empty room. The podium was just a clear glass table. I thought it was a joke. A sick joke that Aunt Hannah purposely put here as a sort of final mockery. I spat on the table and it lit up. I put my hands on the top of the table and a small compartment door in the center of the glass table slid open and a fingertip sized red light pulsed from where the small door slid open. I put my finger over the red light and felt a quick, sharp poke. I pulled my finger back and a small pool of blood bubbled up from my fingertip.

A female robotic voice welcomed Hannah Kerwin. The clear table then turned opaque and images began to form. At first look what I saw didn't seem worth all the bodily fluids required to grant access. The images were just blueprints, nothing out of the ordinary. I tapped through a handful of images which were more blueprints, but something showed up that made me stop. There was a blueprint that displayed structures like our city's, no, identical to ours, but built underground. There were more blueprints that followed showing what appeared to be residential homes in a circle fashion adjacent to underground high-rise structures. The last image displayed an aerial view of the land, and it was encompassed by water and it appeared to have a massive body of water beneath the land.

I began to wonder why Aunt Hannah would go through such great lengths to keep these documents secret. Of course I verified, and there were no public records of any of these prints. It was somewhat of a ludicrous assumption, but it wasn't entirely impossible to think that Hannah was building something. Or, had already built something, some sort of new, secret, self-sustaining civilization.

I thought the idea was too farfetched until the table went dark and bodies started to float up. They floated right up the table like they were floating up from water, belly up. Dead bodies. Piles of them appeared and disappeared before my eyes. I was watching a slide show of death. Bodies tortured, maimed, bloated, stacked on top of one another crudely and with no remorse. I took pictures and uploaded them via Thin Air to the Skeye. Once I did that, there was no turning back. Staring at the dead bodies distended in these images, I noticed my reflection and the corners of my lips were turned up. I didn't feel myself smiling at these images and yet I was, in plain sight for my own eyes to see. I allowed it because no one was there to witness.

The images faded and my smile stamped out. It would only be a matter of time before Hannah realized I have this information. If she is capable of all of this, who knows what else she is capable of.

Puzzle pieces were forming. These bodies, who were they? Where were they? What happened to them? Who killed them? I know in my gut; the images of these bodies are somehow tied to my brother. And when I find him, I can finally ask him why the voices won't go away.

Right before the table projector went blank there

was a split screen image of a man half-dressed who had a distinct scar down the center of his chest and then there was an image of a house. A deep-brown house enveloped by lush greenery. I didn't recognize the man, but I recognized the house. It was mom and Hannah's childhood home, The Connecticut House. I've seen it before in mom's old flip page albums.

With the report and me being able to take advantage of sharing Hannah's DNA, it was unsettlingly easy to find Michael's dad. He was closer to home than I thought. Everyone is linked to Hannah in one way or another. It turns out, Michael's dad is our leading physicist. When I found him, neither of us were surprised by the other. I think he had been expecting me. I saw recognition in his eyes when we met for the first time. He wouldn't be the first to say I look like mom. My face was his confirmation I was who I said I was, and the scar peeking out of his top button was my confirmation that he was who he said he was.

He told me his theories about a 5th dimension in the spacetime continuum. He spoke about their being other realities, outside of ours. Mirror realities, he called them. He said they existed as transient anomalies in space and time and that they would allow for things to exist in alternate realities that should not exist. Meaning there should be ways to move back and forth between mirror realities. He had no data though. How would he possibly collect data on something he couldn't test? I recommended that perhaps he couldn't test it because he didn't have the right test subject. He knew how to find mom and Hannah's childhood home. When I asked him how he knew where it was he told me he once lived down the street. How convenient. When he took me to the house I was blindfolded, and it seemed like we drove in circles for hours. I got the impression he either didn't want me to know how to get there or that he really didn't know how to get there either but being blindfolded really didn't bother me. It gave me an excuse to not have to make small talk with him.

Once we got there and he removed my blindfold I didn't waste any time. I headed straight for the house, but he stopped me and led me a long way through what would've been a backyard into a dense stand of dead trees. He walked us back to a part of the barren woods like he had done this a thousand times before. There was a well, I could see it a few feet away. I tried to keep an open mind but all I could think about was throwing him down just to hear how far down the well went for wasting my time and dragging me all the way out there to do whatever it was he planned on doing. Then came the reward for behaving.

When I looked into the well, what was in there was the last thing I expected to see. Water. He and I walked circles around the mirage waving like idiots at our reflections, only it wasn't a mirage, it was real. I told him he must have somehow filled this up before bringing me here because it was impossible for it to be naturally filled with water. He insisted he had no reason to lie to me. He told me this was the portal. I think I hurt his feelings a bit because I laughed so hard I could barely breathe and when I was done his face was as red as mine, only he wasn't laughing.

I could see why mom didn't stick around with this guy, too sensitive, it's unbecoming. Once I calmed down, I listened to him rattle off a list of items that he tried to send through this portal, to another reality that is. I listened to him lament about how no matter how many times he chucked things into this mysterious water filled well that nothing ever happened. I asked him why he suspected that out of all places this place would be a portal to these other mirror realities that he claimed existed. He told me that this was the only structure in the entire state that not only had moved from its original foundation but that all science says should have been demolished by the Superstorm. He said that every time he went there the coordinates changed. It is unmappable. It exists where it shouldn't and wherever it wants. The house is a transient anomaly, and the well filled to the brim with water is just unexplainable. He was convinced it all had to mean something and that it had to be related to his theories about their being a 5th dimension. He believed that the 5th dimension that would allow someone or something to cross into alternate realities was somehow accessible here.

This may have begun as a theory for him. A part of his role as a leading physicist. It became clear, however, that he wasn't at peace with losing his son. Even more obvious was that he believed Michael was alive, but not here, in our world. He didn't say those words exactly; he actually spoke very little about his child, my brother. But what he didn't say with his mouth he said with his body, and its expressions, and his mind. He was obsessed with finding a way to reconnect with Michael, and I was going to let him lead me straight to him. In this reality or another, I am going to find my brother if it's the last thing I do.

I watched him throw random small objects into the water filled well. Nothing came back out. I suggested maybe the object must be significant to whoever or whatever is in the reality you want to contact. We had a light bulb moment. He left quickly and returned with an old, rusted key. He smiled at me and tossed it into the water, and for a moment I caught a glimpse of what my brother could've looked like. We waited and waited. We waited long after the sun should have set. I wondered, had we already crossed into a different reality and not even noticed? The days do get longer every year, but the sun should have set by the time we started to walk out of the dead woods.

Before we left, he said he wanted to show me one more thing, mom's old room. He said this may be the only time I ever get to see it. I wasn't particularly interested in going inside the dilapidated house. I was fairly certain if I went inside, I wasn't going to come out. It was one strong wind away from collapsing, but something was pulling me in. I agreed and he instructed me how to get to mom's room. He didn't want to go inside either, but I think for different reasons.

Inside the house initially I had to plug my nose the stench was so nauseating but it's incredible what the human body can adapt to. By the time I reached the stairs the smells weren't even noticeable to me anymore. I made it up to the second level and down the first hall to mom's old room. I wasn't taken aback by anything in particular. It was just an empty room and a double doored closet. I would've missed it if I didn't open the doors to the closet. I would've missed it if I hadn't gone into the house. There, on the floor of my mom's childhood closet, was the shell. Unmistakable purple Atlantic calico shell. I had never seen one in person let alone actually held one in my hand but I remember the stories mom told me when I was young about her vacations as a child with grandma and grandpa shell hunting on perfectly white beaches.

When I emerged from the house the first thing I asked was if he had found anything unusual in the house. He said he hadn't. I didn't show him the shell right away, I wasn't sure if it was even real. In the car he blindfolded me again and we began a similar circular drive for hours before he told me to lift my blindfold. It was pitch black outside the car windows, even if it weren't, I wouldn't be able to tell where we were if we were outside of the city's walls. I wanted to believe he was protecting me. Now that I know what he knows, the less I knew probably would've been better for us all. It was too late for that though.

The shell poked me in the leg the entire ride back. The sharp impression it made was a confirmation it was real. I showed him the shell and he didn't seem surprised. He seemed hopeful. He murmured something incoherent about the remnants raids that happened before I was born but he stopped himself, probably because he didn't think I knew anything about what he was trying to say. I told him where I had found it and explained that I wanted to feel certain I could trust him before sharing it with him. He didn't want to let his emotions show but I knew he was excited. It was possible that we had opened the doors to the portal. He said it was the first time he had ever sent something and had anything come back. He said this was the beginning of breaking the walls of reality. I couldn't tell if he thought that was a good thing or not. He said it was imperative that we return to the house as soon as we could because the portal is unstable and could move at any time. We agreed to get a few hours of sleep and return straight away. He told me to hide the shell to make sure it didn't get into the hands of the wrong people. I'm certain he was using the shell as a metaphor. I believed what he said, but I needed some insurance.

His level of secrecy raised flags for me. If breaking down the walls between existing realities on different planes was a good thing, wouldn't it be made public? That there are possibilities of other realities? There was a lot of different directions this could've gone. So why keep it secret? There was something hidden in the realities that he or someone else didn't want people finding out about. So yes, I needed someone on my side if things went bad.

I couldn't make it so obvious that anyone would be able to put the pieces together. It could only be you, mom. You were gone the night I came home. I reset my tablet password in hopes that you would find it first but if you hadn't no one would've known the password other than you. I hid the shell in the only place Pete wouldn't find it, knowing you'd eventually find it. I took your burner number so I could call you without us being traced. Mom, there's no one I can trust but you.

So, if you have found this. It means my plan has

worked, so far. You must have made it here, to your childhood home, and that means you're just one step behind me. It also means he made it through and I'm going through next. I found him mom. I found Michael, and I'm going to bring him home. Whatever you do mom, don't trust her. Don't trust your sister.

Forever together through this life and the next.

Jessica Danielle (J.D.)

Liv

I sift through the pages of my daughter's journal over and over. I look at them, front and back. I read them through again and again. I run my fingers over the last letters she wrote, feeling every indentation.

"*Forever together through this life and the next. Jessica Danielle*," I read out loud.

"What does that mean?" a soft voice asks.

Melanie. I had completely forgotten where I am and who I'm here with. I was in a trance. I finally find my daughter, and she's gone again.

Without looking up from the pages, I say, "It's something the two of us used to say when she was little. It helped her sleep at night when I would leave for work."

I reminisce about the nights I tucked Dani into bed and we said this to each other. She was always so different. She asked about death at such a young age. She had night terrors. She talked in her sleep. She even talked to nobody, to the air, aloud during the day. Once it made sense to her what I did for my career, she became obsessed with death and the possibility of me dying. No matter what I said or did, I couldn't guarantee I'd come home every night, and I didn't want to lie to her. After all, no one is guaranteed tomorrow; I don't care who you are. Instead of pretending death wasn't real, we learned to embrace it. She learned to embrace it. She understood as a young child that everyone and everything dies eventually, from one thing or another. She understood it was my job to help make sure people didn't die before their intended time, and sometimes that meant putting my life in harm's way.

I used to tell her *forever together through this life and the next* to ease her little mind. It just stuck with us, and it worked to calm her overactive imagination.

Until one day she stopped having night terrors. She stopped talking to her imaginary friends. She stopped worrying about me dying every day. Eventually, she stopped talking to me altogether. I thought that's just what teenage girls do.

"It's my fault," I say aloud. I let it happen. I lost my daughter a long time ago.

"Don't worry," Melanie says. "He'll take care of her. If she makes it there, he'll find her, and he will take care of her."

"What do you mean *if* she makes it there? And who will take care of her?"

"Stanton. He's always looked after me. He looks after everyone, dead or alive."

I look at this sweet, filthy, well-intentioned deer in headlights. I smooth my hand over her greasy hair.

"Where did you hear that name?" I feel anger creeping into my fingers. "Who told you about him?" I demand, grabbing the frail girl by her bony shoulders.

My hands shake. I'm ashamed for shaking her the way I am. I'm losing control. I release my offensive grip on her and smooth the hair around her shoulders where I grabbed her. "I'm sorry. I got distracted. I know you're confused by everything. We're going to figure out what's going on." I try to convince myself as much as her.

Undeterred by my erratic behavior, she pulls something out of her pocket. She's surprised by it. "It made it," she says. "Here. Stanton." She holds out to me a worn, delicate, black-and-white picture of a young man, maybe seventeen or eighteen years old. He's tall with a pile of dark hair smoothed over his head. He has a handsome face, a strong jawline. For a minute, I think I'm looking at a picture of his dad. His clothes hang loose and unfitted on his slender frame, and his ankles are bare. His shoes have visible holes and missing shoelaces, and his skin is blotched with black smudges. I wonder if this is a prison photo; it may as well be if he really is where Hannah said. Despite the dirt covering his skin, the lack of color in the picture, and all the missing years, a mother never forgets.

This is my son, my Michael. He's a man now.

I cover my mouth, instinctively trying to hide my emotions. "Where did this come from?" I whisper.

"I brought it with me."

"And where did you bring it from?" I ask, even though I know the answer. If I just pretend this is all a horrible nightmare, maybe her answer will be different.

"From home," she says, matter of fact.

"The Den?"

Her face brightens a bit. "Yes! How do you know where I'm from?"

I look at her, and all the guilt I thought I'd sold to the devil comes flooding back. "You don't remember? Anything?"

She makes no movement but offers, "My mom, she died when I was little. That's my first memory."

"When was that? Do you remember how old you were? When your...mom died?"

"I was six. I know for sure because that's the day I met Stanton."

I fight the emotions, but the anger bubbles up. "Son of a bitch," I say. I put my hand out to her. "Not you. Not you. I'm talking to myself."

I sent Melanie to the Den when she was a baby in the hope she would have a better life there than here. Within a few years, she'd lost another mother. No child should have to lose one mother, let alone three. At least she remembered only the last one. Anger wells in me as I silently judge myself for my past decisions. The anger grows as I think about why Lester didn't report this to Hannah. I stop for a moment, realizing Hannah hadn't mentioned Michael still being alive until today. Eighteen years, and she never once mentioned Michael was alive.

It hits me: they're still working together, Lester and Hannah. How is that possible? What is their endgame? She withheld this for a reason.

"Listen, I need to ask you something. It might be confusing, maybe even offensive, but I need you to know it's not my intention to confuse you or to offend you."

She nods.

"What's your name?"

She pauses before answering, which tells me she's thinking about her answer before responding. Which also tells me she's thinking about lying, but why?

"Melanie," she offers.

I smile gently at her. "That's what I was hoping you'd say. Do you know who I am?"

She pauses in thought again and slowly shakes her head side to side.

"My name is Olivia. Olivia Jones. That doesn't sound familiar to you?"

She makes no movement of confirmation or denial.

"How did you get here?"

"I went through the door."

"What door?"

She looks confused, peering around us. "Here." She lifts her arms, motioning around herself. "The door to this house. It looks different where I'm from, but it's the same house."

I nod my head. She's experienced too much trauma;

286

she's confused and clearly having difficulty remembering how she got here. There's only one way to get to the Den, and only one way to get back. That's how Hannah designed it...

The pages of Dani's journal slip out of my lap. *There's more than one way,* I realize. "Can you tell me what you mean when you say you got here through the door of this house?"

"There was a key. Stanton's dad, Mr. Lyman, gave it to me."

"Lyman? Mich—Stanton's dad? Wait, what did you say?"

"Mr. Lyman, he gave me a key."

I shake my head. "No. No, you must be mistaken. Lyman, he's...he died, sweetheart. A long time ago. He's been dead for a long time," I say, reassuring myself of things I'm maybe not so sure of anymore.

Melanie shakes her head. "No, he's not dead. He gave me a key to this house. That's how I got here."

Hannah, I'm going to kill you, I think. I shove down my emotions. If Lyman didn't die all those years ago, then what happened? Why would he fake his own death? I try to reason with myself. If this, if any of this, were possible and true, and my son is alive in the Den, I want Lyman there with him. But it doesn't make sense because I saw him take his last breath. *Focus Liv,* I repeat in my head.

"Are you okay?" Melanie asks.

Her pale, thin hand is on mine. Her touch reminds me of the last hug I gave her before I let them take her all those years ago. Here she is, a young lady now, consoling me instead of the other way around. There's no world where I ever thought this would happen. Maybe my world, this world, this reality, isn't the right place for me after all.

"I'm not okay, but it's not for you to be concerned with, Melanie."

"You can call me Mel."

That makes me smile. "Mel?"

She nods, mirroring my smile. "That's what Stanton calls me."

"Is that so? Well, Mel, can I ask you another question?"

"Yes."

"You seem pretty smart and very brave. Do you have any idea what's happening?"

"Yes."

"What do you think is going on here?"

"It's simple, Aunt Liv. I'm here because you need me. Your world needs me. I am a message from the Den. So that you don't forget."

"Wait a minute," I say, holding my hand up. "I thought you said you didn't know who I was?"

She takes her hand back. "Your daughter and I, we aren't the same, and yet we aren't all that different. You see, I'm searching for answers also, and like Dani, I

288

needed a little bit of insurance."

I open my mouth, but nothing comes out.

"I needed to know you were still invested in my wellbeing before revealing the truth. Once you've shown all your cards, you can't unshow them. You understand?"

"And I passed your test?" I ask through my teeth.

"It's okay to be angry, but hear me out. She wanted to go to the Den, your daughter, and I needed to come here. Neither of us would have made it if the other didn't go through. The portal needs to be balanced in order to work. Our realities need to be balanced. For something to come out, something needs to go in. It was the perfect plan for us. The key was the sign I was waiting for, and the shell was the sign she was waiting for."

"You lied to me. You used my daughter."

"No, Aunt Liv. We lied to each other. All of us. You've known since you saved my life in the dead woods who I am. You've also known in some way that I've always known who you are. That's why you work nights, why you've always worked nights. Because you can't sleep at night. The guilt, Aunt Liv. The shame you feel. It never let you escape. You sold yourself to the devil for a person who would sell you to the devil if it meant saving herself."

"Hannah," I say, unable to look in my niece's face.

"Your daughter. She's different."

Mel's eyes dart around for a moment, like she's making sure nobody else is listening, her expression unsettled. It's slight, but it's noticeable when she speaks about Dani.

"She was looking for answers, and I was looking for my mother. Dani wasn't going to find the answers she needed here. And, well, we all know I wasn't going to find my biological mother where I was. My real mother, she died before I was taken."

"Sasha."

"Right. You remember Sasha, right? Your best friend?"

Sasha's face comes to me often in my dreams since her murder more than fifteen years ago. She doesn't haunt me so much as just remind me that I wasn't there for her, that I wasn't there for Melanie. I've told myself over and over there was nothing I could've done. There was no way for me to have known what was going to happen. I like to believe that if I could've done anything, at the very least I'd have gotten Melanie out of danger.

The last time I saw Melanie, I accepted that I'd never see her again. We were never supposed to see each other again. But here we are now, Melanie and me, face to face. And in a matter of moments, it has caused me to question everything.

"Of course I remember your mom. She was my best friend. Not a day goes by that I don't think about her.

And you. But how do you know Sasha? You were just a baby when she—"

"Was murdered," Melanie declares.

I nod reluctantly. "Yes, you were just a baby when she was killed. So, tell me, how did you find out about her?"

"I have my sources. Is that what you'd call them?"

I'm done playing games with her. This isn't helping either of us. "Melanie, is this really about Sasha? Or is this about your biological mother, Hannah? I don't want to lose sight of what you've risked coming all this way for. We don't know how traveling between realities effects an individual's DNA. There could be unknown adverse effects. I'm not saying I'd let anything happen to you, but please understand, the Den was never created to have people..." I pause. I can't believe what I'm saying. "To have people go back and forth. You see, Melanie, you were never supposed to leave the Den."

She cocks her head to the side in confusion. "Created? What do you mean?"

I hold a beat. "You know you're not from there."

"I know," she says abruptly. "But what do you mean it was created?"

What the hell? I wonder as I brace myself to tell the truth for the first time in years. "The Den...we created it. Your mom—" I stop myself. "Hannah and her partner created a company called Novyx. They had multiple projects spanning multiple industries. Their focus was creating the Den. It was supposed to be a sanctum. Do you understand?"

She nods, urging me to continue.

"It all started before the Great Superstorm hit us and changed everything. They meant for it to be a place for the elite. Sort of like the ultimate fallout shelter for the top one percent. They were always anticipating the possibility of needing to leave here, and they wanted to be overprepared if that ever happened. Infection rates were soaring, and Mother Nature was trying to wipe us out. Hannah and her people speculated Old Chicago may not be home much longer if everything continued in the direction it was heading, so they created another home to go to."

The bitter memories of Hannah using this as her big push to get voted into office comes to mind as I tell her daughter half-truths about where she's been kept for the last fifteen years.

"She swore she was going to protect those at the top, and the Den was going to be their safe haven." This is where it gets complicated. "The Den wasn't of our..." I try to find the right word, but all that comes out is, "...reality. You see, Hannah had to make sure her plan was airtight before using any resources to break ground. She figured anyplace in our existence here would become just as vulnerable as Old Chicago. She was convinced it was only a matter of time, and that's how

292

she sold her idea. So she and her elite scientists found a way to create a world within our world that wasn't supposed to exist."

"You thought I wouldn't understand the possibility that more than one reality exists? Funny, I thought you would be the one who wouldn't be able to understand that. Go on."

One of the most difficult concepts for people to grasp is the fact that our reality is not the only one that exists, which is part of why other realities, like the mirror realities Dani wrote about in her journal, weren't made public knowledge. At least that was always Hannah's argument. Melanie, however, doesn't need convincing, so there really is nothing left to do but continue.

"The Den was only partially built when the Great Superstorm hit. When the storm finally ended, the only way we could reach the Den was through limited virtual communications, and only Hannah communicated with the Den. We couldn't physically reach it anymore. Imagine a gate or an opening now completely caved in and inaccessible. The Superstorm destroyed our land and shifted everything, completely disengaging our only portal to the Den. There's been no way to get there since, and the Den was the only mirror reality we were able to breach. Which is why, since our portal to the Den disappeared, it goes against all reason that you're here right now. And it really doesn't explain where my daughter has gone. I think it's time, Melanie, for you to start answering some of my questions."

Her pale skin has turned bright red. "Hannah communicated? How? You mean you've been able to communicate with us all along?"

"Tell me where my daughter is, Melanie."

"I've spent my entire life believing the only way to get the truth was to risk my own life when you've been able to communicate with us this entire time?"

The tension mounts as small beads of sweat form along Melanie's flushed forehead. Neither of us is backing down, and neither of us is going to leave here without the information we want. She's a Jones, without a doubt.

"Melanie, calm down. I need to find my daughter. Help me. Where did she go?"

"Why should I help you?" she says defensively, straightening to make herself appear larger than the frail, pale girl she is.

"I did what I thought was right. I can't undo it. I can't change the past. But you...you can help my daughter. You can help me find her."

"Stanton is going through with his plan. I see now more than ever that it's the only answer."

"What are you talking about?"

She smiles viciously at me. It makes me wonder what sort of person my son turned out to be.

"He's going to break the Den."

"What does that mean? Where is my daughter?"

"You're never going to find her. You're never going to see her again," Melanie states between angry gasps.

Shaking my head, I plead with my niece. Fifteen years of pent-up aggression and nothing to lose has made her the most dangerous person in this room. She has the upper hand, and she knows it.

"You." She points her finger at me with spite. "You left me there! You dumped me there, knowing I'd never be able to get out, all while communicating behind my back."

"It wasn't me, Mel. It wasn't me!" Any hope of preservation between her and Hannah is disintegrating. I want Hannah to be the one to put the final stake in her relationship with her child, not me. It shouldn't be me. "I'm sorry. I'm sorry! Is that what you want to hear? I'm sorry I took you from this world and sent you to the Den. I'm sorry. You want an apology for something that won't change anything? It won't change what you've gone through, Melanie. I know you've suffered. I know you've lost. I know you're angry and confused, and you've never been allowed to let any of those emotions out. I know. I know. I understand, and I am sorry. But I'm a messenger too, like you. I promised you and your mom I thought I was doing the right thing. With all my heart, I thought your life would be better in the Den than here. Honestly, I don't know if I was right or wrong. But you…you are you no matter where you are. Do you understand that?"

She collapses on the floor, crumpling into a small ball in the corner of the closet. I reach my hand out to her, and she draws her legs closer to her chest.

"Please, Melanie. Please help me. My daughter doesn't know what we know. She doesn't know how to get back. I need to know where she is. I need you to tell me: how do I get into the Den?"

She lifts her face from between her bony knees and is just about to speak when the sound of a car right outside the house turns both our faces toward the window. We look back at each other, confirming we heard the same thing. She edges closer to me, and I put my arm around her as familiar voices echo through the hollow house.

Stanton

I couldn't stop staring at the thumb-sized photos in the small locket. I had a nagging feeling they were more important than they appeared. Mel had this locket and didn't tell me about it for a reason. We'd never kept secrets from each other. Well, I'd never kept a secret from her; I knew that at least.

The more I tried to wrap my mind around everything that was happening, the more each event seemed less real. No way could Jo be the sacrifice. No way was Mother dead. No way could these articles have gotten here. Yet, I held the worn newspaper clippings and blueprints in my pocket. My sister had been groomed for death. My mother was among John and his people now, and there I was, numb, absolutely and undeniably numb, staring at a photo I didn't know the meaning behind of people I'd never met.

The elevator door threatened to shut, but my foot forbade it. *Thump, thump, thump.* The door accosted my foot over and over. I grabbed it and pushed it with all my strength back into its pocket. Then, I opened my mouth to let out a scream loud enough to wake the dead, a scream that would tell a story, a sound filled with my doubt, anguish, disbelief, and impatience at wanting things I would never get.

My lips parted, but nothing audible came out.

I had suffered in silence my entire life like so many

others in the Den. What was one more day? If it meant pushing my plans forward, then suffering in silence was the best strategy. Silence had been, and still was, my best ally. The elevator door pushed against my resisting palms, and I finally stepped out of its way.

I was back in the long hallway with rows and rows of holding cells. I stood in front of cell 5468 as though I'd teleported there. I didn't remember taking the steps to get to John's door, but his door was in front of me nonetheless. I opened the door to his cell and immediately felt something was off. I couldn't feel John's presence.

He wasn't there. He should be there. Someone had moved him.

Bodies weren't supposed to be moved until I okayed transport. This had to be Lester and the Procreates. But why? Was it possible they knew about my plan? No, if they knew, Lester would've already taken Jo down and put me up in her place. There was no way they knew.

Then who had moved him?

I left John's cell and started to check adjacent cells. Nothing. All my conversationalists were gone. I had five bodies at any given time. Where had they gone? Who would've moved them? I checked the large room at the end of the long hallway. I was the only one with the key; the key was my DNA. It was the most high-tech operating apparatus we had in the Den, at least that I knew of. It seemed out of place considering how prehistoric everything else here was. I put my lips up to the pin-sized filter on the door and let out a breath.

Nothing. The door didn't budge.

I rubbed the filter with the inside of my dirty shirt and tried another breath. Nothing again. I opened one of my newly scabbed-over, self-inflicted wounds and smeared my blood over the filter. Nothing. A warm sensation trickled down my arm. I looked down: my wound had opened completely. A steady, warm trickle of blood from my forearm dripped off my elbow and collected in a small puddle on the floor. I lifted both arms and banged on the door, splattering blood everywhere. Nothing. The door did nothing.

I swallowed my rage and suffocated my screams with blood-covered hands. My mother would be so ashamed if she saw me right now. *Mother.* They would bring her down after medical was done with their job. It would take longer, though, I was certain, seeing as her death wasn't natural. Time didn't exist in the holding cells. I needed to get back aboveground and to the shoreline.

I would wait for Father, even if it took hours for him to come. I would wait.

***

Back aboveground, intending to go straight to the shoreline, I instead found myself retracing my path back to the presentation stage. I held out for any feeling of relief, but each breath felt forced and thin, and each step took more effort than the last. It wasn't dread I felt that made every movement seem so difficult. I wasn't resistant to what needed to happen. I didn't walk in trepidation for those who deserved what was coming. It shouldn't have happened that way, though. Jo shouldn't be made to suffer.

Every year when the sacrifice was presented, the people of the Den carried on with their business as usual, unphased by the life on the line because it didn't matter to any of us. Their soul had already been taken by the sins that placed them there. The annual sacrifice became something we all had to play a part in, a chore.

Everyone knew Jo, though. Everyone loved her. The atmosphere around the dais told me that everyone was fearful for her and her soul. To be living did not mean you were alive, and the Den, where the dead haunted the living, was no place you wanted to send someone to their death unless you were certain they deserved it.

The presentation stage was exceptionally active with Jo on post as our sacrifice. The Den's people left silent gifts for next life as though she were already gone. Kneeling in the mud with their elbows on the makeshift stage, they bowed their heads to pray by her feet. Who were they praying for? My sister? Or themselves, begging forgiveness for the actions they were going to take? If my sister died, we were all fitted for the same fate.

I watched for a while from a distance. I didn't want

to call attention to myself, but I needed to talk to her before I saw Father. After just a few hours on that post, she looked exhausted and frail. Her head hung down in misplaced shame. Her shoulders drew in, making her appear much smaller than she already was. I didn't need to see Jo clearly from where I was standing to know how painful her restraints were. I knew from years of sacrificial ceremonies because after each sacrifice ended, I was the one who unwrapped the chains. I was the one who took the body off the post. I was the one who laid them each to rest, for their final time, bodies bruised and bloodied from the thorny ropes that tied their limbs together, as if the eyes watching them weren't immobilizing enough. Bones crushed, organs perforated from the air-sucking pressure of metal chains repeatedly wrapped around a soft body, crushing it from the outside in.

And then there was the water in the lungs, a keepsake from the Den for their last offering to this earth. But we would all be violence-free for one more year.

I could see the bruises on Jo's wrists from the same sacrificial, thorny ropes. I could see the blood oozing slowly from those bindings, her open skin stinging with every drop of rain. I pictured her insides giving in to the pressure of the chains that would soon confine her to her final resting stage. And the water from the Den that would linger in her lungs, serving as her last memory of her life in this place. No, I didn't need to see her clearly to be able to see all that.

From where I stood in that moment, those visions were as clear as they got.

I worked my way around the back of the housing circle. It was easy to go unspotted with Jo consuming everyone's attention. Silently, I slipped into our house.

Just that morning I'd been there, inside the house, with Mother lying in my lap.

My memory was hazy. I knew I was responsible for what happened to Mother, for everything that happened since, but I still couldn't remember how it all came about. The memory was just out of reach. It wasn't clear; none of it was.

There were blood stains all over the main room and in the bedroom, deep red, like rust-colored paint had been splattered across the walls and floor. It was on the table we shared meals at and on the couch we sat on. A large stain marked where blood must have pooled on the floor between the kitchen table and the couch. I bent down and reached my fingers out to touch the floor. The dirty hardwood had become porous and soft. It pushed in like a sponge when I pressed my fingers into it. Blood pooled around my fingers, my mother's blood. The rock in my chest pounded away as the stains sunk into my skin. Flashes of my mother's death came back in a haze, but standing there in the room where it happened helped the images become clearer the more I remembered.

I saw myself with broken dish shards in my hands. I saw myself covered in blood, flailing around like a man who had lost his sight and his mind all at once. I didn't recognize myself, and it wasn't because of the blood-soaked images. It was the rage. The anger. The violence and hostility that came from my body made me unrecognizable to myself. There was my mother, an innocent bystander, watching as I unloaded eighteen years of repressed infection and violence.

The incident returned piecemeal, some parts clearer than others. One image I couldn't quite make out. Was there…someone else in the room?

Yes! Someone else was there; they had to be. I looked down at my hands. There were only two; I certainly had only two hands. Yet I'd seen a third hand, a hand belonging to someone else. The third hand completed the slashes my hands made in the air, only the unseen person's slashes made contact with my mother.

I watched this nightmare play out before my eyes. Someone's hand killed my mother, but it wasn't mine. It wasn't me. I followed the unknown person's slashes and my own. I swiped at the air; their hand swiped at my mother's body. My hands swiped again, and I made contact, but it wasn't with Mother. I cut them. I cut the person who killed my mother. The rage had overcome me in the moment; I must have entirely dismissed that someone else was in the room with us.

"I see you," I said through gritted teeth. "I see you."

A rush of adrenaline pumped my heart faster, but I was beyond trying to control it. If I was going to drop dead, it just had to wait until I freed my sister. I had no time to save myself anymore. I moved toward the front door, ready to save Jo, but I stopped.

"It's not her," I said, reassuring myself.

But did you see who it was? the voice in my head responded.

"No."

Then how can you be so sure?

I stretched my hand out to the doorknob just inches away. "She is not responsible for this," I said again to myself.

Be sure, the voice in my head said. *No more mistakes. There's no time.*

"I'm sure," I said.

I grabbed the leftover bread from the kitchen counter that Mother had saved for our twenty-first-century living night, which we never got to celebrate, and I made my way out into the rain.

I stuffed the bread in my pocket to keep it dry enough to be edible. I ran to Jo; between the mud and the eyes staring at me, the few hundred feet between Jo and me felt like miles. She saw me coming, and through the sheet of rain, I saw her lift her head high for the first time since being dragged away from our home.

I finally reached her, and the first thing she said to me was, "I'm sorry, Stanton."

I hugged her until I heard a bone crack. I reached into my pocket and pulled out the bread, half of it stale and the other half soggy. She deserved better, but she thanked me over and over as though it was a fresh harvest roast. A person like that did not commit the crimes she was being accused of. I knew it, she knew it, and everyone else knew it.

As I fed my sister what many onlookers likely presumed would be her last meal, I whispered in her ear, "I know it wasn't you."

She slowly swallowed the sticky, stale bread, and with her mouth dry, she whispered back, "I know it wasn't you either."

"I need to do one thing, though," I said, looking at her clothes. "Will you let me?"

She looked down at my hand clutching the last of the bread and nodded.

I rolled up her sleeves and examined both her arms. No wounds. I looked at her for approval before I peered down the front of her shirt. No wounds there either. For the benefit of the piercing eyes behind me, I hugged Jo, peering inconspicuously down the back of her shirt. No wounds. I knelt in a prayer position. My sister's feet were cold and bare and blue. My prayer hands made prayer fists. I willed my hands to release their tension. Where would she go even if she was able to run away?

I snuffed out my encroaching anger; I needed to stay focused. My anger had gotten us here in the first place.

With one hand still in prayer position, I used the other to slowly lift the raggedy ends of her cold, wet pantlegs, examining both her legs but finding no wounds. I knew it wasn't Jo, but this confirmed it. If it wasn't me, and it wasn't Jo, then who was the third person in our house with us when my mother was murdered?

If the Procreates suspected violence was involved in my mother's death, then why wasn't the Den on full lockdown? Everyone was carrying on, business as usual, like my mother hadn't just been violently murdered. Something didn't add up. This had Lester's name written all over it. That heathen had something to do with Jo's detainment, and it was just as likely he'd killed Mother. The entire situation reeked of his filth and lies.

"I'm going to make this right, Jo. You know I'll never let anything happen to you," I whispered in her ear as I embraced her one last time. "I have a plan."

"Don't do it, Stanton. Whatever it is, my life isn't worth the risk you're taking. Don't do it," she pleaded in her soft, innocent voice.

I knew she meant it, but I would die before I stopped trying to save her.

"I have a plan," I said. "When darkness falls, be still and be silent. They will ascend from the holding cells and spread like wildfire through the Den. Keep your eyes shut and your lips sealed. Silence and darkness will be your friend. Don't open your eyes, no matter what you hear. Stay silent and still, and I'll come for you once it's over. This will all be over before the sun rises tomorrow."

"They? Are you...is it what I think it is?" she whispered.

"What do you think I've been preparing for all our lives?" I let go of her and slowly made my way down off the dais.

"Stanton," she said through the downpour. "I'm sorry."

***

I paced up and down the shoreline, scouring the tree line for my father. It wasn't yet sundown, but I thought he'd plan on being there before then to wait for me. I'd hoped to beat him to it. I thought over and over again what I was going to say to him. I needed him on my side. My plan would never work without the support of him and his men. Well, it would work, but not the way I intended it to. It was in everyone's best interest for my father and the militia to be behind me. I never intended this to happen so quickly, but with everything that had transpired in the last two days, I didn't have the luxury of planning things out perfectly. I'd have my next life to question if I'd done things right this time around.

Every sound I heard coming from the forest's edge

caught my attention. Every time I turned, I thought he would be there, but it was only the forest playing tricks on my mind. Just as I began to question my intuition, I heard the distinct sound of branches breaking underfoot. For a moment, I tensed. If it wasn't my father, then I'd have a lot of explaining to do that I hadn't thought out. But it was him, brushing the branches away as he stepped out of the forest and onto the shoreline.

He just stood there on the edge of the tree line, staring at the water's edge. We listened to the undisturbed sounds of the soft waves crashing around my feet. I looked down at the sand that covered my feet with each small crash and then watched the water rush back out, taking all the sand along with it, uncovering my bare, bruised feet. He watched me as a father would watch a son playing in the sand on an ordinary day at the beach, a life I'm sure we both wished we had.

A thunderous blast was followed by a clap of lightening that lit up my father's pale face. From where I stood, his expression could be easily mistaken, but blood or not, we were bound, and I knew the look on his face was one of war. He was as ready as I to break the Den. Perhaps he had been waiting for me all along to be just as ready as he was. We both now had more reason than ever.

We walked toward each other with determination. My bare feet squelched through the wet sand; his booted feet dragged through the drowned forest's edge. We finally came toe to toe. He spoke first.

"I thought I said sundown."

"Are you really surprised to see me here?"

His shoulders sagged and his face along with them. "No. Stanton, you know we don't have much time. There's something I need to tell you."

"There's something I need to ask you first."

He nodded. He already knew what I was going to ask.

"How did you know John?"

My father put his hand on the back of his head and rubbed his neck in his traditional act of self-soothing.

"His name isn't John. It's Ben. Benjamin William Stanton."

My throat tightened. I'd suspected for a long time I wasn't Mother and Father's son by blood, and I'd been okay knowing just that much. But an obvious answer isn't always believable. My father looked at me; his mouth moved, but I couldn't hear anything he said. The only sound I heard was my racing heart. Then, like a reverse vacuum, the silence was swept away, and sounds were injected back to life.

I felt like I was back on the deck of our decrepit boat, staring at the corpse they'd pulled from the water. It was different, now that I knew. He was no longer John Doe. He was my father. He came for me. What did that mean after all these years?

"Let me get you out of this rain, son." Father grabbed my arm and began walking me to the tree line.

I dug my feet into the sand and pulled my arm away from him. "You," I pointed at him. "You knew? All this time?"

"Stanton, let's get out of the rain and calm down."

"No! You played me! Why?"

He stepped in close and grabbed my shirt in his fist. "I am not your mother. I will not coddle you. I am here to protect you to my last breath. That is why I came. That is why I stayed. That is why I'm here now. That is why I didn't tell you."

"Coddle? You're softer than Mother ever was. She was the real soldier of our family!"

"You will not speak to me that way, Stanton. I am your—"

"Father?"

He let go of my shirt and stepped back with his hands up. "You always knew, Stanton. Before she told you, you knew. And I know you're smarter than you're behaving right now. If you calm down, we can talk this through."

"You still haven't answered my question. How did you know Joh—Ben? How did you know him?"

"He came for you," he said with his head hung down low. "Back in Old Chicago."

I felt chills down my spine. "What do you mean?"

Letting out his breath, he said, "The day of the Great

Superstorm. He came to the hospital. He came to claim you."

"What did you do?"

"I think you already know, Stanton. Isn't that why you've been...not yourself since we found him? Isn't that why you've had all these questions? You've been carrying this around...for what? Your mother? She's dead. Your sister? She'll be next, Stanton. We don't have time for this."

"I want to know what you did. What did you do to him?"

"Nothing, Stanton! I didn't *do* anything! Your biological mother, she...she wasn't right. She didn't even tell your biological father about you. He somehow found out, and he came for you. But your mother and I, we'd already made a vow to protect you. He would've taken you back to her. We couldn't let that happen. We couldn't risk anything happening to you. They were not fit to be parents, Stanton."

"Liar," I accused. "He showed me, Father. John showed me his last moments, and I saw you." I pointed an angry finger at my father. "I saw what you did to him."

With his hands up, he stepped closer to me. "Stanton, I swear on my life I didn't do anything to him."

"I saw you drown him. I saw your badge as you held him under," I said pointing to the patch on his arm. "I saw you holding him underwater. You watched him choke on his last breath!"

Shaking his head, he said, "No. That wasn't me. I did not do that. Is that what you saw when you took him down to the holding cell? Did you see a face? What exactly did you see?"

My mind swirled with the images of Ben's last moments that he'd shared with me right before I blacked out the first time we spoke, images of him being held underwater. I saw the hands and the sleeves of the person who held him down. I saw a gold compass on the sleeve, just like my father's. I saw all this, but no face. The confusion only fueled my anger and disorientation.

"Speaking of the holding cells, where is he? I went down there earlier to—he's not there. Why do I feel like you know where he is? You killed him; I saw it. And now you're hiding him to cover your tracks because you know I've uncovered the truth." I couldn't believe what I was saying, and yet the words came right out.

"Stanton, listen to me. You always see their last moments, right? How could it be me? I was here with you, and Mother, and Jo. I've always been right here with you. How could it have been me?"

I paced again, sorting out the lies from the truth in my mind.

"Stanton, he was alive, very much alive, the last time

I saw him. Yes, I used force with him. But I didn't harm him. I didn't harm him."

"Then who did?"

"I know you're looking for someone to blame. I can see that. It's been in your eyes since you returned from the holding cells. I've seen that look many times before."

"What look?"

"Revenge."

We stared at each other, knowing we were each right in our own way. Who was my war with? Was it really with this man who stood before me, who had done unspeakable things to keep me and his family safe? Or was it with this place that was slowly killing us all, one by one? Who would be there to tell my story if no one could speak to me in my forever silence? My father wasn't my enemy, but he had sins he needed to answer for.

"I have made many mistakes," my father said, as if he had read my mind. "Being good sometimes means you have to do things that aren't." He took the quote straight from my mother's book. "I promise I did not do what you think I did."

"You stole me," I said, giving in to gravity and slumping to the ground.

"I did." He slumped down next to me. "We did. Your mother and I, we fell in love with you, kid. What else were we supposed to do? Leave you to die?"

"It wasn't your decision to make."

"Who do you think should've decided? Your biological mom? Trust me, Stanton, I know your biological mom well. Too well. She…wasn't fit to raise you."

"I already know about you and her," I said, feeling my heart finally slow down.

"You do?"

"Yeah."

"Mother told you?"

I nodded my head.

"When?"

I looked up at him sadly. He just nodded his head in response.

"You said he came for me. What happened? Did he say anything?"

Father rested his arms on his knees and let his head fall between his legs. "Not much. He wasn't in control of himself. He was angry with your biological mother. He was scared about everything that was happening during the Superstorm. He had no plan for you and him, and your mother and I were scared. Scared that if we let him take you, he would either give you up once he realized he wasn't stable enough to take care of you on his own or try to give you back to your biological mother. Either scenario, at least in our minds, was unacceptable. So, yeah, we stole you. And it was the best decision we ever made."

"It was you, wasn't it?" I asked, remembering my conversation with John the first time we met. I remembered waking up on the cold ground of his holding cell and thinking someone had come in and moved him. I knew now it was Father who'd come in and moved him, but why? "You came to see John in the holding cells that first day when we pulled him out. I passed out and woke up, and it was obvious someone had been there when I was out. I thought it was the guard searching John for valuables, but it was you, wasn't it? Why? Why were you there?"

Looking out across the water, he answered softly, "I needed to see if it was him. I needed to be sure I wasn't imagining it."

"I know the feeling," I said. "Why didn't you tell me?" I followed my father's eyes out across the water.

"I don't know. I guess a part of me thought that if I didn't acknowledge it was him, then it couldn't be him. I didn't want it to change anything between us."

I bit my tongue, unsure of what to say. My entire life may have been a lie, but I knew in that moment my father had no reason to lie to me. He was trying to protect me, like he always had.

"Well, maybe you can make some sense of this," I said, reaching into my pocket and pulling out the locket I'd been carrying around all day. Just taking that tiny object out of my pocket made me feel a hundred pounds lighter.

My father took it from me with open hands. He instantly recognized it. I could see it in his eyes. He handled it with a delicateness I'd never seen before. He turned it over and over between his fingers as I had when I inspected it. He rubbed the front and the back.

Then he asked me, "Did you open this?"

I nodded. The locket threatened to slip out of his fingers, the rain creating a barrier between it and his skin, but he held onto it as though his life counted on it. He opened it briefly, just long enough to see the photos inside.

"Who is that?" I asked.

"It's your biological mother's sister. Her name is Hannah."

"And who is the other person in the picture with her?"

"What other person?"

"Look again," I said.

He carefully opened the locket once more.

"You need to take the photo out; it's folded up."

He did as I said. The rain was soaking the photo, but Father couldn't stop staring.

He stuttered, looking at the picture of the two women, "This…th-th-this is…your biological mother." His face turned pale like he was remembering a ghost he thought he'd rid himself of. He looked at me, but there were no more surprises to be had. I had put it all together. "Do you want to know her name?"

I watched the rain becoming one with the waves rolling onto the shore. "It doesn't matter. Who's the baby? Is that me?"

"No, that's not you. It's Mel."

Liv

The voices echo through the hollow house. Melanie is glued to my side. I rub her arm, reassuring her everything is fine despite how unsettled I feel. I recognize the voices, but what confuses me is why they're here and how they got here so fast. It's Hannah and Pete, I'm positive. Hannah had just peeled out, leaving Melanie and me stranded; it didn't make sense that she's back so soon. What's more confusing is why and how Pete is here with her.

I'm about to call out Hannah's name when I realize all these thoughts I have don't add up. Hannah said only she knows about the house, and no one else knows how to get here. I put my finger over my lips to motion to Melanie to stay silent and stay put. When I was a child, I could hear a normal volume conversation all throughout the house. But now, with the vaulted ceilings collapsed to single layers, everything is muffled.

I slowly edge out of the closet and worm my way out of the room. At the threshold, I try to make out the voices a little clearer. I spread out on my belly. Even though this house isn't the same, no one knows it better than Hannah and me. We knew every creak, groan, and screech these old boards made, and no one, not even Hannah, was better at eluding them than I was. I make it to the end of the hallway without a sound. To my left, what used to be my father's study, filled with books and doctor décor, is now an empty room with missing windows. I can see my father completing his dictations, seated at his oversized, antique desk. I see him napping on his study couch with a book on his chest and his feet up on the arm of the sofa.

I shake the images away and force them to fade so that I can focus on what's happening beneath me right now. The voices become more audible; they're getting closer. Their tones are argumentative.

"Find them," I think I hear a male voice say. That has to be Pete. "Call out for them." His voice is louder and clearer, definitely Pete's.

Hannah wouldn't bring him to the house. So how did he get here?

"Hannah, if you care at all about anyone but yourself, please call out to them," he says.

"Come on, Pete, you know the only thing Hannah cares about is Hannah." I urge under my breath. "Play at her level. Come on, like I taught you."

"You're hurting me," I hear Hannah retort.

"I'm hurting you? Oh, I'm sorry. How's this?"

I hear Hannah scream.

"Call out to them! Now!"

I stand up, and the floorboards groan under my weight. The house is instantly silent. This is fucking ridiculous. I walk down the hall to the top of the stairs.

"Pete? Hannah?"

Hannah emerges first at the bottom of the broken banister, holding her hands behind her head, followed by Pete. They stand erect at the bottom of the rickety stairs. I don't need to see the muzzle to know Pete has a gun to my sister's back. It makes sense now why she's more submissive than usual. I know Pete, though, and he's not the sort of guy to shoot somebody. Not anymore at least. Although it does make me wonder what he's doing with a gun to begin with.

"Hey, Pete…"

He looks at me with impatience. "You two get your acts together. This shit is unbelievable. Always with the shit, Liv. Can either of you just be honest for once?"

"Hannah, you okay?"

"I'd be better if your partner took his gun out of my back."

Hannah's hair is loose and disheveled, and it looks like her brow and lip are split. "Pete, what are you doing? Put the gun down," I tell him.

He pushes the muzzle harder into Hannah's back, making her arch and grimace. "Tell her," he demands with his voice and his weapon. "Go on, tell her." Hannah drops her hands, and Pete snaps at her to put them back on her head.

I've been creeping cautiously down the stairs, avoiding the missing or broken treads, and am halfway down when this stops me. "Tell me what? Hannah, is there something you need to say?"

She squirms, uneasy about the pistol bruising her back. "I don't know what he's talking about."

She and I both know that isn't true. She's hiding something. We both know it. She's always hiding something.

"Hey, Pete," I say, nearing the bottom of the stairs. I reach out. "Give me the gun."

He draws back a step, dragging my sister with him. "Liv, this isn't about me. I'm doing this to protect you. Trust me."

"How did you get here, Pete?"

"I followed you."

"For how long?"

"You think I was going to just leave you after everything you told me? I knew you were trying to get rid of me for a reason."

"You've been following me since…?"

"The entire time. I've been following you the entire time. Until you just disappeared into thin air."

"So, you waited?" I ask, putting the pieces together.

"Seemed like the sensible thing to do. No one just disappears. You had to come back at some point, I figured. I just thought you'd both be together. When I saw it was just her," he says, pushing the gun deeper into Hannah's back, "I knew something wasn't right."

Even with my hand extended, I'm still an arm's length from them. "How did you get here, Pete?"

"I came with her," he says, holding Hannah tight. "I

saw your car appear just like it disappeared, but you weren't in it."

"The psycho rammed me off the road," Hannah interrupts.

"I'm not the psycho, Hannah."

"Okay," I say, working my way towards them. Pete takes a step back with each step I take forward. "I got it. You guys came back together. Hannah, how'd you know it would work again?"

"I didn't."

Partners put their lives at risk for each other every time they put their badges on. Pete's an overachiever, though. He's already saved my life more times than I care to admit. I'm reckless, and he's reasonable. I get us shot at, and he dives in front of the bullets. That's how it used to be, before we eradicated the infection. He reminded me of a young Lyman when we met; that was why I requested Pete for my partner. Lyman knew better; he didn't catch feelings. He was the coldest motherfucker I'd ever met.

"Pete, please. She's my sister. Give me the gun." I reach out to him.

He has no doubt in his eyes. "No. This animal needs to be controlled. She's not your sister. She's not even human."

"Pete, I think you're confused right now. It's Hannah. You know her."

"I don't know anyone who's capable of what she's

capable of."

"God damnit, Hannah! For fuck's sake, just tell me whatever he wants you to tell me."

"I don't know what he's talking about," she says, stubborn as hell.

"You don't remember?" Pete accuses. "Terry? Terry Goodbread?" He looks at me while still holding the muzzle in my sister's back.

Confused, I look at Hannah for some sort of answer.

"Tell her about Terry. Tell her about everyone. All the missing. Tell her now!"

"What's he talking about, Hannah? Come on, you've got give me something here. Hannah, he's holding a fucking gun to your back. Believe me, he's itching to pull that trigger."

She purses her lips, willing herself to silence, blood oozing from her fresh wound. A noise breaks above us, and we all shudder in our shoes. We look up to the second story.

Melanie. "God damnit," I say.

Pete looks at me with his eyes open wide. He knows I too am hiding something from him. He drops his grip on Hannah and pushes me aside, fleeing up the stairs.

"NO!" Hannah screams. "Run, Melanie! RUN!"

Everything moves in slow motion as I turn to bolt up the stairs after an unstable, armed Pete, Hannah one step behind me. The staircase collapses behind Hannah's heels with a loud crash. We race down the hall, our hair flying wild behind us as we run toward my room.

We slide into each other at the end of the hallway. I grab the cracked doorjamb, and it peels back, sending me crashing into Hannah. She shoves me off, and I pull her back down, putting my body between the door's threshold and her. I hold my arms out in front of her the way our mother restrained us with her arm when she had to stop short while driving. Hannah has always been her own worst enemy; no matter how much she has let me down, by instinct I've always tried to protect her.

She breaks through my arm gate and bursts into the room. She freezes; across the room is Pete, and Melanie has retreated back into the closet.

Pete anxiously awaits an explanation for the strange, dirt-covered girl hiding in the closet. He stares at me in the doorway, then at Hannah, and then back into the closet. I shake my head at him, trying to tell him to put the gun away. He keeps it out but down at his side, his finger tapping the side of the trigger.

Hannah edges closer to Pete. "You've already committed treason," she says. "There's no going back to your normal life, Pete, but I can make the rest of your life bearable. Just give me the gun and walk away."

Pete looks at me again with impatience. He wants to know just how long I'm going to tolerate this charade.

Let her talk herself into it, I tell myself. *She'll find that corner. She always does.*

Thinking she's edging in on him, Hannah advances. "We're the only ones who know what you've done. We can find a solution."

Pete starts laughing. He wipes the sweat off his face with the back of the hand holding the gun. He looks at me but doesn't get the answer he wants. He points his firearm back at Hannah.

"Back off." Still pointing his gun at my sister, he turns his head towards the closet. "Come out of there. It's okay, come on out. We're police officers. You're safe now."

"Don't listen to him," Hannah pleads. "Stay where you are."

I'm suddenly done with her bullshit. "Since when do you care, Hannah? Since when have you cared about anything but yourself?"

"That's exactly what I've been trying to say," yells Pete, who's fixed his focus back on Hannah. "Just fucking tell her what you told me. You can't hide anymore, Hannah. You're gonna get us all killed."

"What's he talking about?"

Hannah, in a rare moment of panic, looks back and forth between Pete and me, realizing she isn't going to break our partnership. Whatever she's hiding is going to have to come out, or none of us is leaving. I step closer to Hannah, who takes a defensive stance, but there's nowhere for her to go, and she knows it. Her

325

plan to abandon me here with her child again has finally failed. She's going to have to begin answering for her past, and it's going to start here and now, in the same room where her sordid past began.

I'm close enough now I can reach out and touch her. I reach toward her chest. "Let me show him so he knows you're telling the truth." I pull down the neck of her shirt so that Pete can see her heart beating through the transparent window in her chest.

Pete's mouth falls open. "What the fuck?"

Her heart races. When it begins to slow, Pete raises his gun at her, but it continues to slow. He points the gun at me, and Hannah's heart returns to an almost normal pace.

Then, he points his gun at the closet, and her heart jolts awake.

"Now talk to us," I say while Pete keeps the gun pointed at the closet. His gaze remains fixed in disbelief on Hannah's heart.

"What do you want to know?"

"What is Pete talking about?"

"Just, please, lower the gun, and I'll tell you whatever you want to know. Just lower the gun. Point it at me, Pete. Come on, it's me you're after."

I look at Pete and shake my head. "I'm sorry, Hannah. I don't think that's a good idea. My partner seems to think you know something important enough for him to throw his life away for. Have you ever felt that way?"

Sweat covers Hannah's face in a fine sheen. I tighten my grip on her shirt and focus on watching her heart, still amped up. "The parade," she finally mutters. "There's going to be an event."

Pete and I exchange looks, this time of deep concern. "What? What's going to happen?"

"Tell her about Terry," Pete demands.

I put my free hand out to Pete. "Please, Pete. Stay focused." I turn to Hannah. "Speak."

"There's going to be an event tomorrow at the parade. It's already in motion. There's nothing that can be done."

"What event, Hannah? Stop stalling. Why does Pete keep talking about Terry? What did you do? What have you done?"

She looks at me with an air of righteousness. "What nobody else could do. I took Terry, and McCauley, and Morris, and Laney...do you want me to continue?"

Pete's grip tightens around his gun as he listens to our missing colleagues' names pouring out of Hannah's mouth. I keep one hand on my sister and the other blocking the gun now pointed at her again.

"Took them where, Hannah? Where did you take them?"

"I gave them meaning. They were lost. Their lives had no meaning left. We tried, Liv. You know we tried. We gave them money. We gave them new careers. It didn't fix their souls. They wanted what they wanted, and they didn't want to do what was best for our city."

"What have you done? Did you…did you kill them?"

"No, of course not. I saved them. They're all alive because of me. And all the people they would have taken out their aggression on are all saved because of me."

"So, they're all okay?"

"Yes," she says. "Better than okay. You'll see for yourself tomorrow."

Pete shakes his head. Something isn't right.

"Are you lying, Hannah?" Her heart rate is steady and constant. She's giving herself away, her heart telling us that she feels in control.

"Where is everyone else then? More people went missing than just good cops. Where are they? Where is everyone else?"

Hannah quiets, and a look of evil spreads across her face. "They had to practice."

"Practice for what?" I ask, but I'm already answering my own question. The horror my sister has executed doesn't even seem fathomable, and yet she did it. I don't want to admit it, but it's undeniable: I've lost my sister. This person who stands before me isn't her. Pete's right, she isn't even human. "You killed them?"

Hannah looks at me with sad, mocking eyes. "Don't sound so sad, sister. They were scum. Treasonous criminals. They were our enemies. I took criminals off the streets and put them somewhere they couldn't harm anyone ever again. I eradicated violence. I created an infection-free era. And you have never thanked me. You have never thanked me once for giving your child unlimited possibilities and a life without fear or danger."

"And what about your own daughter?" I say, my heart heavy. I let go of her shirt. I'm not interested in what her heart has to say anymore.

"Where are they?" Pete asks. "Where are Terry and the others? Where are the bodies?"

With a matter-of-fact expression, Hannah says, "They've been here the entire time."

"Where's 'here'?" Pete asks, his tension mounting.

"They've been right underneath my headquarters. Right where I can keep an eye on them."

The basement, I say to myself. *The labs,* I remember from Dani's journal. That's what was in the rows of rooms. She kept them down there all this time. She hid them where she knew no one could go and find them, but Dani did, and Hannah knew it. That's why Dani left.

She didn't run away. She's hiding.

"I know where they are, Pete," I signal for him to put his gun down. His grip on the trigger is a hair's breadth from lighting up the room.

"Where are the bodies? The dead ones? They

deserve better. We need to bring them to their families. They don't belong to you. God damnit," I say, exasperated. "How did we overlook this? All those people…How have we never seen them? Smelled them? I don't understand how you've gotten away with this all for so long."

"Oh, the bodies aren't there. What did you expect the others to eat?" Hannah says.

Pete involuntarily pulls the arm with the gun back to cover his mouth. My legs betray me and give out from under me. I fall to the floor. I can't feel a thing. "The pictures," I murmur, horrified.

"What are you talking about, Liv? What fucking pictures?" Pete calls out, just as horrified as I at the realization.

The grotesque, violent photos on Dani's tablet…It was Hannah's human meat shop. Hannah had it right beneath our feet the entire time. I look up with a feeling of unmatched helplessness at true evil. Just how much has Dani exposed?

A message…Melanie…She's the message. That's why she's here. Not to reunite with Hannah, but to expose her.

"No, you didn't," Pete says, shaking his head in disgust, trying to convince himself she's lying. "You fucking fed them to…" He can hardly keep his vomit down. He points the gun back at Hannah.

"What's going to happen tomorrow, Hannah?" I ask

as my mind threatens to collapse on itself.

"Since all our secrets are out in the open now, and since there's no way to stop it, I guess it doesn't hurt to tell you. Only I *have* told you, Liv. You're just too single-minded to hear what I have to say."

She moves to stand right above me, to remind me that she is and always will be the alpha.

"I told you, we don't have much more time here in New Chicago. The end of our resources is imminent."

"You said we were running out. You never said how much time we had left."

"Well, I'm telling you now, sister, so listen or don't because I am not going to repeat myself."

"Are you going to stand for this, Liv?" Pete says, repulsed.

I wave him off. "I'm listening."

"You know why we built the Den. What its intended purpose was."

"Yes, but it's not finished. There are...people there. You know that. My son is there and D—" I stop myself. I may not be able to save Dani and Michael, but I'm not giving Hannah both of them.

"It doesn't matter that it's unfinished. Once we inhabit it, we can finish it. We rebuilt our city once when the Superstorm stripped it down to its bones. At least the Den has a foundation. We laid all the groundwork before our access was cut off. What we need isn't what's built there; we need what's underneath it."

"What is she talking about?" Pete asks, his voice taut.

"Underground water, Pete. Massive bodies of water underneath the Den. Allow me to give you a glimpse of who you're fucking with. Before my sister's little boyfriend, I was the best physicist our country had seen. I won't bore you with my list of accolades, but there's a reason my teams of scientists are the best: because *I'm* the best. I discovered what the world had searched for since the dawn of creation. I identified tears in the spacetime continuum and uncovered what I'd always suspected: multiple realities exist all around us. My team theorized that if there were other realities, and if nobody had discovered them, then the possible resources could be endless.

"Turned out Old Chicago sat right on top of what we needed to ensure our survival, but we couldn't access it in our world. Ben found a portal to our mirror reality; that's why we chose that location. We built the Den's foundation right on top of the largest underground lake system in the country. It's untapped, and there's no telling how many resources lie there waiting for us. But it's not going to be enough for everyone."

"How do you know it hasn't been used? Or depleted already?"

"Why do you think I sent Lester there? He's been running the Den until we need it."

"I knew it. You *are* still working together!" My hands ball up into white-knuckled fists. "How could you?"

"Let's not talk semantics, sister. Time isn't on our side."

"You let the devil run the den. Why am I not surprised?"

"That's what always made us different, Liv. You give people the benefit of the doubt who don't deserve it. I've always known who Lester is. Before I met him, while I worked with him, and after I sent him off. But I never thought he was ever anything more than what he is: a liar."

"How do you know he hasn't been lying to you all these years?"

"I don't, but I trust that he wants to live just as much as we do. He knows I hold all the keys for survival, and that's all the devil really wants isn't it? To survive so that he can live among us? He's only intelligent when it comes to certain matters. He's remarkably simpleminded, especially when he's sent to his own playland with free rein of his toys. He's been guarding something that he doesn't even know exists. So that's how I know. It's still there. Still untouched. Still filled with the resources we require to start over."

"What do you mean 'there may not be enough resources for everyone'?"

"That's where your old colleagues become useful.

333

For the last…I don't know, ten, fifteen years, I've held those men and women in cages like wild tigers in captivity. I've given them just enough taste of their own blood and flesh to want more, and I've kept them shackled up just long enough to still have a drive to release all their rage."

"The parade," Pete says. "She's going to release them during the parade."

"You're fucking crazy! And you're a murderer. You're going to kill all these people you've vowed to protect? Just to save yourself?"

"No, sister. To save the elite."

"It doesn't matter, Hannah. You've forgotten there's no way to get there."

"Are you fucking kidding me, Liv? Come on! We have to get the fuck out of here! Let's go!" Pete hollers.

I wave him off once again. Hannah's been thinking she's dominating the conversation. But I have her right where I want her.

She puts her finger in the air. "Ah, yes, that's what we thought. Until your dear old high school sweetheart found a loophole."

The portal from Dani's journal, I think. *The goddamned well.*

"Nobody works for me without me knowing everything they're working on. I followed your old boyfriend. How do you think I found the house?"

"You goddamned—"

334

"Remember, I'm not going to repeat myself."

I bite down on my tongue until I taste blood.

"I'll find him somehow," I say, trying to convince myself.

"Well, when you do, I don't think there's going to be much talking."

My fingers are numb from being balled up so tight. "What do you mean?"

"I had to make sure he was right. After all, he may have just discovered the only way to get back into the Den. But I couldn't risk him exposing everything I worked so hard on just because he decided he wanted to be a dad."

"No, Hannah. No."

"I'm sorry, sister. Ben left me no choice."

Pete looks at me. I can't make sense of all the emotions crossing his face, but I know he's made the connection. He raises his weapon back up towards Hannah.

"You're a fucking disgrace. I can't even look at you." I pause, connecting why it was so easy to get Hannah to come to the house. She meant for me to be here all along. "You brought me here on purpose, didn't you? What was your plan? Were you going to kill me with your bare hands, and my daughter too? To think, *you* made a life. Do you even know what shame is? Remorse? Do those mean anything to you? I guess Melanie was lucky to have been raised by her father

335

rather than you."

"You're still alive, aren't you?" She puffs out a breath of air. "Lester isn't the fatherly type. I doubt he did her any more good than I would have."

We've been so engrossed by our back-and-forth that when we hear the closet doors creak open, we all freeze. Melanie slowly appears from the closet. Hannah falls to her knees and reaches her hand out to Melanie, who carefully crosses the room, circling the three of us.

"Lester? Is that what you said?" Melanie's quiet voice asks.

"Yes," says Hannah, uncertainly.

"He's…my father?"

The color drains out of Hannah's face. She turns to me. "She didn't know?"

Staring through my sister, I smile and say, "In the end, truth will out."

Shock spreads across her face as she leaps towards me. "I'll fucking kill you!" Hannah screams as she tackles me to the ground. My sister holds me down, and between her flying fists, I make out Melanie and Pete standing above us. Pete lowers the pistol. In one swift movement, Melanie plucks the gun out of Pete's slippery grip.

My sister's full weight falls upon me as the smell of gunpowder fills my nostrils.

Stanton

My father followed me silently along the shoreline. I had nothing to say about the locket, or the photos for that matter. I had one thing on my mind: save Jo. Melanie would understand. I'd explain myself to her when I saw her.

We were headed to where I'd seen her last; I was sure I'd find her.

"You're not going to find her there," Father said.

I didn't break stride, but in my head, I stopped at his comment. How did he know what I was thinking?

"Stanton, you asked what you wanted to ask, right?"

I didn't respond. I just kept walking through the wet sand.

"Okay, I'll take your silence as just that. Well, kid…I have a lot to say, but we don't have a lot of time. There's something important you need to know. There's something about the Den you don't know."

I pulled the blueprint out of my pocket and dropped it in the sand behind me without a word. I heard my father run to catch up, which told me he'd stopped to pick up the paper.

"Where did you get this from?"

"I know things too, Father."

He stopped me and turned me around with a strong movement. "Stanton, I know you're upset. You have every right to be. But we don't have time for all your new feelings, not right now."

"New feelings?" I shook my shoulder out of his grip. "When are you and this place going to stop telling me how to feel? And what I can and can't do?" I was starting to shout.

"Never, Stanton! Never! I am your father! Like it or not, I will never leave you, and I will never stop trying to do what is best for you. There's a difference between what the Den has done to us all and what a father does to protect his children."

"It's my time now, Father. It's my time to make my own choices," I demanded, beating my fist on my chest.

He put his hands up again in a gesture of surrender. "I understand, Stanton. Believe me, I do. You've lived a life made of decisions you never had a part in; I get it. If we do this right, if we do this together, you'll have that chance. I promise you, son. I'm not letting you die here; you or your sister. But you need to listen to me."

I turned my back on my father and started walking again, caring but not wanting to show it if he followed.

"You're going the wrong way," he said behind me.

"What are you talking about?" I asked without turning or stopping.

"The house. That's what you're looking for, right?"

I stopped. He still knew more than I did.

Trying to put my ego aside, I turned to face him. "Show me," I said.

I was readying to verbally berate him for wasting our

time, fully expecting him to simply turn us around and head back to where we'd just come from, but he didn't. Instead, he turned to face the water. He took a few steps forward, not bothering to remove his shoes and letting thin layers of water wash over the tips of his boots. He looked over his shoulder at me watching him wade into the water fully-clothed. He nodded for me to follow him into the forbidden waters of the Den's shore.

"C'mon, Stanton. I know you've been able to swim for a long time now. You don't need to pretend anymore."

Without a clue where this was going, I knew that if I could trust anyone, it was my father. We both had much at risk, and we both knew every minute that passed was one more we couldn't get back. I walked to where the water met the sand and let it wash over my bare feet. The water was gentle and cleansing; it felt warm and inviting, like it didn't belong here in the Den and yet held its place. Father was waist deep in the waters and made no movements of slowing down. I trudged into the water and watched as it swirled around me, rising higher and higher with each step. I felt the slight pull of the current get stronger the higher the water rose around me.

My father, now chest-deep, paused to wait for me. We stood next to each other in the water, feeling the same near-weightlessness as the current strengthened and weaved its way between our legs and our bodies, casting the threat of separation between us. He grabbed my forearms, and I instinctively wrapped my hands around his forearms, latching tight.

He said, "Take a deep breath, and don't let go."

I closed my eyes and drew in as much air as my lungs could hold. Dad lowered us under. The water staked its territory over our heads as my father and I, arm-in-arm, slipped underneath its surface. The current came swift and unexpected and propelled us through its depths until it was in complete control of us, rolling us around, pulling us in all directions. The sandy bottom of the lake dropped away beneath us, and we were sucked into a deep, dark vortex.

Just as suddenly as the lake floor disappeared, it returned, and our feet pressed back into the soft, uneven surface. We kept moving along the bottom of the lake until we somehow had walked our way right back up to the surface. My lungs ached for air, and I stretched my neck up towards the water's surface. The lakebed beneath us kept carrying us closer and closer to breaking the water's surface until we finally emerged, gasping in relief.

Where were we? What had happened? I chased the questions flying around my dizzy head, not realizing the answers were obvious if I just opened my eyes. We rose halfway out of the water. My eyes opened and searched our surroundings. What I saw had no explanation, but sometimes that is explanation enough.

Just a held breath ago, we'd stood on the Den's shores; now, I saw a large piece of land in the distance.

A large piece of land with a strip of shoreline and a dense tree line behind it.

"Wait...what the hell?" I said, staring into the distance. "Is that...?"

Father wiped the water from his face, unphased, and answered, "The Den? Yeah, that's it."

"How is that possible? We were under for how long?"

"I used to make a career out of asking questions about things that didn't make any sense. But here, even the answers I *can* find only lead to more questions. I get what I need from this place and nothing more. This place is filled with endless questions. It doesn't matter, Stanton. What matters is what's on the other side of the hill."

"What hill?" I turned away from the distant shore of the Den, and there was, indeed, a hill erected straight out of the waters in which we stood.

"I think this is what you were looking for," my father said, starting to move out of the water.

I followed, and we worked our way up the hill. I noticed the wet sand turn into dry sand. As we neared the top of the hill, the dry sand turned into a pebbly gravel. I remembered that feeling under my feet when Melanie led me to the house the first time.

When we got to the top, the rain stopped. It just

stopped. Even more miraculously, we began to descend, and I felt a new sensation: warmth. My eyes squinted, my skin prickled, my bare feet warmed from beneath. I lifted my head, but the brightly-lit sky forced my eyes shut.

With my eyes closed, the sun appeared to me as an orange haze through my eyelids. I spread my arms out with my face lifted upwards to soak in as much warmth as I could.

"Open your eyes," my father said. "You don't wanna miss this."

He guided me down the gravely hillside until it turned to smooth pavement; before I knew it, we reached the bottom.

"Your eyes will adjust, trust me."

I cracked my eyelids open and blinked wildly as direct sunlight leaked in under them. My vision was blurry and overactive. Every time I blinked, it was like I was seeing one of the negative photos the coffin-dodgers had from the old world. But Father was right: my eyes adjusted quickly. I looked at him; he was looking back at me in a way he never had before. I felt him staring at me, through me, studying me, trying to remember every part of me in this new light. We had only ever seen each other through dull grey layers of rain and poorly-lit rooms. Father looked different to me, too. He looked younger. Pale, but younger. More vibrant.

"Your eyes," he said. "Your mother would be beside herself right now. In a good way! In a good way," he assured me, emotion spread across his face. "Blue like the ocean, no doubt about that."

We lifted our gazes to what stood before us. Astonished and in awe of the transformation we'd undergone, I had no idea how it was possible, and yet there it was, and here we were. Together we stood at the foot of a long, hilly driveway. And at the foot of this long, hilly driveway, there was a house, a brown, deep-wood-colored house.

It was the same house Melanie had led me to the day before, but it had already changed.

"I don't understand," I said, open to explanation. "How did the house get here? It's not supposed to be here."

"I don't think it knows where it's supposed to be, Stanton. Maybe it ends up where it needs to be found." Dad handed me a key. It looked old and rusted. He nodded toward the house. "You're going to need this."

"Is Mel in there?" I asked, staring at this old, unfamiliar relic from a different world, a world I was once a part of but that had always been unknown to me.

"Not anymore," he said, looking at the key. "She went through there, though, to get to the other side. She made it out, Stanton. The locket…"

I felt in my pockets urgently, but I still had the locket. I took it out and held it in my hand along with the new, old key.

Father looked at the contents in my hand. "That's how I know," he said, looking at the locket. "She sent that back for you. To let you know she made it."

"For me? Made it out...to where?" I asked, but I knew the answer. It was what I'd hoped for my entire life: that there was more than just the Den; that my mother and father's stories about my short life before the Den were true; that one day I'd be able to go back there again; that it was real.

That my life was real. That this life wasn't all I'd have before I died.

"Go, Stanton. Go," my father said, looking at the house.

I shook my head. "No. No, Father. I won't leave you and Jo."

He faced me and put his hands on my shoulders. "You must, Stanton. Your mother lost her life to make sure you had a chance to save yours."

You're dying, I heard Mother's voice echo in my mind.

"I won't leave. I'll be okay!" We could both see my heart beating through my damp shirt.

"You won't, Stanton. You need to get to the old world. They'll be able to save you there. I can't...we can't fix you here."

"I don't need to be fixed, Father. I'll be fine...I'll be..."

"Go!" He pushed me towards the house. "You have to go, or all of this has been for nothing."

"This is what's supposed to be! I deserve to die. I can't outrun my heart forever."

"You will die, son, but when you're old, older than me. A lot older than me. And when you've gotten to do everything with your life that you've wanted. Not now, and not here. Don't worry about Jo. Like I've said before, it's not your job to keep her safe. That's my job." He looked away, ashamed at not fulfilling his fatherly duties.

"I can save her, Father. We can save her. She didn't...she would never...There was someone else there when Mother died. It has to be Lester. I know it. I cut him! I cut the person who was there. We just need to find who it was, and then we can save Jo. We can free her. And then we can all go together. Don't make me leave! I won't do it!"

"I know, Stanton. I know it wasn't you. I know it wasn't Jo. And I know you're probably right; Lester may have killed my wife. Your mother. But son, that's not a fight you're going to win. Not here."

"I have a plan! For years, I've been—"

He put his hand up, shaking his head. "Who do you think moved Ben? Where do you think all the rest of the bodies went? Why do you think you haven't been able to get into the incineration room?"

"You...you know?"

"I've always known, Stanton. I'm your father, and I used to be a damn good detective in the old world. Your mother and I have known all along."

"Then there's some part of you that never stopped me because you know it can work! They'll never see it coming."

"But you will. You'll see it. You'll live it. You'll be responsible for it. Trust me when I say this, son: taking lives…it stays with you."

"But they're all already dead."

"They may be, your undead army, but what about the ones you're planning on sending them after? You think they know the difference between our neighbor's children and the Procreates? Do you think they can feel remorse? They don't know, Stanton. They don't know the difference between good and evil. They'll kill every living thing in sight. You can't control them."

"I can control them. They have souls. They speak, I listen, and they do the same. They've all told me, in one way or another, that they want to right the wrongs here. How do you think I've been able to communicate with them? It's not magic, Father. I'm open to them. I'm open to the fact that the dead still have voices even after they can't speak. They may not be alive, but they aren't empty. They still have a purpose."

"I can't let you do it. I won't let you trade your soul for theirs. I'm sorry. You need to save yourself. That's all I and your mother and Jo have ever wanted for you."

"I'm not going without you and Jo. You're all I have. I'm…I'm scared."

He looked almost excited. "Good! You should be! That's how you know life is real. A life without fear isn't a life because a life without fear is impossible. Our hearts still beat here. We still talk, eat, work…but we're dead. We are all dead, Stanton. Imposters. Shells of what we once were. The Procreates have taken away our right to be human. Being human isn't perfect, and none of us are. We were meant to be violent beings, some of us at least. We were meant to protect by any means necessary. We were meant to hunt for survival. We were meant to struggle. But we were also meant to rise up, to be resilient, to experience joy even through unimaginable pain. To triumph and strive and move forward, even when our fates seem inevitable. Although we aren't perfect, we good ones know how to love, and love takes sacrifice. Just because violence is gone, it doesn't mean fear was taken with it. Fear is good son. Fear exists in all of us. Only the brave can admit they are afraid. It means you can feel, Stanton. It means you are alive."

I was fighting my body. Black dots swam around my head; my body threatened to shut down, but I continued to fight it.

As he and I stood looking at each other, unspeaking, a low rumble moved through the ground, and it began to rotate beneath us. Another low rumble made me look up at the sky, and in just a moment's time the glorious, warm sunlight was swallowed up by a forbidding cloud, and a shadow fell over us.

Giant raindrops hit me hard and fast. Cold and harsh, I felt pins and needles all over my body. The ground began to separate, and the beautiful, brown house that lay before us cracked straight through its foundation. An ear-piercing shriek preceded a lightning bolt that tore straight through the center of the house, ripping it into two near-equal pieces. The wind picked up, tossing debris around us, taunting us, trapping us.

"Stanton!" Dad yelled through the sudden storm. "Use the key! Go now!" He grabbed me once more by the shoulders. "There's no more time. I don't know if we'll have another chance!" He pulled me close to his chest and held me; it was all he could do.

The house was crumbling right before our eyes. I did the only thing I thought was right. Looking down at the locket and key in my hand, looking back at my father, and remembering Jo tied to the sacrificial post, I made up my mind.

"I'm sorry, Mel. I'll see you again in this life or the next."

I threw the key as far and as hard as I could. I don't know if the wind caught it, or if it was swallowed up by the crumbling house, but either way, it was gone.

"What are you doing?" cried Father.

"Making sacrifices!"

"God damnit, Stanton! God damnit," he said, hugging me even tighter, not even the storm masking his emotions. It felt good being there with him even if the world was ending. It felt right. It felt real.

"We have to go. We have to get back."

"What's happening?" I shouted through the sounds of the storm strengthening around us.

"I don't know," he said, shaking his head in newfound terror and uncertainty. "We can't stay here to find out."

We turned and grappled with the elements that tried to force us to stay. We needed to get back up the hill, into the water, and back to the shore. My ears perked up at a strange sound. I thought I imagined it, but I heard it again, and when Father turned around, I knew it was real. We stopped at the foot of the hill, standing still and listening between thunderclaps for anything that didn't belong.

There it was again: it was a voice! We turned back toward the house. Somebody stood by the front of the house, in front of the collapsed garage.

"Stay here," Father said, putting his arm out in front of me.

I looked at him, and I could see in his expression that he knew he was better off not trying to outrun me. He nodded, and we ran full-out toward the blurry person in the distance. The heavy rain sounded like radio static at its highest volume; it was a miracle we heard the voice at all.

"Help!" the voice screamed. It was a woman's voice.

We got closer and could see it was a girl.

"Help me!" she begged.

Father and I bent and put one of her arms around each of us. The house threatened to collapse on top of us. We lifted her, and the moment we turned and moved her, the second story of the house crashed down at our backs. Shards of glass, metal, and wood spewed across the drowning driveway. Dad and I ran as fast as our legs could carry us. We ran uphill against the water cascading down on us, moving so fast that one slip could easily tumble us straight back down into the mouth of the storm. We didn't look behind us; we didn't want to see what would happen if we got stuck there. My legs cramped, my lungs burned, and my heart beat so fast I couldn't even feel it beating anymore, but we were almost at the top of the hill.

The girl was barely conscious. Without knowing what had happened to her or where she'd come from, I couldn't tell if she was fading because of shock or trauma. We needed to get her to the shore. We had no capabilities there on that shapeshifting hill. We crested the hill and barreled down to the bottom of the other side where the water faithfully met us and welcomed us back in.

Again, we waded waist deep in the water, only this time there were three of us. Father and I held the girl's forearms securely, triangle-shaped, and without the luxury of a full breath, we plunged straight underwater. Moving together, we gave in to the current that sucked us back into the same deep, dark vortex that had brought us there. Again, we exited the vortex and felt the sandy lake bottom under our feet. The girl was completely limp. We dragged her dead weight through the water, and I felt myself fading, but I knew Father would get us to the shoreline with his dying breath if need be. I knew he would. My chest pulsated as my lungs begged for air and my legs weakened. A strong hand grabbed me under my arms and launched me to the surface of the water.

The air hit my lungs, and I had never been so grateful to breathe the Den's air. I looked around for my father and the girl. A moment passed before he surfaced. He didn't even look out of breath. He still had the girl tucked under his arm. I picked up her other arm, and we swam her to shore. When I stepped out of the water and my knees had to bear my full weight, they buckled. I fell, pulling the girl and my father down onto the Den's sandy shore, exhausted. But Father didn't hesitate.

"Compressions, Stanton," he directed as he tilted the girl's head back and gave her two breaths.

I didn't hesitate either and watched for their lips to part to start compressions.

"Keep going," he signaled between breaths.

I don't know how long we continued. Long enough to start worrying that the girl wasn't going to come back. I watched my father try to breathe life into her. I watched her chest puff up and drop down with each breath without response. I felt myself pushing down on her chest, but she felt cold and rigid. She was close. So, I listened.

"I'm Dani. My name is Dani. Please don't let me die. Not yet."

Someone tugged at me while I was trying to listen.

"I'm not from here," her voice said. "But someone I'm looking for is. Stanton. Michael Sasha Stanton lives here. I need to find him." There was an urgency in her unconscious voice.

Stanton? How does she know my name? Who is Michael Sasha Stanton? Is she looking for me? Why is she looking for me? I thought as her voice began fading.

Someone was pulling me off her.

"Leave her, Stanton. She's gone."

"No, she's not. She's speaking to me. She's not gone yet."

I moved to her head and instructed Father to take over compressions. I breathed out twice, followed by his compressions. Nothing. I breathed again, and a river of water flowed from her mouth. She gasped as water tried to fight its way back down into her lungs. She coughed and rolled over into the wet sand, gasping for air. I sat her up and held her between my legs, striking her on the back to help clear her lungs. Father flopped back on the sand in relief. He looked at me and the girl with a look of confusion. Wasn't he happy? We'd saved her life.

His eyes went back and forth between the girl's face and mine. "What's your name? How did you get here? Was anyone with you?"

"Father," I put my hand out. "Don't. Give her a minute, and her name is Dani."

"How do you…? Oh, I see."

"I told you she was close but not gone."

The girl squirmed in my hold as she lifted her face to look into mine. Her eyes were a deep blue, just like mine. It was like looking into my own eyes.

"Michael? Is that you?"

Confused, I answered calmly, "I'm sorry. I don't think I'm who you're looking for. My name is Stanton."

My dad shifted focus between her and me, moving where he sat, not quite unsettled but unsure of what was happening.

"Stanton? Michael Sasha Stanton?" she asked.

I looked at Dad, shaking my head, unsure of what to make of this stranger's questions. But then I saw it: a look of recognition in his face.

"Stanton," he said. "That's your name."

"I know."

353

"No," he said, shaking his head without blinking. "Michael Sasha Stanton is your name."

I looked down at the unfamiliar face searching mine. "Who are you?"

"I'm your sister."

Liv

My sister's warm blood seeps from her wound and soaks through her thin shirt, spreading on the floor around us. I haven't seen blood spilled by someone else's hand in nearly two decades.

She's facedown. I press hard on her wound, trying to recall emergency procedures for gunshot wound victims, but it's been so long since I've had to take action like this, I'm not sure if I'm doing all I could. She's so thin, and I'm pushing so hard, I think my hand will go straight through her. I look up and see Pete's mouth wide open, trying to get words out, but I can't hear anything. Melanie stands with her arms at her sides, a smoking gun by her bare feet.

There's movement, but I can't sense where it comes from. I see Pete and Melanie's stance shift as they both put their hands out like they're reaching to hold on to something. The movement intensifies, and sound begins to make its way back into my brain. Pete yells for me to get up. The house makes a noise like someone has picked it up and dropped it into a grinder. It strips away before our eyes: panels fall, walls tear away, and the roof threatens to cave in on us.

The fault lines. They move. I remember what Hannah told me.

"Pete!" I scream over the sounds of the house caving in. "The fault lines are moving! We need to get out of here. Now!"

Pete tries pulling me off my sister's body. My hand presses down on her back, and I still feel her breaths moving her back up and down in a slow rhythm.

"Liv, let go. Let go!" he screams, pulling me off her.

I tear away from his grasp, and with all my strength, I flip my sister over and hoist her over my shoulder. "The window!" I shout.

Pete looks at the window, blown out of its frame, and grabs Melanie, who stands frozen like a deer in headlights. He carries Mel to the window and looks down from my second-story room. I jumped out this window many times as a kid. Back then, there was soft grass to break my fall. The concrete is going to hurt, but it isn't going to kill us. If we stay here, who knows what will happen to us.

He yells for me to leave Hannah and go out the window first. I refuse. He puts Melanie down and swings his legs over the window frame. The house shakes, and debris flies around us, making it difficult for him to get a good grip to lower himself out of the window. He somehow manages to get out, and with a dull thud, he lands on the concrete below.

"Pete! Pete!"

He slowly rolls to a crouch and limps to his feet. He puts his arms out for Melanie. She looks at me, holding her bleeding, dying mother, and I see the emotion and the regret in her eyes. It's the look I always searched for in the faces of the violent offenders I incarcerated. With some, I saw nothing in their faces. No emotion. No regret. Those faces, even after all this time living infection-free, those faces continue to haunt me. But looking at Melanie gives me faith. If she feels sorrow for doing what should've been done a long time ago, that means I didn't entirely fail her. It shouldn't have been at her hands though, and for that I will never forgive myself.

I carry my sister on my shoulder and reach my free hand out to Melanie. She recoils into the fetal position. I stumble closer to her, but she makes no movement to stand. If I lay Hannah down, I'm not sure I'll have the strength to pick her back up. I don't have enough strength to lift Melanie too. I'm not her mother, and even if I were, I wouldn't trust myself to have the right words to say to her in this moment. So, I do what comes naturally to me: I lie, and I hope she will find it in herself to forgive me.

"It's going to be okay. I'm going to be right behind you. I know what you did was an accident. We'll make sure everyone knows. Everything is going to be okay. I need you to stand up on your own and go to the window. My partner, he's going to catch you, okay? He's going to make sure you get somewhere safe."

Through the rumblings of the collapsing house, glass shatters nearby, and Melanie finally sits up straight and looks me in the eyes. "Where can we go that's safe?"

she asks, looking at her motionless mother slumped over my back. "You're not coming with us, are you?"

I'm losing my grip on my sister. I tell my niece, "Keep Pete in line for me."

She stands up on her own and walks to the window where Pete still waits for us. I yell down, "You catch her, Pete! You catch my niece, and don't let anything happen to her!"

He motions for Melanie to drop down. She slings her skinny legs through the opening and turns to look at me. I want to hear her forgive me, but she's a Jones: it won't be that easy. We both know we have work to do if we want forgiveness from each other. With heavy steps, I push my way closer to the window. She turns around and lowers herself down the side of the house. I see her delicate hands gripping the window frame. I get close enough to see her eyes gazing at me just below the broken window.

"There's still time," her voice echoes as her fingers disappear.

I hear no thud this time, which means Pete caught her. I breathe a small sigh of relief as I gather all my breath and all my strength. "You can't die on me, Hannah. Not like this, sister. I'm not going to let you haunt me for the rest of my life. You deserve to face your sins. You're going to live if it's the last favor I do for you," I tell my sister's unconscious body.

I peer down from the open window and see Pete

waiting for me. He sees Hannah still slung over my shoulder and shakes his head.

"Get her back inside the fault lines!"

I let my sister's sweat- and blood-covered body slide out of my hands. I watch it fall toward the ground where Pete reluctantly catches her, knowing he can't show up back in the city empty-handed. Albeit barely breathing, Hannah is going to be his and Melanie's ticket to survival. She isn't even conscious, and she's still calling the shots. She needs to survive for Pete and Melanie to have any chance to live. The city needs Pete and Melanie to survive, too, to have any chance of outliving its unknown destiny that Hannah set in motion. Pete is going to have to save the city without me.

"Goddamn you, Pete," I mutter. "I told you to just go home."

"Liv!" Pete calls up through the strange sounds of wood and earth bending and breaking around us. He looks up at me, standing in the window of the second-story room that I used to call mine. He calls for me again with his hands held high. Through the swirling symphony of dead leaves, we lock eyes. He knows my stare says *I'm not finished here*, and I know his stare says *I have you covered*.

We nod to each other through the window, and I watch him carry my sister to the car, her child following along behind him. I wait, not knowing where they'll end up if they even make it out alive, but I need to be sure they aren't going to get stuck here. There's no help for anyone here. He gets everyone in the car, and just like that, they're gone.

I stand there by the open window longer than I should, just staring at the empty, torn-up driveway, as though my mind is playing tricks on me and Pete hasn't just disappeared into thin air with my sister and my niece. I look down at my blood-stained hands. "Dani, I'm coming, baby."

I turn away from the window and face the closet, the last place I know Dani was before she too disappeared. I move my legs in that direction, and for each step forwards, the earth shift, causing me to take two steps back. The earth moves as if sliding through space, dragging me farther away from where I need to go. I fight my way across the room; it seems like an impossible feat, but I make it. I close the closet doors, closing myself away like I did so many years ago. I pretended then that if I just shut out the rest of the world, I'd be able to focus on what I needed to do; here in this tiny room, anything was possible. That's how I felt then, and I feel like that now more than ever. I need to find my daughter, and this is my last chance.

The torn papers from her journal are still scattered on the floor inside the closet. Next to Dani's journal pages is the photo of Michael Melanie had. This is the closest I've ever been to having my family all together in the same room. A weak smile spreads across my face at the irony of it all. I pick up the faded photo of Michael, or Stanton, as Melanie called him. What will I call him if I ever see him?

I turn the photo over, and there's writing on the back. It must be from Mel. It says *The currents will pull you out and bring you back home.*

I flip the photo over again looking for more. My gut tells me this is a message, but it doesn't make any sense to me. "The currents will pull you out and bring you back home," I repeat to myself like a mantra. Nothing clicks though.

The house is crumbling, and the floor weakens beneath me. "Where are you, Dani?!" I cry out as the closet floorboards buckle. "Please, how do I find you? Show me? How do I find you?" I beg the air. My fists pummel the closet walls in helpless frustration. This is it. This is how I die. Alone. Without my children, who will believe I have abandoned them. Without my family, who I never made an honest effort to reconcile with. Without even a body to be found because this house shouldn't exist, and the only people who know about it may not live through tomorrow. This is it.

I stop flailing. It's useless. I feel emotions I haven't let myself feel in years, followed by an overwhelming urge to sob hysterically, which I never allow myself to do, but all that comes out of my body is the most bloodcurdling, agonizing, ear-piercing scream that has ever escaped my lips.

The sound leaves my body, scraping along the inside of my throat as it penetrates the air. I do it again and again until my throat feels scorched by hot coals, until I don't even have the strength to sit up straight. It sounds and feels so different without a pillow stifling it: I like it. It feels necessary. The room and everything around it flake away, piece by piece, shedding itself. It makes sense.

Spent, I collapse, my face inches from the back corner of my old closet. And that's when I see it. It's faded like a ghost image, but I can still make it out: *Long Liv Big Ben* with a heart drawn around it. It was an inside joke between Ben and me when we were just kids. We didn't know what it really meant back then, what it would grow to mean later. What I wouldn't give for one last hug from my old friend. It doesn't belong here, though. It shouldn't exist here, but the world I live in isn't the only reality. I know that's the truth, but until today I've never experienced it myself. This house has somehow manifested memories from my childhood and physically implanted them within these walls.

Ben and I, we've never been in this house together. Not this version.

This house has always been an imposter. This house, The Connecticut House, is just a stand-in for the real thing. It's the same, but it's also something else entirely. Hannah and I named it when our parents moved us out to Old Chicago when we were teenagers. With their one-percent status income, they were able to build a replica of the house we grew up in. There was no way of knowing then that what they thought was best for them would end up being the worst for us.

I've always questioned what might have happened had we just stayed in our quiet, small town. Maybe Ben wouldn't have followed me here, and maybe he would still be alive. Maybe Hannah would never have met Lester and been satisfied leading a life of normal extraordinariness versus the crippling path to unattainable perfection she chose. Maybe Melanie would have had the mother she belonged to, and maybe my son, Michael, would've had a real chance at life. As for my daughter, had none of this happened, maybe she would have the mother she deserves. Feeling failure at its deepest roots, I have one more thought. Maybe everyone would be better off without me.

I turn my head and push the closet doors open. The second story of this shell is disintegrating right before my eyes. The entire face of the house has shed away. Pete's pistol lies on the ground, calling my name. I bellycrawl far enough to stretch out and reach it. I paw it into my grasp, slither my way back into the closet, and shut the doors for the last time.

I feel the weight of the gun in my hands, small, lethal, and purposeless for the last fifteen years. I've heard that in your last moments your life flashes before your eyes. You see your loved ones in a flurry, a last-minute movie of all things important to you.

But when I put the warm piece of metal in my mouth, all I think about is how it tastes like a burnt ashtray, and all I see is my finger pulling back on the trigger.

Click. Click, click, click. The gun mocks me.

My body hasn't been this terrified in years; it doesn't even know how to react. In the absence of violence, I have still managed to become completely desensitized. I should be shaking, I should be sick to my stomach, I should be horrified, but I'm not. I'm just surprised.

I take the gun out of my mouth and open the bullet chamber. Empty. I laugh out loud; that laugh turns into a howl, and finally the tears of a reluctant emotionalist come pouring down my face. I stare into the empty chamber and think of Pete.

He's saved my life again. He loaded only one bullet. He must've thought he'd only need one.

"Thank you, Pete," I say to the air before my tear-soaked face.

I put the gun down and slump back against the closet wall in exhaustion and surrender. I feel the strangest thing. I sit up and slump back again. The wall feels soft. I push on the wall beside me: it's hard. I push again on the wall right behind me: it's soft. I turn so that I'm facing the closet wall directly behind me. I put my hands out, and for a moment I think I've messed with my own head, but what my fingers feel is real.

The wall is soft. It feels…moveable.

I push harder into the soft wall, and it reacts. A panel emerges and shifts out and to the left, revealing an opening. It looks like a small doorway, a portal.

"Is this…?" I say. "Dani! Dani!" I shout into the dark opening.

Without thinking, I go through headfirst.

Stanton

Father paced along the beach, exactly like I had before he came down to meet me. I knew what that pace meant: he was thinking about how to handle this situation, weighing his options with each step.

The girl, Dani, had fallen asleep in my arms. Night had come, and if it weren't for all the adrenaline in my veins, I'd probably be sleeping from exhaustion, too. I carried her back to a tree overhang to let her clothes dry a bit. Her skin was still pruned; she must have been in water before we found her.

"Father," I said. He didn't stop pacing. "We can't let Lester find out about her."

He kept pacing without acknowledging me.

"I can hide her. Until we can come up with a new plan to save Jo…"

He pointed an angry finger at me. "You should've gone, Stanton. You should've gone. I don't know what the answer is right now. I just don't know."

"We'll figure it out together. I need to hide her, Father. We have to get off the shoreline before someone comes looking for us. I'll take her down to the holding cells."

"No, you won't get past the guard. It's too risky."

"I can get past the guard if you call him away."

"If we go down this road, Stanton, there's no turning back."

"What else are we supposed to do? If she is who she says she is, are we really going to let Lester and the Procreates decide her fate?"

He feverishly rubbed the back of his head, soothing himself while he tried to find a way to get us out of this mess. He shook his head. "There's no way Lester won't find out. All we can do is try to buy ourselves some time."

"Jo doesn't have any time to spare."

"I know. I'm thinking. Let me think."

Holding this sleeping stranger brought back the same feeling I had when Jo was little and would fall asleep in my arms. This person was a stranger to me. I didn't know if she was really who she said she was, yet I had an unshakeable desire to help her, to look after her. How was it possible to feel connected to someone I didn't even know?

"I know what we can do. Help me," I said, gently laying the girl down so that I could take my shirt off.

I covered her face and told my father to pick her up. He was right: there was no way Lester and the Procreates weren't going to find out about our shores being breached again. The more I thought about it, the less coincidental it seemed that, within days of each other, two foreigners had made it to our shores. It couldn't be just a coincidence. It meant something. John was a message. I was convinced now more than ever that somehow, when he breached our boundaries, he brought his world along with him. If that were true, if it was possible for his world to collide with ours, then more could be coming: more Johns, more strangers, more people, more possibilities. It was possible I hadn't thrown away my only chance of escaping this world. It was possible that world had already come to us. John's arrival had pierced our world like a balloon, and it was only a matter of time before it burst.

The thought of change elated me. I welcomed it even if it came with risks. But we needed to move this girl and get Jo absolved; theories could wait. Father followed my lead. We were close to the holding cells already; having been on the shoreline, it was a short walk away.

"Stanton, put these on." Father took the shoes off the girl.

"I don't think they'll fit."

"When have your shoes ever fit?" he asked, using a sharp stone from the shore to tear open the toes of the shoes. He pulled the laces out and rubbed wet sand and mud over the shoes until they looked as dirty and useless as my old shoes. "For appearances. The guard will sniff out any inconsistencies. They've been trained for that."

I nodded and put the newly-destroyed shoes on my feet. Although much too small for my feet, they were already more comfortable than any shoes I'd ever worn. We started our walk to the holding cells. I hoped the rain wouldn't wake her before we reached the cells; it would be easier to get her through if we didn't need to explain to her where we were taking her. My shirt, covering her face, quickly became saturated with the heavy rain. Father noticed her breathing had become erratic and removed the shirt from her face.

"Father, the rain…it's going to wake her."

"We can't waterboard her, Stanton. We'll cover her up when we're closer."

"Waterboard? What does that mean?"

"Don't worry about it. Forget I said it." There was a strange tone to his voice, something that suggested pain and resentfulness.

"Okay," I said, putting my hand on his back. His expression was hard when he looked at me, but he let his creased face soften.

The cloak of night didn't slow us down. We both knew the valley's terrain well enough to walk it blindfolded. As we approached the holding cells, we covered the girl's face again and hoped the guard wouldn't question why she was covered. They never had before, but protocol had seemed to change quickly since John's discovery.

The guard saw us approaching. It wasn't unusual for me to show up with a dead body and no board, the same as when we brought John down through the hollows to the holding cells. When bodies were taken through the forest, conventional methods of transportation were often abandoned. My father carried her in his strong arms. He pulled her closer to him the closer we got to the guard. The guard, all four feet, six inches of him, stood with his finger on the trigger of a gun nearly as big as he was.

"At ease," my father called out as we approached.

The guard relaxed the gun at his side, finger off the trigger. He stared at my father and at the body in his arms. For a minute, I thought the guard was going to just wave us by, but nothing is ever that easy. The guard nodded his head in a gesture for us to remove the shirt covering the girl's face. My father shook his head. The guard gripped the Uzi at his side tighter.

Father stepped toward the guard, and I could hear bits and pieces of what he said: "...the Rappaport girl...found her...Procreates..."

The guard bought it. He waved his Uzi at us to enter. Father didn't hesitate; he stepped through the door, and I followed at his heels, feeling the guard's eyes on us as we passed. Father and I both knew one of us was going to have to get to the Procreates before the guard did.

Back inside the elevator, we took the covering off the girl's face. She started to wake while we waited for the elevator to descend. As it squealed to life, she opened her eyes, but unexpectedly, she didn't open her mouth to scream. She looked up at my father, who looked back at her with the same look of recognition I'd seen earlier on the shore. Who was he seeing when he looked at her?

He set her down on her feet. She was weak; she wobbled and reached out for support. She leaned against the elevator wall and looked at the wires dangling from the top corner of the elevator. She ran her fingers over the dents in the silver wall. She listened to the sounds of water trickling down all around her and watched a water beetle scramble up her arm, also searching for something to support it.

Access to the holding cells is limited, so to see someone experience this bullet train for the first time was a new experience for me, too. Things that normal people found perturbing and off-putting, this girl embraced. She exhibited no alarm at her new surroundings, like she felt she was right where she was supposed to be. I envied her. I wanted to feel that way too.

Father couldn't hold back any longer. I knew that look. He wanted answers, and he wanted them immediately. He squared off to her with his back facing the door.

"What's your name?"

Unphased, the girl responded coolly and calmly, "Thank you for saving me. Of course, my name. My name is Jessica Danielle Jones."

Dad's chest sunk in and puffed back out as air moved in and out of his lungs in great gusts. He fell back against the elevator door and laughed out loud. "I knew you looked familiar. I see her in you," he said through his laughter.

I couldn't remember the last time I'd seen my father laugh, but it didn't explain why I felt uncomfortable. He stood straight again, and the elevator bounced and shook crudely right before the door released.

"What are you talking about, Father? Do you know her?"

He smiled at the girl, a warm, genuine smile. "It's not her fault, Stanton. It's not her fault who her mother is. It's not your fault, either. You kids...you can't choose your parents."

"Father," I said as the elevator door began to close. He stuck his heel back and the elevator obeyed, leaving its door open. "Let us out."

He was looking at her, trying to see through her. He glanced at me and then back at her. "Your mom," he said to the girl. "What's her name?"

"Olivia," she replied.

"I knew it," Father said, smiling to himself, but the smile was filled with reservation and uncertainty. The elevator tried to have its way again, but he put his arms out and forced the door back in its place. "Stanton, she's telling the truth. She is your sister."

"Was Olivia your partner? In your old world?" Father nodded. I looked at Jessica. "Mother told me about her, your partner."

"It's not your place, Stanton. That's between

your…her mother and me."

"Wait a minute," I said, searching through my mind's archives. "Your name…Jessica Danielle. Jessica Danielle?" She looked at me with wide eyes, unsure what I was asking. "Jessica Danielle, John Doe, J.D.…wait a minute. If John Doe isn't really John Doe, then the journal…" I saw my fingers running over the gold-embossed letters *J.D.* on John's journal. "You're J.D.? I have your journal," I said in disbelief. I looked at my father, who put his hand up.

"I already read it before we gave it back to you. She hasn't done anything wrong. Not yet. Although it's best we found it before anyone else did. When Melanie told us she found a way out, we didn't know what that meant or what to expect. When I found you, by the house—"

"The house?" We both knew he was talking about the first time Melanie showed me the brown house. "How?"

"I followed you, Stanton. After what happened that night, there wasn't any way I was going to risk you trying again. So, I followed you to keep you safe."

"I wasn't trying to hurt myself."

"I wasn't going to take any chances."

The elevator's mechanism fought my father's grip. Veins protruded from his arms, and his temples pulsated.

"Dad," I reached my hand out to him. "I'm okay.

Trust me. You have to let us out before they start wondering why it's taking so long to go back up."

Relenting, he stood with his back against the door to keep it open for us to exit. He hesitated.

"Are you coming? They'll suspect us if we don't stay together."

He stepped out of the elevator, but it felt like he was leaving more than its empty car behind as it screamed back to life and heaved its way upwards towards the surface.

"Let's take her to John's—I mean Ben's room," I said, trying to convince myself I was comfortable saying that name out loud.

Jessica stopped in the middle of the dark hallway.

"Come this way, Jessica. We're almost there."

"Dani. Call me Dani. Where are you taking me?"

"It's just a room, right ahead. It'll be safe for you to wait there, for now."

"No. No, you said it was Ben's room."

"Yes, that's where we kept his body."

"Oh, I see," she said.

I looked at my father, who looked confused but determined to put the pieces together.

"Sorry, Dani, did you know him?" I asked.

"Not really. A little. Do you know who he is?"

I looked at my father again. "I know enough." She understood what I was trying to say.

"I'm sorry you have to find out like this. That

he…he's dead."

She nodded. "I already thought that. I guess I was just hoping I was wrong." She shook off the confirmation. "I'm the one who should be saying sorry to you; he was your dad."

Father's brow creased as he stepped between her and me. "How did you already know?"

"No more questions," I said, putting my hand on his back to disarm him.

"Let her speak, Stanton. She wants to talk? Let her." He crossed his arms over his chest.

She looked back and forth between the two of us, obviously aware of the tension this place manifested. "I saw him go into the well. He told me to keep my distance because he didn't know what was going to happen. I hid behind a big tree trunk. At the time I wasn't sure why I was hiding. I could've easily just stood a few feet away in plain sight. But my instinct was to hide. Then she came."

"Your mother? Liv—Olivia?" Father pressed.

She shook her head. "No, it wasn't my mom. It was Hannah. Aunt Hannah. I was about to stand and call out to her, but she put a mask over her face, and I knew only one of them was going to be left breathing. She said something to him I was too far away to hear. Ben's arms started to swing in and out of the well. Water splashed out of the well, and Hannah was bent all the way over. When she stood up, she was soaking wet, but the water wasn't splashing around anymore. So, like I said. I knew he was dead."

"Did she have anything on her sleeve?" I asked.

"What do you mean?"

"A symbol or anything like that?"

"You mean her compass insignia?" She asked, pointing to the patch on Father's sleeve. "Yeah. It's her company's logo; she and everyone who works for her wears it."

Father looked at me to gauge my response, to see if I finally believed he wasn't responsible for killing Ben as he'd tried to tell me earlier. I couldn't make eye contact with him. Accusing him, my own father, of murdering someone…there wasn't anything I could say that would make it okay. I should've known he'd never do anything like that.

"You don't need to apologize, Stanton. I used to be somebody who would've done something like that. You always use your instinct, okay?"

I stood dumbfounded. He had literally just read my mind.

He focused his attention back on Dani. "Where's your aunt now? Did she follow you here?"

"No," Dani shook her head. "But she's looking for me. I have something she wants."

"Where is it?" Dad asked, concerned and suspicious.

"I don't have it anymore. Well, I do have it…up here." She pointed to her head. "But nobody will believe me. I'm just a kid. So, I left all the details in writing."

"Your journal?" I asked. "The missing pages?"

"Yes." Her face lit up but then fell again. "But I left them behind." She looked at my father. "For my mom."

Dad's eyes grew wide. "Are you saying your mother was with you?"

"No, but I know she's coming for me."

"What did your notes say for her to do?"

"Well, if you know my mom, you know you can't tell her to do anything."

My dad scoffed at that comment; Dani had clearly connected with him. "That's the truth."

"All I could do was lead her in my direction and hope she made the right choices."

"Which are?"

"To expose my Aunt for what she truly is and to break the Den."

"What did you just say?" I punched out.

"My aunt...she's a murderer, and she must be exposed."

"No," I pushed her against the wall. "What did you say about the Den?"

"It shouldn't exist. It was never supposed to be for people like you. It's part of one of her systems. There's something here she wants, and the only way to keep her from getting it is to break the Den."

I threw my arms around her and held her so tight I

felt her breath push out. "You *are* my blood," I said, squeezing her with all my strength.

Dad was patting me on the back. "Stanton, let her down. She can't breathe."

I looked down: I had lifted Dani clear off the floor. I immediately let go, and she dropped, gasping for air. I reached down to help her up. "I'm sorry, I just...I'm sorry."

"It's okay. It actually felt...sort of good," she said, catching her breath. "Even though you nearly squeezed the life out of me. I haven't been hugged in forever."

That saddened me because I was too familiar with that same feeling. This was a sign that things were going to be different. Things were going to change for the better.

"What's that noise?" she said as she stood.

"What noise?" Dad asked.

She put her hands over her ears. "Jesus, they're so loud. You can't hear that?"

"Dani, what exactly do you hear?" I asked.

"Voices! They're everywhere. They're surrounding us. They're so loud. You don't hear them? I thought...I thought you could help me," she said, dejected.

My father looked at me. For the first time in my life, I didn't feel alone.

"You hear them?" I asked with my jaw open.

"Yes. I hear them all the time. They drive me crazy. But they're so loud here. There are so many voices.

You really can't hear them?"

"I can't," said my father. "But your brother can."

"Make them stop, Michael!" She begged with her hands pressed into her ears. "They're so loud. I can't understand them."

I put my hands on hers and drew them away from her ears, holding them in mine down by her sides. "I can help you. I can help you, Dani."

Her face twisted up on itself. She couldn't separate the voices; they were overpowering her. I knew the feeling well.

"Listen to me, Dani. Close your eyes and listen to me. Listen to my voice. Follow my voice. The other voices will follow. That's okay. Just listen for mine and the others will start to fade away."

"I can't! They're too loud…"

"Hear my voice, only my voice."

"They're too loud," she shook her head as though shaking the voices from her head.

"Listen to me. Listen to me," I repeated.

"I hear you. They're getting quieter. Keep talking."

I looked at my father with wild excitement and disbelief. "Focus, Dani. It's working. Listen to my voice. Hear my voice."

Her breathing calmed. "I hear you. They're whispering now."

"Do you guys mind keeping me in the loop?" Father asked.

She opened her eyes. I had an ear-to-ear grin on my face.

"Why are you smiling?" she asked.

"Because it worked."

"Yeah, I know it worked. You talked me through it, and the voices went away."

"They did. But I didn't say a word. We were speaking to each other without speaking out loud."

"What the hell? Like, telepathically?"

I nodded my head in disbelief. I finally knew what it felt like to meet someone like me.

"Can you teach me more? The voices…they're around me all the time. I can't focus when I hear them."

"When they speak to you, the more you listen, the clearer the voices will become. The more you fight hearing them, the louder and more overlayed they will become."

"Okay. Can we try again?"

"We'll have our entire lives to keep trying," I said, smiling at her. "Right now, we need you to stay down here. It's a long story, but you don't belong here, and we can't let anyone know about you, not yet. And my sister—"

"Melanie?"

Hearing her name come from someone outside of the Den caught me off-guard. "No. Melanie? How do you know Mel?"

"She helped me get through."

"Helped you how?"

"She sent me a message, a shell. That's how I knew you existed, that there was another world out there. They tried to tell me you were dead. I got these reports," she reached into her pocket and pulled out a wad of damp papers. Father reached across me and took the papers from her. As he scanned the papers, she continued, "That's how I got my first clue that you were real. I followed every lead until it led me to your dad, er, Ben...sorry," she looked at my father. "And now here I am."

"But Mel...where is she?"

"She's in my world now. She showed me the way out, and she stayed."

"Why?" I looked at my father, who was still scanning the documents. "Why would she stay?"

Father put the papers down. "Stanton, there's a lot about Melanie that you don't know. I don't think now is the time to talk about it either. It's her business, not ours. Her choice. And we need to go now. There's a lot of work to be done and very little time."

I thought of Jo, left up on the sacrificial post. I had promised her I'd absolve her, and I'd never broken a promise to her.

"He's right," I said to Dani. "We have to go. I'll be back; wait here." I opened the door to John's room.

"You're just going to leave me here?"

"It's the safest place for you right now."

"I can help. Let me help. I owe you both for saving my life."

"It's too dangerous. I'll come back for you."

It was nearly soundproof down in the holding cells, but not entirely. Father looked off; I listened for what he was focusing on, and I picked it up too. It was too quiet. Something was happening on the surface, and we needed to get up there immediately.

"I'm sorry, Dani. We need to go," I said quickly, turning and closing the door to the holding cell behind me.

Father and I ran to the elevator. It never seemed fast enough when we needed it to be. It finally made its way back to us, and we headed up into the eerie silence. There was no guard when we exited. That was a definite indicator something was going on, and it didn't feel right. We moved in the direction of the valley. We had to get through the hollows to get back; it was going to take too long.

"Here," Father yelled.

He clawed at the wet, muddy forest floor. This time, I knew what he was looking for. Underneath layers of mud and wet leaves, we uncovered a hard, cold surface. Another metal door.

"What if someone sees us?"

"It doesn't matter, Stanton. Get in. Hurry."

We climbed down into the underground tunnels he'd led me through before. I had more questions but knew there wasn't any time to ask. We moved through the dark, using instinct to feel our way through the tunnels. Father stopped abruptly, and I collided with his back, but it didn't slow him down. I heard a clinking sound move upwards; he had found a ladder and was heading up. He threw open the hatch above us, and the dull, low light of the cloud-covered moon shed some light in the tunnels. We climbed out and were on the edge of the housing circle. My father put his arm out to keep me back.

Jo wasn't on the sacrificial post. But someone else was.

Who was it? Through the rain, we could make out figures lined up around the post.

"Who is that? What are they doing? It's not time, why are they starting already? Where's Jo?"

"Stay down, Stanton," Father said in a low voice. "Stay down."

It was so silent. Through the downpour, the sacrificial chains rattled, and the eerie sound of metal on metal made my entire body cringe. Father and I crouched low, trying to make out the person on the post. There was movement off to the side, and I let out a sigh of relief when we saw Jo. The relief was only temporary, though; Lester and the Procreates followed right behind her.

"I'm going."

He pulled me back down. "No, don't move." He

looked into the distance. "How can it be?" I heard him say. The figures started to move, and the metal chains clattered louder as they circled the sacrificial post. They were starting the sacrifice, but it wasn't time yet. It wasn't supposed to happen until tomorrow. There was supposed to be time still. What the hell were they doing and who the hell was on the post?

Dad stood up, and I followed his lead. We didn't make a sound, but several of the figures turned in our direction, like they'd been expecting us. The rattling stopped, and so did the movement. We walked forward, exposing ourselves to the open space of the housing circle where the sacrificial post was displayed. As we walked closer, the figures' faces started to come into focus. Whether with shame for themselves or shame for us, no one made eye contact with Father and me.

Jo stood to the left with Lester and the other Procreates. I still couldn't see who was on the sacrificial post, but on her shirt, a name caught my eye: Trojans.

*Look for the Trojans...*I heard John's voice in my head.

That same look of recognition was in Father's face again, but this time it looked like all his blood had rushed out. He couldn't turn his face away from the unknown sacrifice. Lester was the first to make a move. He stepped in front of Jo. His movement broke Father's trance; he stared up at Lester, balling up his hands into thick fists.

"C'mon out," Lester yelled through the rain. Father and I stood our ground.

Father called up, "We're right here!"

Lester yelled again, "Come out! Show yourself!"

We realized he wasn't calling out for us. We turned around; Dani stood behind us.

"God damnit," Father spat.

"What are you doing? We told you to wait," I hissed at her.

The person on the post screamed something through the rain.

Lester gestured with his arm in large sweeping motions over his head for Dani to approach. She looked at my father and me and pushed past us. All of a sudden, she broke out into a full run, screaming, "Mom! Mom!"

I looked at Father as I took off after Dani. He was too shocked to move, but he let it take hold of him only for a moment. He ran after me, a few paces behind. We broke through the line of figures that surrounded the sacrificial stage. We stood before the crowd, panting, unsure of what was happening, unsure of what to do next. Dani clawed desperately at the woman on the post, trying to rip off her shackles, pulling at the chains only to tighten them around the woman's legs. Dad just stood, like a stick in the mud, looking up at the woman who couldn't stop staring at him, too. I saw him mouthing something through the rain.

I stared at his lips. "Olivia," he was saying.

Olivia, I thought. The name was familiar. *Dani had said…her mother. She's her mother!*

She's…my mother.

My heart swelled inside my body until I couldn't stand. I felt crippled. Helpless. I felt like I was failing everyone.

"Lyman!" the woman on the post called out to my father. "Lyman!" she called out again. "Save my son! Save my son!"

Father turned and caught me just before I hit the ground. "Stanton!" he yelled. "Stanton, stay with me!"

He held me close to his chest. The rain bounced off my face, cleansing me, forgiving me, preparing me. *Go now,* it said. I looked at what lay before me and around me. My father clutched my soul, this strange new girl who claimed to be my sister clutched the soul of her mother, my mother, and Jo, expressionless, emotionless, watched on, Lester's hand resting hostilely on her shoulder.

No! I screamed at myself. *I won't go! I won't let you beat me.*

Father watched me stagger to my feet. "Stanton, please, sit back down. Your heart…"

I stepped away from him. "My heart is strong, Father. Stronger than ever. Can't you see that?"

He let go of me, and I walked to Jo. I put my hand

out. "Jo, come with us."

"She's not going anywhere," Lester said. "She belongs here. She belongs to me."

Dad heaved himself at Lester; militiamen stepped in front of him and forced him back.

"Are you all crazy? Have you all lost your minds? You should be ashamed of yourselves," he said, disgusted that his men had allowed Lester to recruit them. I pulled my father back to stand next to me.

"You didn't think you were going to get away with this all, did you?" Lester sneered.

"What are you talking about, Lester?" I growled.

"Your plan. Your little plan with your little army."

I looked at Father but got no response. "How did you know?"

A sound made us turn. In the distance, a mass was moving towards us. That mass grew larger. As we watched, silent and aghast, the mass came into focus. The person leading it was shirtless, exposing a visible scar in the middle of his chest. Through the sheets of rain, a wave of unsteady and decrepit bodies stood behind him as far back as we could see.

"John?" I said. I turned to Lester. "How did you do that? You've turned them into machines."

"I have some tricks up my sleeve too, Stanton," Lester hissed.

I looked closer at John; something blue glowed within his chest. From that distance, it was hard to tell, but it looked like…a heart. A mechanical heart that pulsed right through his chest for all to see.

"You didn't think you were going to have all the fun, did you? I have my toys too, Stanton. This is my house. Above and below. Everything here is mine." Lester moved his filthy hand from Jo's shoulder down to her belly, exposing a large gash on his forearm. Father and I both noticed the wound immediately. Lester turned to my father. "Seeing as your boy couldn't fulfill his duties, somebody had to step in."

"What are you saying? Get your hands off her," Dad demanded, a disoriented look to his face.

"Oh, you didn't know, Lyman? Your boy didn't complete his eighteenth-year duty. Treason cannot go unanswered, Lyman. You know that better than anyone. You see, Josephine…she's mine now, and so is what's inside of her." He licked his lips and locked eyes with Father. "She is loyal to me and to her home. She knows her place, and it's right here, in the Den, with us."

"I'm sorry," whimpered Jo through the rain.

She tried to tell me earlier. She tried to tell me she was sorry, but I didn't listen. I didn't hear her.

"You're fucking dead!" Father tore through the line of guards in front of Lester.

And that's when I realized: It was all a set up.

The newspaper clipping, the blueprints, the diagram of the artificial heart…He planted those things. He'd been mocking me the entire time. Lester found out my plan, and he planted everything I'd need to think I had the upper hand. He had us right where he wanted us.

I opened my mouth to yell for Lester's guards to let my father go, but a voice behind me shattered the atmosphere.

"Let him go!" the voice screamed out.

It was the woman on the post, Olivia. Dani was working to release her. She was screaming for them to release Father. "You know me, Lester! You know me! You know I will destroy you! It's over, Lester! You know by me being here that it's over!" she screamed.

He laughed with his face to the sky, howling at the moon like the madman he was. He walked to the post where Olivia was tied.

The militiamen released Father, and he grabbed Jo and dragged her through the mud away from the dais. He lifted Jo on his shoulders and carried her to me.

"Take her," Lester howled as he waved us off. "There's nowhere you can take her that I won't find her." We watched Lester address Olivia.

He peered up at her and said, "You've been here five minutes and you think you can call the shots? I've been here for eighteen years! Eighteen long years. This isn't your world, Olivia. This is my world."

"My sister should've killed you when she had the chance, you evil son of a bitch. Being exiled here was a blessing for you. She shouldn't have shown you mercy. She should've let me slaughter you. You shouldn't be alive. Who do you think sent me here? She knows, Lester! She knows you fucked up. It's over, Lester!" She spit in his face.

Lester wiped her spit from his cheek. "Your sister? Merciful?" he scoffed. "You think I'm evil? Your sister Hannah is no comparison. She's colder than any hell she could exile me to. You don't know her like I do."

"The same goes for you," Olivia spat back.

A tremor shook the ground, and it brought us all to our knees. The dais collapsed, and the post Olivia was tied to toppled over; she fell to the same ground before me. She stared into my eyes, and I into hers.

"Blue like the ocean," I said. Like mine and like Dani's.

"Michael?" she said. Another tremor erupted, and the ground ripped open. Water spewed up from underneath. We struggled to our feet. With the post no longer secured, Olivia slithered out of her bonds. "We gotta move," she said.

It was like she knew exactly where to go. She led us away from the housing circle, Lester and some of the militiamen following as they regained their footing. We ran over the bridge spanning the water we'd pulled John from. The water looked like it was boiling. It bubbled up higher and higher. Something was coming from the water. We looked closer. Father and Olivia held us back as we stared in horror at the awakening water.

Heads emerged from the boiling river.

"Oh my God, Pete. What have you done?" Olivia said in disbelief.

"You're never going to make it out of here!" Lester screamed from the other end of the bridge. "You'll leave over my dead body!"

Bodies scrambled, people ran in every direction, screams pierced the air, masking the sound of the Den's downpour.

"How does it feel, Lester?" The water boiled over the bridge, cutting off Lester's path. Bodies rose up from the water. "How does it feel to know that your own daughter would rather see you dead than save you?" Olivia taunted.

Lester's undead army marched toward the bridge, John leading the way with his glowing heart.

"I have my insurance, Olivia," he shot a look at Jo. "You tell that bitch Hannah she'll never outrun me."

"I have my insurance too, Lester!" she called out as the bodies emerged from the water. "This is what Hannah wanted. She doesn't care about you. She never did!"

"You're a liar, Olivia! A liar!"

"You'd know, Lester! You are the best."

Olivia grabbed Dani's hand and mine, pulling us away from the overflowing river of bodies. The river rose up over the bridge, and the bodies spilled over onto the banks. They scrambled and wiggled around like a pot of worms dumped out onto the pavement. The bodies didn't know what to do. They were disoriented, shocked, ready to fight for survival. They were so rabid I couldn't tell if they were dead or alive, but no matter what they were they weren't like John, and they weren't like us. They were something else entirely. They were monsters, monsters from another world, and the Den had given them life.

John and the undead army moved as one towards us. The squirming bodies, newly birthed from the Den's waters, rapidly enveloped John's undead army. They ravaged their decayed corpses as the rain turned to blood, painting the ground red, flowing over our feet and back into the water. John and I made eye contact seconds before he launched himself toward the pile of squirming bodies.

"Ben," Olivia said to the air as she watched his undead shell crudely dismember one of the living monsters that floated up through the water under the bridge. "Let's fucking go," she said, looking over her shoulder.

"Wait." I pulled my hand away. "We're just going to run?" I watched the carnage between the living and dead unfold.

"No, we aren't running. We are surviving. They're fighting a battle we cannot win ourselves. Someone needs to be here when the war is over to rebuild."

Jo broke away from Dad and ran toward the mass of

dismembered bodies.

My vision. I thought of the image of the masses of bodies. I was right. My vision was right.

"Jo!" Father yelled. "Jo, stop!"

"Lyman!" Olivia screamed, trying to call her old partner back.

I broke out after Jo. If my vision was coming true, that meant Jo was going to be killed here and now. I fought my way through the rain and the mud, but no matter how fast I ran, I couldn't catch up to her. She was almost at the mountain of dead bodies when I realized she wasn't heading toward the mass; she wanted to get *through* the mass. Lester stood on the other side of the mountain of corpses, somehow pulling her back to him, and she ran to him like he had possessed her. I gained ground.

Jo was almost within arms' reach when a figure exploded out from the mountain of corpses. A shiny, bloody blade glistened above me. The figure dripped blood as he flew through the air toward my sister. His chest emitted a blue glow. It was John. I vaulted through the air with every ounce of energy and all my power and stretched my body in front of Jo. I was flying just like John when suddenly I dropped to the ground like a lead hammer.

"Stanton!" Jo yelled my name. Her voice faded in and out. I heard her cry out again, "Stanton!"

The rain was smothering me, trying to drown me,

trying to keep me down. Faces filled with terror circled above me. Father, Jo, Olivia, and Dani blurred in and out as they hovered around me.

"Get him up! Get him up!" Father yelled. I felt my arms wrap around him and Olivia as they dragged me to my feet and moved me as fast as they could away from the killing pit.

"Jo," I coughed out. I tasted blood in my mouth. Why was there blood in my mouth? My head drooped down.

A large, dark stain spread across my shirt from the steel end of the knife protruding from my chest.

We finally stopped moving. I looked up and saw Olivia's face, my head in her lap. She was yelling out orders to Dani. None of it made sense to me. None of it mattered. All that mattered was whether Jo was alive.

"Jo," I called out again. I turned my head to my father, who was holding Jo.

"She's all right, Stanton. She's okay. Listen," he said, trying to cover up the panic in his voice. He held his hand against my chest. "You're hurt, Stanton. Very badly. We need to get you help right now. We need to get you out of here," he pleaded with me with Jo in his arms. She was silent, just staring up at him.

"Let's go," I said between gurgled breaths.

"Shush," Olivia said. "Don't talk, Michael."

My name is Stanton, I wanted to say, but I couldn't get it all out. "Dad," I reached for his hand.

He took my hand, and I heard him say, "You save my son. You owe me."

Bodies melted into each other, water poured into land, and land poured into water. My sight blurred; I started to see double and then flashes of light and dark.

Another voice said, "He's my son, too. I'll get him home with my dying breath."

And everything went dark.

***

I awoke to water droplets falling on my face and a voice saying, "Wake up. Your work isn't finished."

Acknowledgments

Thank you…

To Andrew. For believing in me. For the interminable sacrifices you took upon yourself so that I could follow my dreams. But even more so, for being my muse and for always reminding me that it's okay to put myself first. I love you more than words.

To Nik DeKasha. For encouraging me to not sell myself short. For your undeniable, crazy talent. You truly are one of a kind and a master at your craft both as an editor and as an author. You brought this book to levels I wouldn't have been able to reach without your guidance and expertise.

To Mom and Dad. For giving a little girl from another world a second chance at a life filled with beauty, opportunity, and love. Without you, there would be no me.